D1527212

*Caught in a Web of Passion*

I drew only a fraction away from him. "We musn't," I whispered. "The servants?"

"None are here," he said. His dark gaze bore into my soul and he clasped onto my shoulders and yanked me fiercely to him. My hands were pressed hard against his chest and I could feel his thundering heartbeat against my palms. My feelings were a raging battle inside me.

"Gavin," I cried softly, but his mouth closed hard upon mine. He drew me into a torrid embrace, crushing my breasts into his chest. My senses reeled in drunken pleasure as his kisses inflamed me with burning passion, with wanton desire. I couldn't deny him to my throbbing heart, but how could I trust him . . . ?

# *LOVE'S LEGACY*

# LOVE'S LEGACY

## CASSIE EDWARDS

A SIGNET BOOK

**NEW AMERICAN LIBRARY**

NAL BOOKS ARE AVAILABLE AT QUANTITY DISCOUNTS WHEN USED TO
PROMOTE PRODUCTS OR SERVICES. FOR INFORMATION PLEASE WRITE TO
PREMIUM MARKETING DIVISION, NEW AMERICAN LIBRARY, 1633
BROADWAY, NEW YORK, NEW YORK 10019.

SIGNET, SIGNET CLASSIC, MENTOR, ONYX, PLUME, MERIDIAN and
NAL BOOKS are published by NAL PENGUIN INC., 1633
Broadway, New York, New York 10019

First Printing, November, 1987

1 2 3 4 5 6 7 8 9

PRINTED IN THE UNITED STATES OF AMERICA

*With much love I dedicate* Love's Legacy
*to my dear nephew, Andy Raymer, of Humble,
Texas, and his sweet wife, Cathy.*

# One

*T*he wind howled across the roof, rattling the loose shingles and banging a shutter in a steady rhythm against the side of the house.

Caroline Burton awoke with a start, fear quickening her heartbeat. She feverishly gazed around the room, then drew a breath of relief. She was safe, though in a setting only vaguely familiar. Her assigned bedroom at Twin Oaks, her Uncle Daniel's grand plantation house, was serene by day, but by night an ominous, almost sinister presence seemed to occupy the room.

In the twilight glow of a candle burned almost to its wick, Caroline stepped from her bed and pulled on a robe, tying its belt about her waist as she fit her tiny feet into soft slippers. She couldn't shake off the paralyzing dread that seized her after experiencing yet another nightmare.

Combing her fingers through her waist-length, fiery red hair, Caroline tried to make sense of the recurring dream she'd had since her arrival at Twin Oaks a week ago. She had never before been plagued by such nonsense and she was beginning to fear going to sleep at night.

She tried to remember the details of the nightmare, but nothing materialized. As always happened when she was fully awake, all that remained of the terrifying dream was a drawn, worn-out feeling that stayed with her the rest of the day.

She knew not where the seed of the nightmare lay.

7

The room in which she slept was charming enough. Before her arrival, the walls had been freshly papered in pale gold and white stripes, filling the air with a clean smell of newness, and gold velvet drapes hung lustrously from the one window in the room.

A massive, four-poster bed with its huge, soft mattress, spotless coverlet, and canopy had been readied for her as well as cheerful, flower-patterned washstand china and a large, solid oak armoire with a sparkling mirror.

Beside the bed stood a nightstand where the candle now flickered, its wick floating in liquid in its brass holder. Caroline withdrew another long, white candle from the drawer of the nightstand, lit it, and then positioned the new candle in the brass holder. Taking the taper with her, she walked softly across the bare oak floor to the window and drew aside the thick, heavy drape.

Morning light shone dimly into the room and everything within eye's reach outside was shrouded by a dim haze of fog. Caroline blew her candle out, unable to control a slight shiver as she watched the fog slowly begin to lift, revealing a house only a short distance away. The mansion plagued Caroline's remembrances of another time, another place. When she was five years old, she had spent one month with her Aunt Meg in a house similar to the one she now viewed through the fog.

Caroline was now twenty, and the month spent with her aunt in that quaint southern Illinois town suddenly surfaced in her mind, encased in mystery. Although she only remembered a few details of her trip, she associated an uneasiness with the house. Yet the only truly unpleasant side to her visit had been her twelve-year-old cousin, Todd.

Todd had been devilishly mean to her and his cruelty lingered in the back of her mind. She remembered him twisting her arm behind her back with his long, bony fingers. His gray eyes always watched her, and Caroline sensed their coldness even now.

She shook her head to clear her thoughts. Something more terrible than a twisted arm must have happened to her at her aunt's house, but whatever it was had been blocked from her mind.

The fog was nearly across the lagoon which separated her uncle's Twin Oaks Plantation from the manor called St. Clair. She could now make out the complete silhouette of the old house. Her overwhelming impression was one of dreary bleakness. The mansion was heavily covered with climbing, clinging vines. Any clapboard siding left exposed was colorless. Clearly the house had been ravaged by weather, age, and neglect.

Thick shrubbery formed huge looming shapes against the rambling fence that ran around the house and the gabled stable, which had its double doors boarded closed.

An iron gate guarded the gravel path leading to the desolate house but as Caroline gazed across the lagoon this morning, a new sight graced the familiar landscape. A lone horseman rode up the drive, pausing before the porch steps to look up at the house.

A light tap on the door behind her drew Caroline from her surveillance of the ghostly manor and the mysterious man on horseback. She swung around, her cheeks pale, her green eyes wide with wonder. She had a frail appearance, yet her inability to sit and idle her days away with embroidery or books attested to her restless spirit and sense of adventure.

With hardly a sound she moved to the door where she found Rosa Lawrence, the one remaining maid at Twin Oaks, standing in the corridor wringing her hands, her round face intense with worry.

Caroline ushered Rosa into the bedroom. "Is it Uncle Daniel?" she asked anxiously, placing the candle on her nightstand. "Has he worsened during the night, Rosa?"

"I'm not sure, ma'am," Rosa said in a slight voice that didn't match her buxom figure. Her thick waist and hips filled out her floor-length, fully-gathered black dress with its long sleeves and prim white collar and cuffs. Her coal-black hair had been drawn severely back in a tight bun and her large, dark eyes were even more pronounced by her olive complexion.

"What do you mean, you're not sure?" Caroline persisted. "You have checked on him, haven't you?"

"Yes, ma'am," Rosa said, lowering her eyes.

"Then what, Rosa?"

Rosa's eyes raised, meeting the challenge in Caroline's. "I looked in on him a moment ago," she said in a rush of words. "He . . . he's so still. I'm afraid to try and awaken him. What if he's . . .?"

Caroline's heart skipped a beat. "I'll go see to Uncle Daniel myself," she blurted, brushing past Rosa and into the softly lit corridor. Candles hung in wall sconces along the wall and Caroline had to watch her step in the dim light.

Her thoughts were troubled about her uncle, yet she couldn't help thinking about Rosa at this moment. She was not the best maid, yet Rosa was the only servant Daniel Burton had retained during one of his angry rages against his employees. She was one who stirred sympathetic feelings in even an elderly, dying man. Her husband, Elroy, had been wounded during the battle of Vicksburg in the Civil War and was now half crippled.

Caroline's Uncle Daniel had given them one of the vacated slave's cabins rent-free as their living quarters. Elroy worked at Twin Oaks doing odd jobs that included house repairs, riding into Charleston for supplies, and tending a small garden of fresh vegetables. He also took care of their three-year-old daughter, Sally, while Rosa worked. Caroline had seen Elroy a few times, though they had only spoken once. His gruff manner made her wonder what Rosa had ever seen in the man.

Breathless, she entered her uncle's bedroom and looked down upon his mask of predeath. She had traveled from Boston to be with him as soon as she had received the wire with his personal request. For as long as she could remember, she had been his favorite niece. He had liked her spirit, which seemed to match his own.

She had only recently learned that she had been named the sole heir in his will, and the knowledge still surprised her. Yet since her aunt's disappearance many years ago, there was hardly anyone left in the Burton family to Uncle Daniel's liking. He would only entrust his beloved plantation, which had been nearly ruined after the war, to Caroline.

The plantation was not as Caroline remembered. The slaves were gone, the cotton fields lay rotting and untouched. Her uncle's wealth, which had been preserved in New York banks during the war, had ensured Twin Oaks's survival, though now not even money would restore Daniel to his former self.

Wasting away to only bone, Daniel Burton had never given up his hopes for Twin Oaks, but he had ceased to expect the safe return of his wife. Amelia had been gone ten long, heart-wrenching years and now he did not even care whether he lived or died.

The dark and austere room was lit only by a flickering candle on the nightstand beside the bed. The drapes were drawn over windows whose closed shutters blocked out sunshine and fresh breezes. The aging, dying man had ordered them closed, not wanting to see his once thriving fields laid to waste. He said they now seemed to be an extension of himself, shriveled, useless, and bereft of dreams.

The aroma in the room was medicinal. Dust covered the massive, carved pieces of furniture. The bed seemed to dwarf the man asleep on the wide spread of mattress.

Covering her mouth with her hand to stifle a sob, Caroline looked down at her uncle in his loose-fitting cotton night sack. He was a shell of what he once had been: his skin was drawn tautly over his high cheekbones and long nose. The veins in his hands were swollen in purplish blues and his eyes were hollow sockets.

His red hair was all that remained of his youthful days, having stubbornly refused to fade along with his spirit and body.

With trembling fingers, Caroline reached out and straightened his quilt, pulling it up to cover his arms and hands, leaving it to rest just beneath his sharp, pronounced chin.

Suddenly his green eyes blinked open and in them Caroline saw the mirroring of her own. She smiled reassuringly down at him.

"Good morning, Uncle Daniel," she murmured. "I just thought I'd check in on you before breakfast."

"No need fussin' over this ol' bundle of bones," he managed in a low growl. "Caroline, I didn't ask you here to Twin Oaks to keep you hidden away. I wanted you here to understand what's yours when I die. Other than that, you need to get out in the fresh air and sunshine."

He removed a trembling hand from beneath the quilt and lifted it toward her, gesturing toward the door. "Go get some color in those cheeks today. You're much too pale."

"But, Uncle Daniel . . ." Caroline said, rescuing his waving hand and easing it back beneath the quilt.

"No buts," he said. "If my recollections are accurate, it's May, and May is the time for lovers. Since the war, Charleston is buzzin' with handsome gents, most gettin' rich. Ride into town. Maybe you'll latch onto one, Caroline. Maybe even Randolph Jamieson, my lawyer. He'd be a prime catch for any lovely lady."

A blush suffused Caroline's face. "Uncle Daniel, what a thing to say." She softly laughed. "But I'm glad you did. Your lighthearted teasing is welcome. Perhaps my being here at Twin Oaks has cheered you up, at least a bit."

"You're worryin' over me much too much," he said, frowning. "Now you must promise to take a walk in the sunshine after breakfast."

"If there *is* sunshine," she said, remembering the gray gloom of this early morning and the brisk winds rattling the loose shutters. She wouldn't let the recurring nightmare linger in her thoughts, nor would she let herself wonder further about the foreboding house which lay across the lagoon.

She looked toward the closed drapes, then back down at her uncle. "Uncle Daniel, you're the one who needs sunshine. Please allow some light and fresh air into your room this morning," she said. "I'm sure it would make your day much more pleasant."

He flashed her a sour look. "Just leave me to spend my last days in my own chosen way."

Caroline shook her hair from her shoulders and bent low over him. "All right," she sighed. "If you insist." She eased a hand beneath his head and lifted it from his pillow. "Though you must at least allow me to plump your pillow."

She saw his eyes soften and smiled warmly down at him, grateful for his special feelings toward her. She had lost so much in her life these past five years and needed the activity which he and Twin Oaks afforded her.

Caroline had lost her parents in a tragic train accident three years ago and before that the man she had secretly chosen to marry, when she was a child. She had been ten at the time she fell in love with twenty-year-old Harold Hicks, and had been fifteen when Harold died at the battle of Richmond in 1865. Since Harold's death she had behaved like a widow, not socializing, remaining at home. Her visit to Twin Oaks had reminded Caroline of the outside world and of her duty to those other than herself.

"You didn't promise, Caroline," Daniel said thickly as she eased his head back down onto the softness of the pillow.

Caroline once more smoothed his quilt. "Promise?" she said. "Promise what, Uncle Daniel?"

"That you will take that walk today," he said, taking her hand in his. "For color in your cheeks. You must, Caroline. To make me happy?"

Caroline's heart ached with pity as she felt the

knotted boniness of his fingers. She blinked her long lashes, forcing back the tears gathering in her eyes.

"Yes," she murmured, "I promise. A walk would do me good. And I'd do anything to make you happy."

She squeezed his hand before he withdrew it from hers, turned his head, and pointed a trembling finger toward his nightstand. "Then do something else for me this morning, Caroline," he said, his voice now weaker than it had been. "I've something to show you."

He lifted his head slightly off the pillow and nodded. "In the drawer," he said. "Open it. There's a jewelry chest in the drawer. I want to show you a few things of importance to me, Caroline, because they should also be important to you. They were your Aunt Amelia's. They'll soon be yours."

Swallowing back the lump in her throat, for she knew how hard it was for him to speak of his missing wife, she inched toward the nightstand and slowly opened the drawer. The gold chest caught the light of the glowing candle and reflected it back in Caroline's eyes.

"Place it on the bed where I can see it," Daniel said hoarsely. "I want to share some memories with you, Caroline. It's best now. Later might be too late."

"Please don't talk like that," Caroline softly scolded. "Why, Uncle Daniel, the way you're acting this morning, so full of life and talk, I'd say you're much better."

A low chuckle rose from deep inside him. "If it makes you feel better thinkin' that, just go right ahead," he said. "But as I was sayin', Caroline, let's share a look or two inside this chest." He patted the bed. "Sit down." He nodded toward the chest. "Open it. See what's inside."

Caroline eased herself onto the edge of the bed, placing her fingers on the lid, then paused to once more look up into her uncle's eyes, seeking approval, though it had already been given her.

"Go ahead," he said. "When you get my age, any time wasted is too much. Open the damn chest."

She smiled weakly, then slowly lifted the lid. When it was fully open and the candlelight revealed the abundance of jewels that lay inside, Caroline softly gasped. She had never seen such an assortment of jewels in her life. Diamonds . . . rubies . . . sapphires! Their dazzling beauty drew her breath completely away.

"Bring the chest closer," Daniel said, his head wobbling as he once more attempted to raise it from the pillow. "I want to show you what was at one time Amelia's favorite necklace."

"I think I know," Caroline said softly. In her mind's eye she could see her ravishing Aunt Amelia, whose golden hair had fallen across her shoulders in waves like spun silk and whose face had an almost angelic glow at all times. Aunt Amelia had worn only the latest of fashion, exquisitely displaying her hour-glass figure even at the age of forty.

She had always worn one favorite necklace, preferring it over all the sparkling diamonds and other gems she possessed. Daniel had given her a cameo necklace on the night of their marriage and Amelia had said it was a symbol of her love for her dear husband.

Caroline moved the jewelry chest closer to her uncle. "Uncle Daniel, surely the necklace isn't here," she softly suggested. "Aunt Amelia . . . didn't Aunt Amelia always wear the necklace?"

Daniel's eyes took on an embarrassed, wounded cast as he glanced up at Caroline. His pale, narrow lips lifted into a nervous smile as he dropped his head back onto the pillow. "How foolish of me to think it was there," he said. "Just shows how my memory fades in and out. Of course, it would be with Amelia. She never parted with it." He looked away from Caroline. "Take 'em away, Caroline," he choked. "She's never comin' back. The jewels are yours now. Take 'em away."

Caroline closed the lid on the jewelry chest, biting her lower lip in frustration and wishing she could somehow ease her uncle's loss. But nothing ever had. Nothing ever could. His beloved wife had left for a leisurely walk on a lovely spring day years ago and just hadn't returned. No trace of her had been found and even today her clothes still hung in her wardrobe, awaiting her return.

Knowing her uncle would still want to steal an occasional peek at the jewels to see Amelia in their reflections, Caroline placed the chest back inside the drawer and closed it. Then she rose from the bed and tiptoed to the door, sensing her uncle had talked enough this morning and would doze back to sleep.

"Get color in those cheeks, Caroline," he suddenly said, breaking the silence.

Caroline turned with a start and stared at him. "I will, Uncle Daniel," she murmured. "I promise."

"Don't walk too far, though," he warned, his gaze meeting hers. "Stay away from that ol' St. Clair place. No one lives there now, not since that loony George St. Clair passed away. Crazy as a loon he was, even if he did have a way with women. He painted, you know. And mostly women, from what I used to hear. Amelia never went near that shameful place and you shouldn't either. That ol' coot's ghost is still probably in that damn house, paintin' away."

Caroline laughed softly, then went back to her room and to the window. The St. Clair place intrigued her more by the second, as did the rider she had glimpsed earlier, though he had obviously left as quickly as he had come for his horse was gone and St. Clair Manor looked as deserted as ever.

What could it hurt to go and take just one peek into the windows? Ghost indeed! She knew she had only the living to be wary of . . . and her dreams only turned to nightmares while she slept. . . .

# *Two*

*T*he sun had melted the fog away, and the wind had died to a gentle breeze. Uncle Daniel's collie, Lucky, ran ahead of Caroline as she strolled away from Twin Oaks while Princess, the coal-black family cat, scampered along beside the dog.

Caroline laughed to herself, watching the dog and cat at play. They were as old as Methuselah, having been her uncle's pets since before the war. She welcomed their company—their presence made her feel not so alone on her morning venture.

A sudden noise behind Caroline made her stop and turn with a start. She was still tense from her nightmare. When she found only Rosa's three-year-old daughter, Sally, following her, she smiled and emitted a quivering sigh of relief.

She bent on one knee to make herself Sally's height as the little girl bounded closer, her blonde hair bouncing on her shoulders. "You must be Sally," she said, extending a hand in friendship. "I'm Caroline. It's a pleasure meeting you, Sally."

Sally stopped and smiled, but ignored the offered hand. "Pretty," she said, pointing to the cat. "Kitty cat."

"Yes. Princess is pretty," Caroline said. "But so are you in your lovely yellow dress and black slippers. And my but aren't you a lively one so early in the morning?" She laughed softly. "I wish *I* were as energetic."

17

Sally ignored Caroline, her eyes still on Princess. "I want the kitty cat," she said. But just as she stopped to pick up the cat a dark shadow fell across her, frightening her into standing again.

Caroline's eyes jerked upward and found a pair of malevolent gray eyes beating down upon her. Finding herself face-to-face with Sally's father, Elroy, she recoiled and rose hurriedly to her feet.

Caroline noticed how Elroy leaned his full weight against his cane. The cane was a constant reminder of the wound to his leg that he had received during the war. Other than that one flaw, and the iciness reflected in his eyes, he was a handsome man.

His ruggedness was displayed in a face of sharp contrasts. His jaw was square, his cheekbones high, and his hair, the color of summer wheat, hung shaggily to his shoulders. The breeches he wore were faded, molded to his long, lanky legs, and his cotton shirt was threadbare, both reflections of the fact that his lot in life was to struggle from day to day, just to exist.

Straightening her skirt, Caroline met Elroy's steady stare with a challenge that she felt was warranted by such insolence from a man under her uncle's employ. Out of kindness, yet hesitatingly so, she offered him her hand.

"Elroy, I'm Caroline Burton," she said. "I'm glad to make your acquaintance."

As Sally had done, Elroy ignored Caroline's outstretched hand. "I ain't got time for small talk," he said flatly. "Come along, Sally. I've chores to do."

Caroline gaped openly at him as he steered Sally away from her. She didn't know what to make of his utter coldness. An involuntary shiver raced across her flesh, for she had never met a man who made her as uncomfortable as this man did. He was rude as well as unfriendly. She wondered why.

Yet now was not the time to worry about it. She had been on her way to St. Clair Manor, seeking some

adventure in her colorless existence. She would see
about Elroy later.

Yet did she even care to? He and the way he had
looked at her added to the uneasiness already awakened in her by her persistent nightmares.

Feeling foolish for letting anything unnerve her so,
Caroline turned and again started toward St. Clair
Manor. Leaving the brilliant spring flowers and sum-
mer-green lawn behind at Twin Oaks, she inched her
way through scratchy brambles, avoiding the murky
edges of the lagoon. She seemed to have entered a
different sort of world.

She ducked beneath gray beards of Spanish moss
which hung from the gnarled, wide branches of live
oak trees. She gasped in pain as briars pierced the
tender flesh of her legs through the skirt of her dress.
She fussed at her choice of apparel, a delicate, pale
yellow muslin dress with puffed sleeves, a low bodice
displaying the soft flare of her breasts, and a fully-
gathered skirt which emphasized the tininess of her
waist. She should have worn a heavy skirt to protect
herself from the weeds and briars.

Stopping to get her wind and stretch her back,
Caroline checked the velvet ribbon which she had tied
to hold her hair back from her face. Yes—it had
withstood the scrapings of the lower limbs of the trees
and still hung in a perfect bow above the long fall of
her red hair.

Once more, she surveyed the gloomy bleakness of
St. Clair Manor and its tangle of high, untended
shrubbery. Her gaze moved slowly to the stable which
stood behind the house. When she saw the boarded-
up doors, something stirred uneasily in her mind. But
she knew not why she felt so apprehensive, and so
dismissed the feeling.

Again she studied the house with its tower and
gables. Such a house seemed displaced here in the
south where most were pillared mansions. Wondering
if its interior were even more curious, she decided to

look through the windows. Perhaps doing so would enable her to forget her morbid thoughts about the place. Perhaps her nightmares would even go away. For some strange reason, she felt as though this house had caused her sleepless nights. It did resemble a haunted house. Her uncle had even made reference to ghosts when speaking of it!

No matter how foolish she knew she was being, she couldn't help but feel dispirited and uneasy as she resumed battling the thick tangle of trees and brambles which now nearly obliterated the fence that outlined the St. Clair property.

But suddenly she found herself face to face with a massive iron gate. It loomed before her, tangles of vines weaving their way up and over its rusted surface. Wiping the perspiration from the palms of her hands onto the skirt of her dress, Caroline tried to raise her courage to push the gate open. Yet her grandfather's warning caused her to hesitate. Hadn't he told her to stay away from the St. Clair estate?

But what could it hurt? The man her grandfather had briefly spoken of was now dead, and as yet, no one had chosen to take his place as master of the manor. She knew that her worries were ridiculous. She would take a quick look and then leave, and no one would be the wiser.

The gate gave a loud groan as she opened it. A musky smell of thick shrubbery and rich earth met her in an unpleasant pungentness as she stepped inside, onto a dark weedy path. To her left she could see the larger gate that she had viewed from her bedroom window. Strange that it had fallen to the ground. Earlier it had been standing in place, protecting the graveled path before the house. But perhaps the gate had given way only this morning to its rusty hinges. . . .

With a sense of uneasiness still hovering over her, she pushed her way onward and through the overgrown weeds. She lifted the skirt of her dress above her ankles, cringing when her delicate slippers oozed down into muddy mire. She was glad to finally reach the three stone steps that led up to the porch of the house.

Stopping to take a nervous breath, Caroline strained her neck to look up at the monstrous edifice. Its many uncleaned windows resembled large, accusing eyes, looking back at her, causing a crawling sensation at the nape of her neck. Then her gaze moved to the stark, lonely tower that rose up, away from the rest of the house.

Caroline hurriedly climbed the steps to the porch. The wooden flooring creaked ominously beneath her feet. She barely breathed as she inched her way along. And when a gust of wind rattled a window at her side, she jumped as though shot.

Swallowing hard, she placed a hand to her throat, then emitted a soft laugh. She was still letting this house intimidate her.

The temptation of the window and the secrets it held behind it were too close to be denied. Caroline cupped her hands over her eyes and leaned against the glass. The room was dusky behind the grimy window, yet once her eyes adjusted, she slowly began to make out objects.

The room was huge, deep, and cavernous. The rich fabrics of the overstuffed chairs and loveseats all gave evidence of wealth and taste and surprisingly showed little ill effects from having been neglected for so long.

Caroline's gaze traveled about the room, taking in the heavy rolltop desk, a tea table, wing chairs, and a large stone fireplace. Then something in particular caught her eye. She peered intently at several paintings stacked against the far wall, one against the other. The top painting was the portrait of a beautiful lady. . . .

Something grabbed Caroline's insides. She grew coldly numb when she recognized the angelic face of her Aunt Amelia, the gold of her hair, and her beloved cameo necklace about her long, thin neck.

The sound of hoofbeats on the gravel path drew

Caroline around, momentarily forcing her to forget her shocking discovery. She paled and cowered against the house as a man on a beautiful roan stallion approached. She surmised that this was the same mysterious horseman she had seen earlier. Why was he there? Was he too intrigued by the house's ghostly presence . . .?

The man reined in the stallion at the foot of the steps. Sitting tall in the saddle, he was more handsome than any man Caroline had seen since Harold Hicks. She found this disturbing, even more so when she looked into his penetrating dark eyes beneath their even darker arched eyebrows and thick lashes.

In one quick glance she took in his straight, aristocratic nose, full lips, and square jaw. He wore long side whiskers and was hatless. His midnight black hair, which he wore to his ruffled collar, was windblown from his countryside gallop.

Impeccably dressed, he wore his tight fawn breeches and glistening black boots well. His broad, muscled shoulders filled out his white linen frock coat worn over a ruffled white shirt void of a tie or cravat.

"Who are you and what do you want here?" he suddenly asked, leaning forward in the saddle. His eyes played over her in an almost insolent survey.

Caroline felt a flush rise to her cheeks, yet lifted her chin haughtily, trying to discount the attraction she felt for the stranger. But there was no denying the rapid beat of her heart.

"Who am I?" she said icily. "I might ask the same of you, sir." She caught the shine of a pistol belted at his hip.

He gave her an engaging smile, one of amusement. "Oh? So she does speak?" he chuckled. "With spirit to boot."

"Of course I can speak," she snapped, taking an angry step toward him. "But it seems you are avoiding my question. Sir, why are you here? You surely are trespassing. And twice in one day?"

"Me? Trespassing?" he said incredulously. "And

what do you call what you're doing?" He quirked an
eyebrow at her. "And what did you say about my
having trespassed twice in one day? Where do you
view my uncle's property from?"

Caroline blanched and took a quick step backward.
"Your uncle's . . .?" she gasped. "You . . . you are a
St. Clair?"

"Gavin St. Clair. And may I reword what I just
said. Where do you view *my* property from?" he
asked, again smiling almost wickedly down at her.

"Your . . . property . . .?" she softly asked.

"Quite mine," he said matter-of-factly.

"I didn't know," she murmured, wishing he would
quit staring so openly at her, as though memorizing
her every feature.

"Now you do," he mocked, resting his hand on his
pistol. "And it seems I didn't catch your name, miss,
eh, what did you say?"

"I didn't," she said flatly, tossing her head haughtily, yet realizing it was she who was the true trespasser.
Seeing his hand on the pistol made her initial uneasiness return, yet she couldn't let him see this.

"My name is of no concern of yours," she quickly
added, eyeing the steps that were blocked by his horse.
"If you would kindly guide your horse to one side, I
shall take my leave."

When Gavin's horse didn't move and he didn't
speak, Caroline's gaze moved slowly upward and once
again their eyes locked, setting her pulse racing. She
knew that something uncontrollable was weaving
between them, for in his eyes she could see the same
unspoken passion that she was feeling.

She nervously fluttered her lashes and firmly set her
jaw, knowing that nothing could be allowed to happen
between them. Gavin's uncle had had a reputation of
being a womanizer. Surely this nephew was from the
same mold, already flashing arrogance in his mocking
smile and flirting eyes!

"Your name," he persisted. "And why are you here?
Surely you see that I have the right to ask these

questions. You are on my property. Trespassing is dangerous business. Usually I shoot first and ask questions later."

If his eyes weren't twinkling so, Caroline would have taken him much too seriously. As it was, she knew that he was more than likely enjoying the chance to tease her.

"My uncle is Daniel Burton," she said in a rush of words that surprised even her. She hadn't wanted to be tricked into saying anything to him, much less confess her name. She flinched when she saw a shadow of sorts mask his handsome face and wondered why he seemed so disturbed by the fact that she was from Twin Oaks.

"So you are a Burton," he said smoothly, looking at her and then across his shoulder in the direction of Twin Oaks. Then he studied her once more. "I heard that old Daniel is ailing. You've come to be with him, I gather."

"Yes. He wired me. He requested my presence at Twin Oaks," she said softly. "I traveled from Boston as quickly as I could." She hated herself for letting him drag words from inside her. What was this power that he somehow had over her, as though she was compelled to please him . . .?

A frown lined his brow. "If you came to be with him, why are you here, snooping around St. Clair Manor?" he growled, gesturing with a hand toward the house. "What did Daniel tell you to intrigue you so much about this house that you took it upon yourself to come peeking into the windows?"

He looked over his shoulder at the fallen entrance gate. "And did you have to deface the property by knocking the gate down?"

Caroline's insides flamed with anger. She doubled her fists and glared at him. "My uncle said nothing of St. Clair Manor," she hissed, lying. "And, sir . . ."

"Gavin . . ." he interrupted, correcting her.

"*Sir,*" she emphasized, "I did not deface your

property. That gate was already on the ground when I arrived. And you can have this ghoulish house. I much prefer Twin Oaks!"

She gave his horse a slap on the rear and laughed smugly as the roan whinnied and ambled away from the steps. Holding herself haughtily erect, Caroline stepped from the porch and stomped away, leaving Gavin to stare after her in wonder.

She almost tripped as her uncle's collie bounded from behind a shrub, frightening her. "Lucky!" she scolded, steadying herself.

"And keep that damn dog away from here!" Gavin shouted. "Whatever your name is!"

Fuming, Caroline turned and glowered toward him. "Caroline is my name, though it certainly is none of your business, *sir,*" she snapped. When she saw a slow smile lift his lips, her face grew hot with embarrassment. She wondered how on earth he had managed to get her to say her name.

Turning on a heel, she grabbed Lucky's collar. "Come on, boy," she ordered. "We *both* are trespassing. We mustn't do such a terrible thing as that. We just might dirty this man's immaculate property."

Out of the corner of her eye Caroline could see the big roan stallion kicking up clods of earth as Gavin rode away. Caroline wondered if she would ever meet him again. She couldn't deny wanting to, yet at the same time she so wanted to dislike the man. He surely was an arrogant rogue, nothing like the gentle, sandy-haired Harold Hicks of her past.

Lucky barked and scampered alongside Caroline as she left through the same gate she had entered. Then she suddenly stopped, her eyes wide as she remembered the portrait that she had briefly seen through the window.

Releasing her hold on Lucky's collar, she swung around and peered intently toward St. Clair Manor. Surely she had been mistaken. The portrait couldn't have been of her Aunt Amelia. Uncle Daniel had said that Aunt Amelia had never gone near St. Clair Manor, let alone stayed there long enough to pose for a portrait!

Hearing Gavin's roan's hoofbeats fading in the distance, Caroline was tempted to return to St. Clair Manor to take another look, but decided that now wasn't the time. As it was, she had already been gone too long. There was no need to worry her uncle. Tomorrow would be soon enough to visit the manor again. And even if she did discover that her Aunt Amelia had shamefully posed for the portrait, what then could Caroline expect to do about it? She could never tell her uncle.

But perhaps the portrait could be a clue that might explain her aunt's mysterious disappearance. . . .

# *Three*

*T*he room lay in shadowed darkness. Only a vague trail of light escaped where Caroline had left the drapes partially open at her bedroom window. Now fully awake, she pushed the blanket down from her body, perspiration glistening on her brow like morning dew. She had experienced the frightening nightmare again, and it had left her limp with frustration. She couldn't understand why she was being plagued by such horrifying dreams.

In her sheer nightgown and with her hair long and loose down her back, Caroline scooted up and sat huddled against the headboard of her bed, choking back tears. What was happening to her mind? Were these frightening nightmares an omen, warning her of some future danger? Surely they had to mean something!

Caroline realized that this morning was different from those past. She could *vividly* remember portions of the nightmare. Closing her eyes, clutching her knees to her chest, she trembled as remembrances fully engulfed her. . . .

She was running! She could hear the low growl of a dog close behind her as it continued to chase her. Looking back over her shoulder she saw blood dripping from the dog's fangs. Desperation seizing her, Caroline turned her eyes away from the dog and ran harder and harder, working her way through a dense fog. Then she suddenly fell against the same boarded-up doors that had begun to materialize in her previous nightmares. She began clawing at the boards, trying to pull them away. . . .

Caroline's thoughts returned to the present. She muffled a cry. Her fingers ached even *now.* Holding them before her eyes she studied them. She turned them back and forth, looking for scratches or bruises, finding neither.

She then thrust them down away from her. She had to busy herself to help her forget all this nonsense about nightmares. She couldn't let them rule her day *and* night!

Remembering how she had caught a glimpse of a portrait that had resembled her aunt at St. Clair Manor, Caroline's gaze moved to the window. A sudden idea was forming inside her consciousness. She had just thought of a way to busy herself. Her eyes lit up with a thrill of adventure. She would return to St. Clair Manor and take another look at the portrait.

Then in her mind's eye she recalled something else that she had encountered at St. Clair Manor—Gavin St. Clair and his absolute handsomeness. Even now Caroline felt strangely disturbed while remembering his penetrating dark eyes and commanding, teasing smile.

But she also recalled his arrogance. That was enough to dissuade any further thoughts of him and lessened her fear of meeting him again should he catch her at St. Clair Manor studying the portrait.

Eager to get away from her bedroom and the nebulous gloom of her nightmares, Caroline hurried into a heavy skirt and a white, long-sleeved blouse. By wearing protective clothing, she felt her skin would be shielded against the briars and low-hanging branches of the live oaks. But she understood that she would not be protected in any other way from anything or anyone who might endanger her.

She dismissed such a thought with a half-hearted shrug. She ran only a few strokes of her brush through her hair. As she stepped into the corridor, her hair lay lustrously loose about her oval face, looking like red satin. Her green eyes were like a cat's, penetrating the faint light about her. Golden sprays of candlelight played upon her as she tiptoed to her uncle's closed bedroom door. Placing her ear to the door, she listened. When she heard the steady drone of snoring, she knew that her uncle had won another victory over death, at least for one more night.

Up and about earlier than usual, Caroline suspected she had time to do her exploring before her uncle awakened. She fled on outside. The risen but still-veiled sun gave the eastern sky the cold glow of stone-ground iron. And when Caroline looked toward St. Clair Manor and again saw it fully in all its dreary gloom, she shivered. In this first blush of dawn, the manor looked even more ghostlike than usual. She felt as though she might see bats emerging from the tower windows.

Her gaze went to the stable which stood back of the manor. The wind was blowing tall, dew-dampened weeds against it, making them cling like fingers to the boarded-up doors.

A chill warning gripped Caroline, causing her to stop and stare at the all too familiar stable. An image materialized in her mind. Her eyes widened, and she covered her mouth with her hands, stifling a gasp. Suddenly, she remembered a portion of the nightmare that had been plaguing her. She could see it now as she had during so many restless nights.

She was seeing . . . boarded . . . up . . . doors! She paled. What could it mean?

Then her gaze returned to the foreboding, ghostly manor. She sensed warily guarded secrets hidden there, secrets that she might not want to learn. For a moment she shrank from the thought of going on to the manor. But she knew she must. Now that she had seen the portrait, nothing could stop her from making sure it was her aunt.

Determination to solve the mystery made her push onward until she was again standing in front of St.

Clair Manor. Its square tower, whose windows had stared out at her as she had approached, cast a ghostly gray shadow over her. She could almost feel the shadows touching her with icy fingers. Shivering, she hurried up the steps to the heavy oak door.

She paused to look cautiously about her for fear of being caught, but saw no one nor heard anything out of the ordinary. She tried the doorknob but it refused to turn.

She continued to work frantically with the door-knob, then softly stomped a foot as she took a step backward, realizing that, yes, the door *would* be locked. Wouldn't Gavin St. Clair have made sure of that? He had seemed *too* protective of this relic of a house, hadn't he? He had probably even locked the door and thrown away the key!

That wouldn't stop her. She would find entrance. Somehow.

The window at her right side drew her attention. She had seen the portrait through that window. Maybe one more look was all that was needed to place her mind at ease. Her Aunt Amelia would *never* have posed behind her husband's back. She had been dainty, sweet, and devoted. . . .

Stepping gingerly up to the window, Caroline placed her nose to the glass and peered inside. Her heart lurched and her throat went suddenly dry when she realized the portrait was no longer in the parlor. In fact, there were *no* portraits. None.

In an instant Caroline knew Gavin had moved the paintings. But why would he purposely remove them unless he was trying to cover up for something?

Now even more intrigued and determined than before, she stomped from the porch and followed the perimeter of the house around to the weather-beaten cellar door. Her heart thumped like a hammer against her chest as she stopped to grab the rusted handle of the door. Tugging and pulling, she began to raise it, one squeaky inch at a time, until finally it was leaning fully open against a twisted shrub, revealing rotted steps that led downward.

The lacework of cobwebs that lined the stairs on both sides caused Caroline to shudder. But she was determined not to let anything stop her now. She had to know if her eyes had deceived her. And if so, then she would leave St. Clair Manor to its ghosts and owner, Gavin St. Clair.

Willing herself not to feel the cobwebs as they reached out for her, Caroline descended the steps, afraid they might give way beneath her weight. They creaked and popped, but finally she stepped into the cold vault of the cellar. Brushing aside the cobwebs that clung to her in sticky strings, she inched toward a set of steps that led upward.

The damp air brushed against her face, feeling like death itself. The stench of mildew and rot crept inside her nose and down her throat, making her gag. She stepped over fallen debris and finally reached the stairs. She paused only long enough to bring her nervous breathing under control. Looking at the dark void of the staircase, she wished she had a candle to guide her way.

The sudden sound of creaking boards overhead made Caroline's heart jump and the pit of her stomach become queasy. She wasn't alone! Someone was in the house!

Immediately, she thought of Gavin. But it surely couldn't be him. She hadn't seen his horse. Or had he arrived after she had found entry into the cellar?

Then everything was quiet once again. She couldn't hear footsteps overhead. She couldn't even hear the wind in the pines or the cries of the birds outside the manor. It seemed that everything about her had suddenly been robbed of all sound. She felt isolated . . . *too* alone. Even Gavin's presence would be welcome. At least he had no intentions of harming her. Or, did he . . .?

Barely breathing, she moved on up the steps. When

she reached the top landing, she slowly tried the door, fearing that like the front door, it too would be locked. But to her relief the door opened easily enough. She eased her way on inside, into a dark hallway.

Caroline again wished for a candle as she felt her way along the wall, peering through the darkness for signs of light. A low scraping noise ahead caused her heart to plummet. She stopped and stared in total horror as the spark of a match ignited. The chill about her heart grew and spread through her body. She watched, transfixed, panic rising in her throat, fearing who she might be alone with. Should it be Gavin, even *then* how should she feel . . .?

The golden glow of a candle was reflected in a pair of dark, accusing eyes and then revealed the full handsome features of Gavin St. Clair.

"You!" Caroline said in a near whisper, her eyes wide with discovery.

"You!" Gavin growled, holding the candle closer to Caroline's face, fully lighting it.

His voice reached her like a lifeline, though Caroline didn't want it to. Deep down inside her, she new that she truly didn't fear this man. He hadn't given her just cause to. She only wondered what he had done with the missing portrait.

"I see that just a look through the window wasn't enough," Gavin snapped, his dark eyes branding Caroline as he continued to scorch her with an accusing stare. "You had to further trespass and break into my house?"

One of his brows lifted quizzically as he looked on past Caroline and then again questioned her with his eyes. "How *did* you get in?" he asked. "I thought I saw to it that all doors were securely locked."

Caroline took a step backward, feeling as though she had stepped into a much larger web than those she had found in the cellar, and was getting more entangled by the minute. Gavin's accusing stare was making her feel extremely uncomfortable.

But, oh, didn't he look handsome? Though he still sported a holstered pistol, his attire was more casual this day. He wore a white shirt, unbuttoned halfway to his waist revealing fronds of chest hair, and ivory-colored breeches which fit him like a clinging glove.

It was hard to stand up to him with harsh words. Caroline wanted to be anything but angry with him. She had felt something weaving between them from their very first meeting, but she had yet to place her finger on just what. . . .

"Seems you forgot locks on *two* doors," she said, lifting her chin defiantly. "Entrance into one led easily through the other. Your cellar door was quite void of any sort of lock."

Gavin lowered the candle down away from her. "Why do you persist in trespassing?" he asked in a lower tone. "Is it because you are bored at Twin Oaks? Or is it something else? God, woman, do you know the time of day? It's too damn early for mischievous play, wouldn't you say?"

"Mischievous play?" Caroline gasped, her shoulders squaring. "What do you think I am? A . . . a . . . child . . . ?"

Gavin's lips lifted into a humorous smile, his first this morning. He raised the candle before Caroline, closely studying her and admiring what he was seeing, though he hadn't forgotten one lovely inch of what he had seen earlier.

"No, I don't think one would be accurate in calling you a child," he chuckled. "You're anything *but*, unless my eyes deceive me."

Then his smile faded. "But that's beside the point," he added. "What I'd like to know is why you're at St. Clair Manor a second time and why you had the need to break into my house? Weren't you taught good manners in Boston?"

Gavin's close scrutiny of Caroline continued to unnerve her, his handsomeness already having disturbed her too much in ways unfamiliar to her. But now her throat was tightening for another reason, though she had known she would eventually be asked the critical question of why she was there.

What could she say? She couldn't give him her true reason, for if she told him of her suspicions about the portrait she had seen, she would be revealing that her aunt might have been wantonly unfaithful to her husband. She had to protect the family from disgrace, especially her beloved Uncle Daniel!

"Sir, my manners are quite intact," Caroline said dryly, clutching her hands nervously together behind her. "It's just that I found your house so . . . uh . . . quaint, so unlike any others I've seen in these parts. I just wanted to take a better look. Surely you can't condemn me for admiring what until yesterday I thought was abandoned."

Her eyes took on a wicked glint. "Surely you do understand, since it's your manor and you do seem so protective of it," she added.

A shudder rippled through her as she looked over her shoulder at the dark void of hallway, again feeling the ghostly neglect of the house as it loomed behind her.

She turned her eyes slowly back to Gavin, showing a daring in them. She hugged herself. "Yet though you're protective of it in one sense, you aren't in another, which quite confuses me. This house shows much neglect."

Gavin flicked a drop of melted candle wax from the brass holder. Again he challenged Caroline with a set, quite disturbing stare, then lifted his lips into a magnetic smile. "So we both are full of questions about each other." He chuckled, moved to Caroline's side, and placed a hand on her elbow. "I think it's time we change that. You want to see my house? I see no true harm in that. Let me show it to you firsthand while we become better acquainted."

He stopped and questioned her with his eyes. "That is . . . if you *wish* . . ." he quickly added.

Caroline smiled up at him, knowing that at this

moment she would approve of anything he might suggest. He was different from any other man she had ever met. There was a mixture of characteristics in him that made her heart race and her insides strangely weaken. He was not only handsome, he was intriguing . . . quite a man of mystery.

She felt as though being with him could never be boring. And wasn't his suggestion just too perfect? If he willingly escorted her through the house, she could take this opportunity to watch for the portrait.

But his sudden change puzzled her. First he acted as though he wanted anything but her in his house . . . and now he even invited her to linger . . .?

She eyed him suspiciously, then smiled as she quickly dismissed all suspicions and just as quickly agreed to the private tour. "I'd love to see your house," she blurted. "*All* of it. It's so kind of you to offer."

Gavin leaned down into her face, so close she caught the masculine scent of his expensive man's cologne and felt the heat of his breath on her cheek, stirring something akin to passion inside her.

"I'll do the honors on one condition," Gavin said, his dark eyes gleaming.

Caroline's smile faded. She regarded Gavin narrowly, setting her lips in a straight, stubborn line. She had been too quick to dismiss suspicions of him. Of course he would want a reward for being so suddenly attentive to her. And most men wanted such rewards given them by women to be anything but innocent. Hadn't she seen his dark eyes charged with more than just appreciation of what he saw when looking at her?

"And, sir, what might be required of me?" Caroline hissed, placing her hands daringly on her hips.

"That," Gavin said, gesturing with his hand.

"What?" Caroline stormed. "What are you talking about?"

"The fact that you continue to call me sir," Gavin groaned. "Surely you haven't forgotten my name all that easily. It's Gavin. Caroline, I may now be lord of this manor, but I don't care to be treated as such. I'm anything but stuffy. Given a chance, I'd prove that to you."

Caroline's eyes widened and her lips relaxed into a faint smile. "That's what you want of me?" she murmured. "That's all? That I call you by your name?"

"Surely that's not asking too much," he sighed, his eyes imploring her.

Caroline laughed softly. "No. Not at all," she said. She combed her fingers through her hair, smoothing it back from her face. "Gavin, I'd love to see your house. But I only have a few moments. I must return to my uncle's bedside soon. I've yet to see him this morning."

Placing his free hand on Caroline's elbow, Gavin began leading her down the hallway. "Except for your worry about your uncle's health, how is your stay in South Carolina? Are you truly exploring at St. Clair Manor because you're bored? If so, perhaps I could find a remedy for that. I could give you a tour of the grand city of Charleston, or should I say what is left of it after the war."

The touch of his hand seemed to set fire to her arm through the thin material of her blouse. She gave him a sideways glance and then quickly looked away, swallowing hard when she found his dark eyes watching her, melting her. The feelings were too new to her. If there was to be a man to fill her lonely nights in the future, surely it was not *this* man. His handsomeness made him roguish . . . perhaps he took a different woman to his bed every night. When Caroline loved, she wanted to solely possess the man!

"Would I accept the invitation from you for a tour of Charleston?" she blurted out, her tongue feeling oddly thick. "I think not. It wouldn't be wise to get that far from Twin Oaks. My uncle is my sole purpose for being in the Carolinas. I mustn't neglect my duties of him." She dared him another glance. "But of course you understand?"

Gavin lifted his broad shoulders in a casual shrug. "Not entirely," he said. "I have never had an uncle who deserves such a kindness. Old Daniel is lucky, to say the least." He nodded toward a soft spray of light ahead that reached out from rooms on either side of the hallway. "If my courtesies to you can only include a tour of my house, then I guess I will have to accept that. We are approaching the part of my house that I have only recently decided to renovate. The dust-covers have only been removed from the furnishings of a few rooms. The others will come later."

"I don't want to appear any nosier than you already think I am," Caroline dared to say, her cheeks pink with anticipation of perhaps seeing the portrait again. He surely hadn't removed it from the premises. "But might I ask, Gavin, if you plan to make St. Clair Manor your residence once it is livable again?"

She didn't want to care about anything that he did. But the nervous pounding of her heart gave her true feelings away. She would simply die if the chance to see him again was stolen from her. Soft panic rose inside her. How was she to quell her heartbeat . . . to keep her insides from turning to liquid when he looked at her? And his touch! Oh, how it did disturb her!

Gavin guided her into a large room and threw back the old, heavy drapes covering the windows. She looked about the room, seeing the furnishings were expensive, as those in the parlor that she had seen through the window had been. Her eyes moved quickly about, looking for traces of the portraits but seeing none.

Disappointment assailed her. Then her thoughts were drawn elsewhere as Gavin placed his hands on her tiny, tapering waist.

"You asked if I was planning to make my residence here at St. Clair Manor," he said hoarsely, his eyelids heavy with obvious desire. "I confess the idea occurred to me only recently. But the more I am here, the less I think that I would wish to live here—alone.

The manor is quite spacious. A woman would have to accompany me here, to fill the empty spaces."

Caroline looked up at him. "A woman?" she dared to say. "You are not married?"

"No particular woman nor the time for one has yet fitted into my busy schedule," he said, his eyes gleaming.

Caroline was strangely relieved to learn his marital status, yet she was reading too much in his eyes and hearing too much in his words, even feeling the possessive press of his fingers into her waist. A yearning was ebbing through her body, and it was like nothing she had ever experienced before. It was like a fire simmering. If he lowered his lips to hers, she might even be lost.

She would not let this happen. She would not be just another woman that he could brag of possessing. She now wished she had stayed at Twin Oaks as she should have. She was finding a danger here that she had never thought to encounter.

Pushing his hands away, Caroline spun around and ran her hands along the fine lines of a high-back chair. "Yes, St. Clair Manor is quite spacious," she said, wishing the heat of her face would lessen. He could surely tell that he had almost won his way with her. It showed in the flush of her cheeks. "But as I see it, much must be done before anyone can live here." Her nose twitched, smelling the mustiness of the room. "It needs an airing, don't you think? Yet the furniture will surely retain the musty smell."

Gavin laughed lightly, seeing that she was struggling not only with her words by trying to make small talk, but also with her feelings. His gaze raked over her, seeing her as he had that first time. She was lovely beyond words, tiny, even possibly frail, yet she held her posture well. And as she held her shoulders so stubbornly squared, he was able to see that she had not been spared at her bust as she had elsewhere. Even completely covered by the drab, white blouse, he could see where her womanly curves swelled out in front, where her breasts strained against the cotton material.

His gaze moved slowly upward and studied the perfect lines of her face and the crisp green of her eyes. Her hair shone like expensive satin and was the color of a gorgeous sunset, spreading its burst of red flames across the evening sky.

He knew that she was a threat in more ways than one. If he let himself, he knew that he could fall in love with her. Up to this point in his life, he had not taken any woman seriously, having spent more time developing his career than developing relationships. But now? Would she make his life change? Could she even make it richer . . .?

Caroline was growing continually uneasy under his close scrutiny. She clasped her hands tightly behind her back. "Is this the only room your personal tour includes?" she asked, looking unconsciously away from him, trying to force herself to see more than him, though the masculine scent of him lingered even now on her clothes where he had touched her.

What she saw was a dining room with a milk glass chandelier that hung over a spacious oak dining table, and crystal in a china cabinet that twinkled back at her in faint purples and blues beneath the light that escaped through the two dusky windows.

The leaf design on the wallpaper had faded to pale greens and the floor was bare of carpet and dull, having lost all its luster and coats of wax through time and neglect.

"If you will follow me, ma'am, I shall show you to the second floor of my humble abode," Gavin said in a teasing voice. "You have already seen my parlor by way of the front window. And all other rooms on this floor leave much to be desired."

A warning went off inside Caroline's head as she saw the fire in his eyes and heard the seduction in his voice. The only rooms that she would expect him to show her on the second floor would surely be those that offered a bed. She knew that she should be wary of him, yet she couldn't refuse this one more opportunity to look for the portrait. That *was* her only reason for being at St. Clair Manor, wasn't it? She would not give up until she found it!

"Why, I would be honored, sir," she said, trying to keep her voice as light and teasing as his. She could take care of herself if by chance he did have a seduction on his mind. No man had yet touched her wrongly. Neither would Gavin St. Clair!

Smiling devilishly down at Caroline, Gavin presented her with his arm. She slipped her arm through his and smiled just as devilishly back up at him. His heart began to thud against his ribs and his loins began a slow ache, now wondering who would be seducing whom? She was the first woman to ever make him feel awkward. Even as he began guiding her from the room he felt all feet. He had to gain control of himself or look the fool he was beginning to feel.

"Now watch your step," he said, hating the huskiness that had entered his voice. He lifted the candle higher, letting its glow light their way upward.

Caroline's smile faded as she looked ahead, seeing the broad staircase disappear upward into nebulous gloom. The interior of this house and its furnishings reminded her of her Aunt Meg's house in Illinois, where she had spent that one dreadful month so long ago. The dark corners reminded her of her cousin Todd. She felt, even now, that she could expect him to jump out at her at any moment, grabbing and pulling at her. Oh, how he had terrified her. She was glad that it was Gavin with her now and not Todd. She drew closer to Gavin's side and clung more readily to his arm.

Gavin sensed her fear, but dismissed it when he guided her on up to the second floor landing and down the hallway which extended, long and dark, away from the staircase.

"It's so dark," Caroline murmured, unable to quell a chill that tremored across her flesh. She looked from side to side. "But of course all of the doors are closed.

That's why. If I had anything to say about it, I would most certainly change that. This house needs light as badly as an airing."

Gavin stopped and eased his arm from hers so he could open a door. "I agree," he said, swinging the door open to reveal a room splashed with sunlight from the curtainless windows. "So we shall open this door and let the sunlight escape on out into the hallway."

He moved into the bedroom, blew out his candle, and placed it on a table. His eyes swept around the room, admiring what was his. "It shows signs of having once been magnificent, wouldn't you say, Caroline?" he said, watching her as she stepped meekly into the room to stand beside him.

"Yes. I would gather this is the master bedroom," she said, almost shyly. Her gaze took in the great bedstead, canopied in lustrous orchid velvet edged with fine, yellowed lace. The bedspread was of the same fabric as the two high-backed chairs flanking a fine oak, drop-leaf table, which displayed a beautifully decorated, Waterford hurricane lamp.

An ornately-framed mirror big enough to reflect a crowd, hung opposite the bed. Caroline's cheeks flamed with color as she imagined the sensual scenes this mirror must have witnessed throughout the years. She looked quickly away and turned her full attention to a fireplace on the opposite, outside wall. Its black marble facade almost took her breath away.

"I sense that you approve of this room," Gavin said, chuckling at her blush upon discovering the mirror and then her gasp over the magnificence of the fireplace. He gestured with a hand. "Which of the features of this room do you approve most? The bed, the mirrors, or the fireplace?" His gaze lingered on the bed before turning back to her.

Caroline strolled over to the fireplace and ran her fingers over the smoothness of the marble. "Why, I don't think I've ever seen anything as beautiful as this," she sighed, then let her gaze travel on about the room. This moment gave her the opportunity to look for the portrait, yet she knew she would not find it there. Gavin had surely, purposely, moved the portraits, and he wouldn't lead her where he had hidden them. Somehow she would have to return later, and resume her search alone.

"A woman's touch in my renovations would come in handy," Gavin said, giving Caroline a half glance. "Your appreciation of what you've seen thus far at St. Clair Manor makes me wonder if you might wish to give me a few suggestions here and there on choice of wallpaper or drapes."

"What . . .?" Caroline gasped.

"It would please me to hear any suggestions you might have," he said. "Surely you have time on your hands, or why are you even *here*?"

Gavin went to her. Caroline's heart skipped a beat when he took her hand. There was no denying the tingling that his touch was causing. She wanted to experience more of the same, yet knew that she shouldn't. But when she saw his face lower to hers, she didn't turn away. . . .

Gavin's lips were soft and warm, his hands and arms demanding as he drew her against his hard, taut body. Caroline was at first too stunned to act, but when she felt herself responding to his kiss, she became afraid and began pushing at his chest.

But he wouldn't set her free. He held her as though in a vise, kissing her with a lazy warmth that left her weak, a kiss that was now burning a path to her heart. She felt his hunger in the increasingly seeking pressure of his lips.

And when she again began to answer his kiss with a need of her own, and an incredible yearning spread through her, threatening to blot out everything else, she yanked herself free and stood in a half daze. Finally she came to her senses and began edging backward, to the door.

"You had only one thing on your mind when you invited me to see the rest of your house," she said shakily, wiping her lips dry of his kiss. "I knew to expect it of you and I was *right*." She turned in a flurry of skirt and swirl of red hair and jerked the door open. "Well, *sir*, I'm sorry to disappoint you!"

Fighting back tears of frustrated anger and shame, Caroline fumbled through the dark hallway, down the even darker staircase, and on outside, welcoming the fresh air and freedom. She didn't look back. Even when she heard his voice shouting her name and apologies in the same breath, she didn't look back. She wanted to leave behind not only him, but also the feelings that he had awakened inside her.

But she knew it was impossible. She would never forget the thrill of his kiss, nor the rapture that it had aroused inside her. . . .

# *Four*

The lagoon seemed silent and still until a red-winged blackbird arrived with its clackerlike call. Caroline ran along the glistening mudbank, her shoes slipping and sliding. But this route of escape had been the quickest, leaving the bother of the tree limbs and sticky briars behind.

Lifting her skirt, she continued her flight, still swimming with emotions that Gavin had aroused. She had dreamed of one day finding a man who could fill the void left by the death of her childhood love, Harold Hicks—but not Gavin St. Clair. There was too much about him that she would never understand. And hadn't he just made a fool of her by tricking her into his master bedroom, all along planning to seduce her? He wasn't the type to lose one's head nor heart over. Her Uncle Daniel would most surely not approve of such a man. Gavin would surely always be compared to his uncle, a rogue in his own right!

Caroline stopped to look back over her shoulder at the gloom of Gavin's house. An involuntary shiver coursed through her again at the sight of it. Why did the place disturb her so much?

And then she remembered Gavin's having briefly asked that she offer suggestions while he renovated the house. This intrigued her, yet she could not take him seriously. It had only been a ploy to make her relax for his planned seduction!

Frowning, Caroline proceeded on her way. She would not bother herself this morning with any more thoughts of the ancient house nor Gavin. She must return to her uncle's bedside, not only to check on his condition, but also to reassure him that she was there, as he had requested. Should her uncle ever find out that she had spent time at St. Clair Manor *and* with a man, she knew not what to expect of him. Surely he would be sent into a rage beyond words. He might even have another heart attack, one that he would not recover from.

She knew that she must, at all cost, keep her Uncle Daniel from finding out that she had disobeyed him. She looked up at the closed shutters of her uncle's bedroom windows. Wasn't it enough that one Burton had gone secretly to St. Clair Manor, let alone another? For surely the portrait was of her Aunt Amelia. Who else could look so much like her? And the necklace worn by the woman in the portrait was so much like the one her aunt always wore. Wasn't this just too ironic?

Caroline would never fully rest at night again until she was absolutely, positively *sure*. She had to return to St. Clair Manor. But the next time she would make sure that Gavin wasn't there. A repeat performance between her and Gavin could not be allowed to happen. It could not. It *would* not.

Leaving the mudbank of the lagoon behind, Caroline stepped on the thick stand of grass which stretched out to Twin Oaks. The sun was warm on her face, and the sky was piercing blue overhead, void of clouds. Only a slight breeze broke the stillness of the morning, lifting Caroline's red tresses to flutter about her shoulders.

Lifting her skirt higher, baring her thin tapered ankles, Caroline broke into a soft run. The angle of the sun revealed that morning was fast escaping her. Should her Uncle Daniel awaken and ask for her, what could Rosa tell him? Caroline's morning escapade was known only to herself and Gavin. It would surely worry her uncle should he be told that she was not there, within calling range.

Yet it was he who had told her to get fresh air. Yes. That would be her excuse, should he ever question her.

A sharp bark drew Caroline's devoted attention to a bundle of flying fur as her uncle's collie bounded toward her. Caroline smiled warmly as she stopped to meet the dog's approach. She gathered him into her arms and hugged him, running her fingers through fur that felt like spun silk.

"And now you also know what I've been about this morning," Caroline giggled, feeling the cold wetness of Lucky's nose as he nuzzled the palm of her hand. She framed his long face between her hands, feeling the devotion in the dog's dark and trusting eyes, though they had only recently become acquainted. "But you can keep a secret, can't you, Lucky?"

Uncle Daniel's black cat Princess came scampering along the green lawn and pounced playfully against one of Lucky's muscled legs. Caroline's hands left Lucky and scooped the soft bundle of black fur into her arms, pressing the cat's face into her cheek. "And you too, pretty thing," she whispered. "Don't you tell a soul, do you hear?"

The sound of footsteps advancing toward Caroline made her rise quickly to her feet, yet not because she was afraid of being discovered by more than pets this morning, but because the footsteps were too light to be adult. She wondered who . . . then smiled warmly when she saw little Sally come into view as she ran from behind the corner of an outbuilding only a few feet from Caroline.

Caroline placed the cat on the ground and watched Sally as she came closer, her tiny face twisted into a strange sort of smile. Caroline quickly observed a difference in Sally. She was not as lively as she had been yesterday; she even appeared sluggish. Caroline wondered if Sally was ill. If so, Elroy must be told.

Sally bent and picked up the cat, ignoring Caroline.

Caught up in wonder of her, Caroline bent to one knee before her and lightly brushed some of the child's loosened locks of hair back from her brow. "Hello, there," she murmured, smiling warmly. "Remember me? I'm Caroline. Are you all right, honey?"

Sally stood mutely quiet. Caroline thought that perhaps the little girl was too absorbed in petting the cat to respond. Or perhaps at age three, she had not yet learned the art of being polite. But Caroline couldn't help but be instantly drawn into loving this small child whose world only reached as far as Twin Oaks, who had no other children to play with, to fill her lonely days. A father was not a good substitute for playmates her own age.

"Do you like the kitty?" Caroline persisted, so wanting to make friends with the child. She began running her fingers along the soft fur of the cat, hearing her contented purr. "She *is* pretty and soft, isn't she, Sally?"

Sally finally responded. She nodded her head yes, then she cried out in pain as the cat tried to wriggle free and in doing so scratched her on the hand. She released the cat and her eyes filled with tears. Whimpering, she rubbed the wound.

Caroline drew Sally into her arms to comfort her, but her coddling was drawn quickly to a halt when Elroy came and cast a long, dark shadow over them. Caroline gave the little girl an affectionate pat, then rose to her feet and met Elroy's steady stare. She recalled his earlier coldness yet again attempted to make his acquaintance.

"My Uncle Daniel has told me much about you, Elroy," she said. "I'm glad to make your acquaintance."

Elroy's lips pinched into a straight line as his gaze raked slowly over her. "And what did Daniel say?" he said in a low growl. "That I'm a cripple not fit for more than runnin' errands like a damn errand boy?"

His eyes rose upward and she saw a quiet anger in them as they locked with hers. He slapped his lame leg. "Ain't pretty, is it?" he grumbled. "Got that fightin' the damn Yanks." Taking a step forward, teetering as his cane became caught in a clump of grass, he glowered even more strongly down at Caroline. "You're one of them, ain't you? You're a damn Northerner. Cain't figure out why Daniel would want you here. His loyalties damn well were to the Southern cause."

"Elroy, the war is over," Caroline said tersely. "What good can come from bitterness? The fact that I am from the North and you are from the South should no longer matter. It was not I, personally, who instigated the war."

Though she hated to, she again offered him her hand. "Can't we put the past behind us and try to be friends?" she murmured. "Rosa and I are friends." She looked down at tiny Sally, who was now clinging to her father's good leg. "Even Sally and I are going to be friends, aren't we, Sally?" She wanted to tell him that his daughter appeared ill, yet she didn't feel free to. He would say that she was interfering. And surely he would notice the difference in Sally. He should know her habits well since they were constant companions.

Elroy glanced down at Sally, then back up at Caroline. A slow smile lifted the corner of his mouth. "Yeah. I guess it won't hurt none," he said, taking her hand and giving it a hardy shake. "I guess I get carried away sometimes." He released her hand and again patted his lame leg. "But it's this damn leg. I have bitter moments when thinkin' how much the war took from me."

Caroline nodded. "Yes, I guess I can understand that," she said softly. "Perhaps I would be just as bitter." Then her thoughts went to Harold Hicks and the fact that he hadn't returned home from the war, alive. Hadn't she lost as much as Elroy? Perhaps even more? And she didn't go around carrying a chip on her shoulder. She had learned to accept her loss. Perhaps in time, Elroy would also.

"So what do you think of my girl?" Elroy said, groaning as he bent his lame leg so that he could squat beside his daughter. "Ain't she just somethin' else? So pretty and all. Just like her dad." He chuckled and winked up at Caroline.

Caroline's eyes widened in wonder at how his personality could change so quickly. Were all men so complicated? First Gavin . . . now Elroy. . . .

She sighed heavily and leaned over to pat Sally on the head. "Yes. She's just lovely," she murmured. "And, no, she doesn't resemble her mother at all. Yet, I'm not so sure I could say that she resembles you." She laughed lightly, seeing that he had caught her teasing tone.

Elroy placed a hand on his lame leg as he straightened it so that he could stand. He looked across Caroline's shoulder toward St. Clair Manor. "I seen you comin' from the old St. Clair place," he said, frowning. He peered intently into her eyes. "I don't think Daniel would like it if he knew you were messin' around that old place. He and old man St. Clair were anything but friends. Seems they were constantly in competition with one another for one reason or another."

Caroline stiffened. She paled. She thought immediately of Aunt Amelia. Would Elroy know . . . ? "What do you mean? What sort of competition?" she asked.

"Nothing in particular that *I'm* aware of. Only speculation on my part." Elroy shrugged. "There was the land to argue over. And horses. Anything that either possessed."

He inched away from Sally, drawing closer to Caroline. His gray eyes began twinkling, the coolness now replaced by a flirtatious warmth. "But why are we talkin' about two old geezers when we could talk about *you*," he said thickly. "You ain't wed yet. Why?"

Taken aback by his abruptness and hardly believing that he was actually now flirting with her, Caroline squared her shoulders and lifted her chin. "Why, that is none of your business," she said icily.

"Widowed because of the war? Is that why you're not wed now?" he persisted, positioning himself more comfortably against the cane.

"Elroy, I am not wed, I have never been wed, and don't plan to be in the near future," Caroline said, heatedly stomping away from him. She stiffened when she heard his low, mocking laugh behind her.

"Guess Daniel will be glad to know that," he said, falling into step beside her, limping. "But I wonder what he'd say if I told him you were at the old St. Clair place? Think he'd be so eager to pass his wealth on to you? Someone who sneaks around behind his back?"

A heated flush rose to Caroline's cheeks. She stopped and turned to boldly face him. She circled her fingers into tight fists. "How would you even know that he doesn't want me there?" she hissed. "Do you eavesdrop, Elroy, as well as pester? You *are* annoying me." She looked up at her uncle's closed shutters, so glad, at least now, that he never gave his consent for them to be opened. If he were witness to this morning's antics, what would he say or do?

Elroy raked his fingers through his long, golden hair. "You have some temper, don't you?" he chuckled. "Miss Burton, after you know me better, you'll discover the teasin' side to me, and hopefully the charmin' side as well."

"Oh!" Caroline said, stomping a foot, now more confused than ever by this man with the obvious split personality. She turned and began hurrying away from him, now truly feeling as though she couldn't trust him. If he told her Uncle Daniel about her visits to St. Clair Manor. . . .

"Caroline! Wait!"

Caroline's insides became a strange melting sweetness when she heard the familiar voice of Gavin St. Clair behind her. She turned on her heel and saw him hurrying her way, past a staring Elroy, to stand directly before her. She looked up into his eyes, nonplussed by his presence there. Yet shouldn't she have expected him? He had shouted apologies to her after her heated departure. Was she ready to accept an apology? Her heart said yes. Her stubbornness said an adamant no.

But then, she had more than apologies to worry about. Oh, lord, what if her Uncle Daniel had heard him shouting for her? How would she be able to explain . . .?

Before even asking Gavin why he was there, and ignoring Elroy's continuing gape, Caroline grabbed Gavin by the elbow and rushed him toward the garden at the back of the house. She would at least have some privacy there in where she could clear up this mess in which she had found herself. What a tangled web it was! It continued to weave its snare around her. Why, oh, why . . .?

"What the hell are you doing?" Gavin demanded, composing himself as she released her wild hold on him. "Is my presence at Twin Oaks all that annoying that you must whisk me away to the garden? Or is it that you don't wish old Daniel to see that we've become acquainted?"

"You are right on *both* counts," Caroline said flatly, trying to catch her breath. She then stood on tiptoe and spoke directly into his face. "Wasn't it enough that you tried to seduce me at St. Clair Manor? I've never been so . . . so . . . humiliated, to think that I seemed to you a woman who would so easily be bedded. Why, I only wanted to . . ."

Gavin's eyes were charged with dark emotion. "You only wanted to *what*?" he asked. "What aren't you telling me?"

Caroline clasped a hand over her mouth, paling. She had almost blurted out to him her *true* reason for being at St. Clair Manor! What was there about him that drew words from inside her? Why couldn't she control the trembling of her hands in his presence? His magnetic gaze was so disturbing, her knees felt as though they might not even hold her up.

She swung away from him and began walking toward the back door of Twin Oaks. This was not the time to try to talk to him. There was too much magnetism between them that she did not understand. When he looked at her some sort of heat starting deep inside her licked little fires throughout her. And by the look in his eyes, she knew that he was experiencing the same.

"Caroline, damn it, stop," Gavin growled, hurrying after her. He grabbed her by her wrist and swung her around to face him. "You're not going to leave me again without first accepting my apology for having behaved like a cad at St. Clair Manor. It'll never happen again. I'm sorry it happened at all."

"Why did you?" she asked, her eyes turning up, drinking in the sight of him, though she hated herself for it. She swallowed hard, not even caring that he still held her in place with a tight grip of his hand. "Surely it was because I appeared to be . . . the . . . sort who would let you."

Gavin was captivated anew by her innocent loveliness. He placed his hands on her cheeks, framing her face, letting his thumbs circle down beneath the delicate curve of her chin. "No," he said thickly, knowing that what he had just spoken had been a part lie. He *had* wondered about a lady who roamed so freely at will in another's house, especially a house that belonged to an unmarried man. He *had* thought she might be an easily bedded romp. But now he felt ashamed for having ever thought so little of her, for she was truly a lady of breeding. He had found that out and now he wanted her even more!

"It was your loveliness that caused me to behave so badly. Only your loveliness," he quickly added. "Please believe me, Caroline. I would be honored to be able to see you again in whatever capacity that you wish, if only that you *would* see me."

He had to fight the urge to kiss her, knowing that to do so would make his words seem a lie. But the sweetness of her lips was beckoning, only to be denied. . . .

Caroline's feelings were raging a battle inside her. She wanted to believe him. Yet, should she trust him enough to say yes to what he asked? And there was her uncle. How could she openly see Gavin without alarming her uncle too much?

No. It seemed impossible, though now that she knew that Gavin would behave only honorably toward her, her heart ached to have to refuse him.

Caroline lowered her eyes. "I think not, Gavin," she murmured. "My uncle comes first just now. And he . . ."

"Caroline, you surely don't mean that," Gavin said, dropping his hands to her waist, drawing her close to him. "Tell me that you don't feel something for me. Deny that you care though we've only just met."

Caroline tried to push his hands away. "Gavin, you promised," she softly cried. "Aren't you a man of your word? Unhand me this instant."

"Being in a garden is not the same as in a bedroom," he growled. "A stolen kiss here is not an invitation to a full seduction. And kiss you I must."

His mouth closed hard upon hers. He drew her into a torrid embrace, crushing her breasts into his chest. A delicious shiver of desire ran through Caroline as he kissed her ardently, weaving a web of rapture around her heart. She felt herself surrendering to him as he anchored her fiercely against him, but a stirring of leaves from somewhere close by jolted her reeling senses to awareness and she knew that someone was watching.

Wrenching herself free, Caroline stood breathless and blush-cheeked, looking wildly about her. And when she saw Elroy in the shadows of a live oak, watching, she felt a slow panic rising inside her. He already knew too much. Oh, if he went to her uncle, she was doomed!

"Gavin, I must go inside to see to my uncle," she

said, rushing on away from him. "Please go home. Please!"

Gavin placed his hands on his hips and stared openly after her, finding it hard to understand her. He had felt her respond to his kiss. But he had seen a strange panic in her eyes and felt that perhaps for now it was best to leave her be. If she felt that her uncle should come first, then how could he fight that? Yet he would not give up so easily.

Running, he caught up with her before she reached the house. Grabbing her gently by a wrist he pulled her around to face him. "I was serious when I asked for your suggestions for renovations at St. Clair Manor," he said thickly. He thrust a key into her hand. "Go anytime, Caroline. The key is yours."

Stunned, Caroline watched him turn and leave. She stared down at the key she held in the palm of her hand, suddenly aware of its meaning. He thought enough of her to entrust her with the key to his mansion. Did this mean that his feelings for her were sincere?

Then her gaze moved slowly upward and toward St. Clair Manor. She folded her fingers over the key, smiling. She could now come and go from St. Clair Manor as she pleased for any reason. She would find that portrait. She would!

Feeling eyes watching her, Caroline looked to her right and found Elroy staring at her. Swallowing hard, she rushed on into the house. Had Elroy seen Gavin give her the key . . .?

# Five

Relieved to finally escape inside Twin Oaks, Caroline stood at the parlor window, getting her breath before going upstairs to check on her uncle. She tried to will herself to be calm, to clear her mind of everything but her duties to her ailing uncle. His days were surely numbered and he depended on her.

Her gaze swept the parlor. Soon this would all be hers. She couldn't feel anything but sadness at the thought. At this moment she wanted anything *but* the responsibilities of such a monstrous house. Though she did love a challenge, she wished it was possible to board the next train to Boston. It would be much simpler than trying to solve a mystery of a lost portrait and a missing aunt.

But she couldn't leave her feelings behind . . . feelings that were now tormented by a man who plagued her every waking moment.

She opened the palm of her hand, seeing proof of why she couldn't put Gavin from her mind. She now had the key to his house! What mysteries would the key unlock for her? Would it even gain her full entry into Gavin's heart?

Closing her fingers about the key, she sighed, again forcing her thoughts from Gavin. The early morning sun slanted away from the windows shrouded with heavy, faded draperies, giving the room a gloomy cast. Its hand-pegged oak floor was bare of carpet, its ceiling was high, and its walls were of bleached pine decorated with tarnished gold and silver hangings.

The room was crowded with massive pieces of oak furniture and upholstered divans and chairs, none of which were to Caroline's liking. The air was close and heavy. She felt all alone and found the silence full of depression and melancholia.

The sound of a horse-drawn buggy approaching outside on the gravel drive caused Caroline's heart to lurch, her thoughts once again on Gavin.

But then she realized that it couldn't be he, for he had just left by foot.

She fled to the dining room whose windows were more accessible to the front drive. Twin chandeliers of Waterford crystal hung majestically at each end of the room. An oak dining table, reeking of a fresh polishing and displaying a fresh bouquet of roses, took up the center of the room. An exquisitely carved cherry sideboard and a china closet stood at the far end of the room, displaying row after row of sparkling china pieces and tall, delicately stemmed crystal glasses that caught the light.

Drawing a drape aside, Caroline peered outward and saw a lone male driving the approaching buggy. She sighed with relief as she recognized Randolph Jamieson, her uncle's lawyer.

He seemed to be a likable enough man, but Caroline hadn't yet talked at length with him. He slipped in and out of Twin Oaks without much flurry, though when he *had* talked with her, she had seen a keen interest in her in his eyes. She would now have to avoid him at all cost. An involvement with one man at this time in her life was more than enough. What would she do if two pursued her?

But at least this man seemed more of the gentlemanly sort, one who most surely wouldn't try to take advantage of her first, then treat her like a true lady second.

The crash of the heavy brass door knocker echoed throughout the house. Caroline waited for Rosa to go to the door to greet the lawyer. When the knocking persisted, she went to the dining room door and leaned out to look both ways down the hallway, yet still did not see Rosa.

To Caroline's chagrin, Rosa persisted in ignoring the banging at the door. Caroline was going to have to go the door after all. Looking down at her attire and seeing mud spattered on her skirt and caked on her shoes, she felt anything but presentable. Even her hair was surely mussed!

But she had no choice but to go to the door, though it was not like Rosa to neglect her duties.

Still clutching the key in her hand, Caroline proceeded down the long, dark hallway. She combed her fingers through her hair and softly bit her lower lip to redden it. Feeling that she was as presentable as possible, she went to the door and flung it open. She smiled warmly at the man outside—a man of her same height, a man who wasn't handsome but who radiated charm in his smooth smile.

Randolph Jamieson was dressed immaculately in a white linen frock coat and beige, double-breasted brocade vest, his white shirt spilling ruffles from beneath a crisp white linen cravat. His brown plaid breeches were sharply creased, breaking over all but the toes of boots that were so polished that one could almost see one's reflection in them.

He carried a fashionable, ivory-topped walking stick in his right hand, and had a brown leather briefcase tucked beneath his left arm. He greeted her with a lift of his leghorn straw hat banded with wide, grosgrain ribbon, revealing collar-length sandy hair prematurely threaded with silver.

He bowed from the waist. "Good morning, ma'am," he said, straightening to smile warmly into her eyes. "It's rare that I have the honor of seeing you, Caroline. You seem to always make yourself scarce when I arrive to discuss business with Daniel. To my pleasure, I am luckier this morning. I must thank Rosa for neglecting her duties."

Caroline felt a blush rise to her cheeks as his gaze slowly raked over her and she saw a look of puzzlement in his pale blue eyes. She now knew to change shoes and skirt before visiting her uncle. The splatters of mud would not only raise his eyebrows, but also his temper should he pull answers from her that she didn't want to reveal.

"I must remember to scold Rosa," Caroline quickly blurted, then hated herself for this slip of the tongue when she saw how shocked Randolph appeared at her bluntness. She must remember that she wasn't dealing with a roguish cad like Gavin St. Clair. Randolph Jamieson was a man who hadn't given her cause for such behavior. He deserved a returned kindness.

Stepping aside, Caroline gestured toward the hallway. "I'm so sorry, Randolph," she apologized. "I seem to have forgotten my manners this morning. First I forget to invite you into Twin Oaks and then I nearly snap your head off with my sharp tongue." She smiled awkwardly. "Please do come in. Is Uncle Daniel expecting you? He failed to mention it to me."

A playful smiled lifted Randolph's lips. "Well, yes and no," he said. "I guess you could say that my visit to Twin Oaks this morning has a dual purpose."

Caroline's eyes widened. "Oh? I see," she murmured, though she didn't and was now quite curious.

Randolph stepped past Caroline and into the house. He placed his hat on a table and left his walking stick leaning against the wall. Turning, he gave her a lingering look. She looked beautiful even in her plain skirt and shirt. Her eyes were as green as the softest moss found in the forest and her lips spoke of hidden passions that surely had not been awakened.

Looking lower he saw how the perfect, ripe outlines of her breasts strained beneath the cotton fabric of her blouse. The war had been long and had denied him the freedom to pick and choose among women. Now he was glad, for now he had met Caroline.

He shifted his briefcase from one arm to the other. "Caroline, I first need to meet with your uncle. Then I wish to talk with you about a ball that I am giving at my plantation."

He began walking toward the staircase with her. "But as I said, I must go and see to your uncle first," he said smoothly. "He's expecting me. I mustn't keep him waiting."

Caroline nodded, but was disappointed that Randolph couldn't tell her about the ball now. Though Randolph Jamieson was not the man to leave her uncle's bedside for, she was intrigued by the mention of a ball. She had kept to herself much too long. Surely it wouldn't hurt to leave Twin Oaks for a few short hours. The thought of wearing a beautiful ball gown and dancing the hours away thrilled and excited her.

Yet she had no feelings whatsoever for Randolph Jamieson and she would not want to make him think that she did by accepting his invitation. Strange how life had its twists. The war had made men scarce when she first ripened into womanhood and now there were more than she could handle!

Rosa came waddling down the stairs, her dark eyes full of apology. She wrung her hands nervously as she looked from Randolph to Caroline. "I'm so sorry, Miss Burton, that I didn't get to the door quickly enough to see to Mr. Jamieson," she said in a flurry of words. "But I was watching my daughter from the upstairs window. She's not herself. She appears ill."

Caroline climbed the stairs beside Randolph, lifting her skirt with her hands. "Sally?" she said, frowning. "What about Sally worries you?"

Rosa's eyes took on images of shadows as she looked from Randolph to Caroline. "I'm not sure what I'm looking for in her behavior," she said thickly. "She's just different, strange somehow."

"Actually, even I thought I saw something different about Sally this morning, Rosa," Caroline said. "She seemed lethargic. Is that what you are talking about, Rosa?"

Randolph stopped momentarily to offer Caroline a hand as they followed Rosa upstairs. Rosa turned.

"Your Uncle Daniel is awake and freshly shaved," Rosa said from across her shoulder, obviously purposely ignoring Caroline's question. "He's been awake for some time, asking for you, Miss Burton."

Caroline stiffened. "And what did you tell him, Rosa, when you found me gone?" she dared to ask, giving Randolph a half glance when she felt his eyes on her. Again she was reminded of her appearance and knew that she must not let her uncle see her now, though she knew that he was probably, at this very moment, still wondering about her strange absence of early this morning. He was used to her checking on him first thing. How could she tell him that she had even done that, but silently, listening to his lazy snores outside his closed door, that having been enough for her to know that he was all right.

She would have to let Rosa make excuses for her while she changed into something more presentable so her uncle wouldn't have the chance to question her about the mud on her shoes and skirt. It had been enough that Randolph had seen and silently wondered!

Rosa stepped up onto the second floor landing and turned and gave Caroline a mischievous grin. "I told your uncle that you were still sleeping," she giggled. "I saw you leave. I knew that you wanted to have time alone. This house is sometimes depressing in its silence. Was I right to not worry your uncle, by not telling him that you were up so early, wandering?"

Caroline sighed with relief. "I appreciate what you did, Rosa," she murmured, stepping away from Randolph as they also reached the second floor. "And, yes, you were right not to worry Uncle Daniel. Though he has, even himself, encouraged me to get out in the sunshine, I fear he worries too much about me when I do."

Randolph cleared his throat. "Rosa, is it all right if I go on into Daniel's room? Is he up to talking business this morning?"

Rosa waddled to Daniel's door, slowly opened it, and peered inside. Then she nodded toward Randolph. "He's as well as can be expected, sir," she murmured. Then she glanced over at Caroline. "But, Miss Burton, maybe you'd best make an appearance first."

Knowing that was the last thing she wanted under the circumstances, Caroline gave Randolph a sweet smile. "You go on ahead," she encouraged, nodding toward the door. "I'm sure Uncle Daniel is more anxious to see you than me. He can see me every day. Please do go on in, Randolph."

"Would you like to see Daniel with me?" Randolph asked, offering Caroline a hand.

Caroline clasped her hands together behind her back. "No. I think not, Randolph," she murmured. "But if you would be so kind, just please inform my uncle that I will be in to see him after you leave."

She looked down at her attire, then back up at Randolph. "I do believe I must change my clothes and shoes. I feel that I have tracked enough mud into the house." She laughed softly, a forced laugh. "These walks that I take around the lagoon must stop. I could quickly ruin several pairs of shoes."

"Not only that," Randolph said hoarsely. "I would think that it would be unwise to leave the Twin Oaks Plantation premises. There are many questionable characters in these parts since the war. Some even make mention of Yanks who still might be hiding out in the swamps and don't even know the war has ended."

He took Caroline's arm. "Someone as pretty as you could attract trouble, Caroline," he said thickly. "Just be careful."

Caroline didn't appreciate his sudden attempt to make himself her keeper. She took a step away from him. "I have always taken quite good care of myself, Randolph," she said dryly. "There is no need for you to concern yourself." She looked toward Uncle Daniel's bedroom door, hoping her uncle hadn't heard the discussion of her wanderings. Yet, since he was partially deaf in his old age, she doubted it.

"It never hurts to have a man worrying over you," Randolph said smugly. He gave her a lingering look which bespoke more than kindness then swung around and disappeared into Daniel's room and closed the door behind him.

"My word . . ." Caroline whispered, raising her hands to her throat. "Men!"

Rosa approached Caroline, smiling warmly. "He's a nice man," she whispered. "And I hear he's quite wealthy. Why, his plantation is one of the finest! Surely you don't mind that he's interested in you, Miss Burton. He would make a fine husband."

"Oh, bother!" Caroline fussed, storming away from Rosa to her bedroom. She placed Gavin's key in a safe place, away from wondering eyes, not even sure yet that she should be glad to have it. She began unbuttoning her blouse as Rosa came bustling after her.

"Rosa, please don't talk anymore of Randolph or *any* men," she fumed. "Just prepare me a hot tub of water and pour a whole bottle of bath oil into it. I want to just soak and relax. I have had quite a trying morning. I hope I don't have more of the same the rest of the day or even tomorrow."

"Yes, ma'am," Rosa said, catching Caroline's clothes as Caroline tossed them away from her.

Wrapping herself into a soft robe, Caroline looked questioningly at Rosa. "Rosa, you never did explain why you are worried about Sally," she said guardedly. "Won't you tell me? Maybe I can help."

Rosa immediately became flustered. Nervously biting her lower lip, she gathered up the last of Caroline's discarded clothes and walked toward the door. Caroline hurried after her and stepped in her way.

"Rosa, why are you acting so mysterious about this?" she questioned. "If something is the matter, perhaps I *can* help. But you'll have to confide in me."

Rosa glanced toward the window, then back to

Caroline. "I don't know myself," she murmured. "It's just that . . . that . . . Sally ain't herself. That's all."

Caroline frowned. "Perhaps Elroy tires her out by keeping her with him so often while he does the chores," she said softly. She patted Rosa on the arm. "But if that's all you're worrying about, I'm sure she's all right. She's quite a healthy three-year-old. Anyone can see that."

Rosa softly shrugged. "Yes. I'm sure I'm being foolish," she said, then walked away, leaving Caroline with her own troubled thoughts. She went to the window and peered toward St. Clair Manor, seeing Gavin's horse reined at the side of the house.

She touched her lips, still feeling his kiss, hungering for another, yet fighting, even fearing her desire. . . .

Randolph eased down into a chair beside Daniel's bed. He opened his briefcase and withdrew a legal document.

"Are the papers in order?" Daniel asked, smiling weakly over at Randolph, his head propped up by a pillow. "You are a man of punctuality. I knew I could count on you. Your father would've been proud of you."

Unfolding the document, Randolph placed it before Daniel. "I've made the minor changes that you requested," he said. "Caroline is assured a future of security, thanks to you, Daniel."

Daniel lifted a shaky hand and pushed the document aside. "My eyes are too weak to read," he grumbled. "Take it away, Randolph. I don't need to read it. I know I can trust you. You *are* your father's son."

Daniel gave Randolph a lingering look, barely able to see him in the dim light of the room. "I've missed having children. Especially sons," he murmured. "But I have Caroline. She's filled the void in my life these past few weeks. She's deserving of my inheritance."

Randolph smiled over at Daniel and placed the

legal document back in his briefcase. "And she's quite a lovely substitute, if you don't mind my saying so," he said.

"It pleases me that you are attracted to her," Daniel said, reaching to pat Randolph's hand. "You see, though the will is written as dictated by me, there are some things left out."

"Oh? Are you saying that you want even more changes?" Randolph asked, lifting an eyebrow quizzically.

Daniel laughed throatily. "No. Not exactly," he said. His eyes gleamed as he caught Randolph's gaze and held it. "I can't have it written into the will that I would hope for Caroline's future to include you. That wouldn't be proper, now would it, Randolph?"

Randolph was not surprised by his announcement. He knew Daniel well. He had grown up knowing Daniel, since Daniel had been his father's best friend. "No, I don't think it would be to Caroline's liking to have you mention me in your will." He chuckled. "Especially since I am the one who has drawn it up." He cleared his throat. "And it will even be I who will eventually present the will to your niece."

"Yes. I understand that would be awkward," Daniel sighed. "But, Randolph, I would rest in peace if I knew you were looking after Caroline's welfare after I am gone. There's much meanness in this world. And she's so frail."

Randolph cocked an eyebrow, envisioning Caroline as he had last seen her. The mud spatters on her skirt and shoes had indicated to him that she was adventurous. "I don't believe you have to worry about Caroline," he said, leaning closer to Daniel. "I don't believe she's as frail as she appears. I'm sure that beneath that dainty facade lies quite a feisty lady."

Daniel's eyes widened. "And why would you say that?" he asked, his voice cracking.

Randolph lifted a shoulder in a casual shrug. "Oh, nothing in particular," he said. "It's just that most tiny women are feisty in one way or another, to make up for their smallness. I imagine Caroline is not the exception. But I wouldn't know. I've yet to be around her all that much."

"And when are you going to change that?" Daniel said in a growl. "As you might notice, I don't keep her tied to my bedposts. She's free to come and go. All you need do is ask."

Randolph straightened his back, and his eyes took on a faraway cast as he focused them on the burning, flickering candle on Daniel's nightstand. "I intend to do just that," he said softly. He gave Daniel a determined look. "Even tonight, Daniel. I intend to invite Caroline to my charity ball. But only if you feel that you could spare her for a few hours."

"Spare her?" Daniel spat. "What do you think I am? A jailor?" He looked toward the closed door. With as much strength he could conjure up he yelled for Rosa. When that didn't get her attention he rang a bell placed beside his bed for that purpose. And when Rosa finally arrived to his room, he ordered her to go for Caroline. . . .

Refreshed and smelling jasmine-sweet, Caroline tied a ribbon in her hair to secure it back from her face. She had replaced the drab skirt and blouse with a low-swept silk dress and a froth of petticoats that lay about her ankles. Her face was pink from its fresh scrubbing, and her bare shoulders gleamed.

When Rosa came into the room, Caroline turned with a start. She knew that Randolph was still on the premises. She had listened and not heard his departing footsteps outside in the hallway.

"I see that you are finished with your bath," Rosa said, nervously twisting the tail of her apron between her fingers.

Caroline's eyebrows lifted at Rosa's uneasiness. "Yes, I guess you can very well see that I am through," she said, laughing softly. "But is that cause for nervousness, Rosa? What's the matter?"

"It's your Uncle Daniel," Rosa said, brushing her

apron down, straightening it. "He's in one of his ranting moods. He's demanded that you come to his room. You'd best go. Now."

Caroline paled. "Did he say why he wanted to see me now?" she murmured. "Isn't Randolph still in my uncle's room? I didn't hear him leave."

"I have no idea why Mr. Burton requests your presence while Randolph is still with him," Rosa said in almost a whine. "But please go on. I don't like it when Mr. Burton yells at me. I fear . . . fear that he might send me away while he's in one of his ugly moods, dismissing me like he has all the others. Even Elroy would be let go then. I just know it. Where . . . where would we go?"

Caroline put her arm about Rosa's thick shoulders and comforted her. "There, there . . ." she sighed. "I'm sure Uncle Daniel meant nothing by yelling at you. I'm sure it's my fault for not having gone to see him yet this morning. Now don't worry, Rosa. I wouldn't let Uncle Daniel send you away. Why, he wouldn't even want to. You're the only one who has ever pleased him. He knows this. Please don't worry so."

"Just go on, Miss Burton," Rosa continued to fuss. "Just do as he wants."

Caroline stepped away from Rosa, her eyes filled with worry. "Why would he want me now, while Randolph is still there?" she murmured. "Perhaps he sees a need to change his will? Why else?"

"I don't know. Just please go," Rosa urged.

Caroline nodded and left the room. The chance that her uncle might change the will did not disturb her. She had never liked to think about acquiring wealth because of someone's death. Though she had accepted the fact that she was going to be the one to inherit Daniel Burton's estate, she hadn't labored over it, feeling no way in particular about it. She had only been concerned about her uncle's welfare upon her arrival at Twin Oaks. She hadn't expected to be sidetracked by a portrait and Gavin St. Clair. . . .

Stepping up to her uncle's door, she paused to get her breath, feeling more shaken than she had thought herself to be at the thought of seeing him while Randolph Jamieson looked on. She didn't want an audience if her uncle was in a scolding mood!

Her chin held high, she hurried on, squinting as she entered the dimly lit room. A candle burned beside her uncle's bed, providing only enough light for her to see Randolph Jamieson sitting dutifully beside the bed and her Uncle Daniel propped up by pillows, his green eyes following her entrance and slow approach to his side.

"So you have finally awakened?" Daniel growled, lifting a bony hand and offering it to her as she reached the bed. He glanced over at Randolph. "We have us a sleeping beauty here, don't we, son?"

Randolph gave Caroline a knowing look, then smiled slowly. "Yes. I guess you might say that." He stood, offering Caroline his chair. "But perhaps it's best that she got added rest today. It could give her more energy for, let's say, the upcoming ball at my plantation?"

Caroline nodded in thanks to Randolph as she eased down into the chair. She took her uncle's gaunt hand affectionately in hers. "I hope I didn't alarm you too much by my absence, Uncle Daniel," she murmured. "I didn't mean to cause you any undue worry. I'm sorry."

"Rosa explained," he grumbled, his green eyes flashing. "But I did miss seein' you, hon. You know how snappish I get when I worry."

Caroline giggled. "Yes, Rosa said that you weren't in your best of moods," she said, giving Randolph a half glance. She decided not to respond to his invitation to the ball just yet. She didn't want to appear anxious. She first had to know if her uncle truly approved. More than that, she had to know that he was well enough for her to leave him.

"Let's not talk about my moods," Daniel growled, eyeing Caroline with almost an evil glint. "I think

Randolph has something to say to you, Caroline." He looked over at Randolph and gave him a slow wink. "Don't you, Randolph?"

Randolph straightened his cravat. He scooted a chair beside Caroline's and sat down. "As I mentioned earlier, I'm giving a ball at my plantation," he said, eyeing her speculatively. "It's in truth a charity ball, as the monies from those who contribute will be distributed among the poor of Charleston who are still struggling because of the aftermath of the war."

He implored Caroline with a steady stare. "It would greatly please me if you would come as my personal guest. I would see to it that you would enjoy yourself. I would introduce you around to my friends and to those who know and admire Daniel."

"Yes, Caroline, you must go," Daniel interjected, nodding. "It will do you good, mixing with those of your own age. You stay cooped up too much here at Twin Oaks. And you would not find an escort more pleasant than Randolph. So the decision is made. You will go."

"Uncle Daniel, it is so kind of you to want me to go," she said softly. "And I would love to attend Randolph's ball. But don't you see? I mustn't travel that far from Twin Oaks. You need me here, to watch after you."

She looked over at Randolph, feeling pulled in two directions . . . wanting to attend the ball, and yet ashamed for wanting to leave her uncle for a full evening. "Randolph, it is commendable of you to help the poor by planning such a ball, but I hope you understand why I must be sure that it is all right with Uncle Daniel that I attend. He comes first. Always."

Randolph's face shadowed, for he knew that earlier this morning Caroline's uncle hadn't been foremost on her mind. What had she been up to? Was she the restless sort?

Daniel's green eyes flashed. "Hogwash!" he scolded. "There's no need for you to play nursemaid to me. Go to the ball, Caroline. I insist."

"I would love to go," Caroline said anxiously. "But only if you truly don't mind, Uncle Daniel." She knew that she wanted to go for more reasons than one. She hoped to see Gavin. She even secretly wished that Gavin had invited her instead of Randolph.

But Randolph was giving the charity ball, not Gavin. Gavin probably didn't have a charitable bone in his body! The only reason he had given her the key to his mansion was surely for his own selfish gains. She must remember that. Always.

Daniel flailed a hand in the air. "Then go, damn it," he shouted. He nodded at Randolph. "She's going. You can count on it."

"Good. Good," Randolph said, smiling over at Caroline. He then pulled a slim gold watch from his waistcoat pocket and consulted it. He rose from the chair, slipping the watch back into his pocket. "I must be going. Caroline, I will send details of the ball by messenger very soon. I am so pleased that you will be attending. All the men there will be in awe of you."

Blushing, Caroline rose from her chair. She offered Randolph a hand but felt nothing when he kissed it. "I look forward to the evening," she murmured. "Thank you for inviting me."

"It's my pleasure," he said, tucking his briefcase beneath his left arm. He gave Daniel an easy handshake, then walked to the door. "Don't bother to see me to the door, Caroline. That won't be necessary. I can see my own way out. You just spend some time with Daniel. That's what's important."

"Yes. I guess I've neglected Uncle Daniel too much today," she said, smiling down at Daniel.

"I will see you soon, Caroline," Randolph said. "Take care of yourself, Daniel."

Daniel grumbled a reply, then closed his eyes, yet too stubborn to confess his weariness.

"Should I leave you now so that you can have a quick nap?" Caroline asked, sensing that too much conversation had weakened him.

"No. I don't need a nap," Daniel snapped, forcing

his eyes open again. "If I slept any more during the day, I'd turn into a damn owl."

Caroline giggled, then grew sober. "Are you sure about my attending the ball?" she asked softly.

"Caroline, how many times do I have to tell you that you must mingle?" he scolded. "You're young. You're beautiful. You would be the belle of the ball. You *must* attend. Though I wouldn't be there, personally, to show you off, everyone would know that you are my niece."

He begged her with pleading green eyes. "You will go," he said in a softer tone. "You'll go for *me*. I want everyone to see you, to know that you're my beautiful niece."

"All right," she said. "And I do look forward to it."

Daniel closed his eyes peacefully. His head bobbed as he fell into a restful sleep. Caroline eased his head down onto the bed and drew his quilt snugly beneath his chin. Her thoughts strayed to Gavin. Would he be at the ball? She knew that she shouldn't want to see him again, but deep down where her desires were formed, she knew that she couldn't lie to herself and say that she desired less than being with him again. . . .

# Six

*E*verything had been readied for Caroline's evening at the ball. Rosa had pressed her gown, jewels had been chosen, and Caroline's hair had been washed. But the waiting was unnerving Caroline. It was early afternoon. The house was quiet. Caroline had just checked on her uncle and found that he was asleep. She now stood in her bedroom studying Gavin's key which she held in the palm of her hand. She still hadn't used it. Perhaps this was the time. It could be a way to pass a few restless hours. And she still hadn't been able to put the mystery of the portrait from her mind.

In a walking dress with its looped up skirt long in back but up to the ankles in front, Caroline rushed away from Twin Oaks. The day was gray, the wind was whistling through the distant pines, and the air was cold and clammy. Her hair blew in the breeze, her nose crinkled in distaste. Her hands were cold and tight.

But the sight of little Sally playing among the flowers in the garden drew Caroline's lips into a pleasant smile. The child surely wasn't ill. She seemed so vitally alive this morning. Her heart warmed when Sally waved to her. She returned the wave, then hurried onward, leaving the security of Twin Oaks and its grounds behind her.

She passed by St. Clair Manor's boarded-up stable

doors and found herself at the mansion's front door. Stepping up on the porch, Caroline reached inside her skirt pocket and removed the key, a sense of uneasiness hovering over her. Though Gavin had given her not only his permission to enter the manor but also the use of the key, she still felt like an intruder. And how lonely the wind sounded, as though it was in search of a lost soul as it whistled around the corners of the house.

With trembling fingers she struggled with the key, then sighed in relief when the door finally creaked open. Dropping the key back inside her pocket, she tiptoed into the vast hallway and stood peering around her. Shadows and silence seemed to close in on her. A shutter banged. She jumped nervously. She could hear the pounding of her blood in her ears.

But her determination to explore drove her onward. She lit a branch of candles, and each flame reached out to light the darkest corners of the hall. But even with the warm glow of the candles lighting her way, Caroline couldn't shake the sense of evil lurking all about her.

She couldn't imagine why Gavin would want to live in this house. She knew that she couldn't. The very sight of it made her flesh crawl with chills.

She looked slowly about her, wondering where to search first for the portrait. The shadows and silence seemed to close in on her, and she again wondered about Gavin and why he had been so eager to give her the key. What kind of advice would he expect her to give him on renovations?

But she hadn't come to St. Clair Manor for that purpose. Once she found what she was after she would never go to St. Clair Manor again. And she would tell Gavin exactly that, when he asked.

Unable to control her trembling and fearful of this gloomy monstrosity of a house and its past secrets, she went into the parlor. To her surprise, everything had been rearranged. The room even had an empty

look to it. Then she realized this was because some of
the furniture was missing.

Wondering about the other rooms, Caroline went
back into the hall and tried another door which
opened into the library. It seemed untouched. And
then something caught her eye. She went to the desk
and found several bolts of material and a catalog of
wallpaper samples.

Caroline smiled, turning the pages of the catalog.
Suddenly, helping Gavin didn't seem so undesirable.
She liked the new smell of the bolts of material and
she enjoyed looking at the wallpaper samples. It
wasn't hard to envision herself pointing out different
samples to Gavin, seeing if their likes and dislikes
were the same.

It wasn't hard to see herself measuring windows for
drapes. It could be fun, even rewarding. . . .

A sudden noise behind Caroline drew her quickly
around. She paled when she saw Elroy standing in the
doorway, staring at her.

"Elroy!" she gasped. "What are you doing here?"

"I could ask the same of you," he said flatly.

"I had a key," Caroline snapped. "How did you get
in?"

Elroy nodded in the direction of the front door.
"The door was open." He shrugged. "I walked right
in."

"You shouldn't have," Caroline said icily, now
recalling that she had left the front door ajar. "You're
trespassing, Elroy."

"And you're not?" Elroy said, limping on into the
room, leaning against his cane. "Oh, I forgot for a
minute. You said you had a key." He went to the desk
and ran his hand over a bolt of fabric. "So *this* is why
you've got a key. Gavin St. Clair gave it to you. You're
helpin' him choose fabrics for drapes, aren't you?"

"What I do or why I do it is none of your business,"
Caroline said, fuming.

Elroy's eyes danced as he looked over at Caroline.

He laughed sarcastically. "Maybe it's none of my business," he said. "But I bet your Uncle Daniel would think it was his."

In her anger Caroline had forgotten to worry about the threat that Elroy posed. "You wouldn't," she gasped, paling, remembering the other time Elroy had threatened to tell Uncle Daniel about her having been at St. Clair Manor.

"Why shouldn't I?" Elroy said, shrugging.

Caroline went to him. She pleaded with her eyes. "You mustn't tell him," she said, her voice weak. "Please don't tell him. He's not a well man."

"It ain't my problem. I only came here to look for Sally. She's always chasin' your uncle's damn cat," Elroy growled. "I'd best get back to my chores."

"Then you won't tell him?" Caroline asked, hating to be put in the position of taking Elroy into her confidence in any capacity. But it was necessary. She wouldn't want to be forced to explain to her uncle why she persisted in going to St. Clair Manor. If news of the portrait reached his ears, it could even be fatal.

"Maybe I will . . . maybe I won't," Elroy taunted.

Frustrated, Caroline followed him to the door and out onto the porch. Her gaze went immediately to Sally. She was squealing, running, and chasing Princess. When Sally saw her father she obediently took his hand and walked away with him, giving Caroline and Princess a look from across her shoulder.

Caroline took a second quick look at Sally as their eyes locked. Though Sally was full of energy, there was now something strange about her eyes. But Sally turned her eyes too quickly away for Caroline to study them further.

"Miss Burton, you'd best get back to Twin Oaks, don't you think?" Elroy shouted from over his shoulder. "We don't want to worry ol' Daniel, do we?"

Caroline tensed. She wanted to shout angrily back at him but knew that she mustn't do anything to cause him to go to her uncle and tell of his discovery. Instead, she went back inside the house and looked slowly about her. Its utter bleakness robbed her of the brief pleasant thoughts she had experienced while admiring the bolts of fabric and wallpaper samples.

A scraping noise overhead caused her to jump with fright. She moved her gaze slowly upward, then inched her way backward to the door. A low whistling noise then drew her eyes to the parlor. And when the sound grew more pronounced, Caroline turned and stumbled out to the porch, hardly able to steady her fingers enough to lock the door.

She turned with a start, her eyes wide with fright. The whistling sound seemed to have followed her from the house. She stiffened and looked about her, then sighed with relief as she suddenly realized that it was only the wind, blowing from around the corner of the house, so hard it lifted her skirt almost to her knees.

Laughing nervously, she ran across the lawn and past the rusted fence, anxious to leave this ghostly manor behind her. But she still must return. She hadn't yet looked for the missing portrait!

The hours had passed quickly enough after Caroline's return to Twin Oaks. Upon looking into the mirror and seeing herself dressed in her sumptuous gown of green satin, Caroline was even more anxious to attend the ball. Perhaps she could forget the portrait and St. Clair Manor. Perhaps she could even forget the dread that accompanied her at night. The nightmares! Surely after a night filled with a gay crowd she wouldn't be plagued by another foreboding dream.

She whirled away from the mirror and grabbed her lace-trimmed cashmere shawl. Why did she have to think of the nightmares now? Why did the portrait continue to haunt her? Why did St. Clair Manor obsess her?

But finding the portrait wouldn't put an end to her wondering about St. Clair Manor. Not since she had been kissed by Gavin St. Clair, its owner!

Swirling back around, she gazed at her reflection in the mirror. If Gavin were at the ball, would he approve of how she looked? Her shining hair fell from a center part into long coils of red, her smooth, bare shoulders were gleaming, her eyes and sensually cut lips bright.

The bodice of her dress dipped low, displaying her full breasts, and a glittering diamond necklace and delectable diamond earrings with long, graceful pendants, chosen from her aunt's fine collection of jewels, sparkled against her skin.

Lace draped the skirt and bodice of her dress, matching the edging on her lovely shawl. Her froth of lacy petticoats swayed provocatively as she swung away from the mirror, hearing a carriage approaching Twin Oaks.

Having received word that Randolph would be sending his own private carriage for her, Caroline swept her jeweled handbag up anxiously and hurried out into the hallway. She knew that she had to bid her uncle good night before she left. And wouldn't his eyes shine when he saw her lovely attire?

Quietly opening his door, Caroline peered inside the dark room and looked at the fragile figure lying beneath a layer of blankets on the huge bed. Never had he looked as small, as he did now. It seemed that he became smaller each day, as his skin continued to draw more tautly over his aged bones.

Caroline tensed when she heard her uncle suddenly gasp for breath. And when she saw his hands emerge from the covers and flail in the air, as though fighting some unseen villain, she knew that he was in some sort of agony. He was having trouble breathing! Perhaps he was even dying!

Panic rose inside Caroline. Her heart pounded against her ribs and her knees grew weak as she rushed into the room. Dropping both her shawl and purse on the foot of the bed, she went to her uncle and threw his blankets quickly away from him. She lifted his head from the pillows, now seeing the wildness in his eyes and the paleness of his lips as he continued to gasp for air. He began clutching at her arms, fear etched across his face, his cheeks and eyes so sunken that he already looked dead!

"Uncle Daniel!" Caroline softly cried. "Oh, what am I to do?"

And then his breathing became more controlled and his eyes lost some of their fear. Caroline eased him back onto his pillows. She reached for a cloth, wet it in a basin of water, and began bathing his perspiration-laced brow. She sighed heavily, relieved to see that whatever sort of spell he had just had, had passed. She smiled warmly down at her uncle as she felt his eyes assess her appearance.

"Caroline," he growled in a weakened voice. "What are you doing here? You're supposed to be at Randolph's ball. You're dressed for it. What is detaining you?"

"Uncle Daniel, the carriage has only just arrived," she said, wiping away the slow stream of spittle that was running from the corner of his mouth. "I had come in to say good night when I found you . . . having difficulty breathing." Her eyes implored him. "Uncle, what was the matter? Can you explain to me what caused the problem? I was so afraid for you."

He patted her hand reassuringly. "There is no cause for alarm," he softly laughed. "Old men like me just sometimes have these spells. As you saw, they quickly pass. Nothing to worry your pretty head over."

Caroline placed the cloth back in the basin, then drew her uncle's blankets back up and over him, resting them just beneath his chin. "Nothing to worry about?" she softly argued, wanting to tell him that he himself had worn a mask of panic while struggling to get his breath.

But she understood he did not want to reveal his true fear of approaching death. She would not let him know that she had seen it in his eyes. She knew that he was too proud. She would not destroy his pride!

"I'm as fit as a fiddle," he boasted, licking his

parched lips. "Now you get along with yourself, young lady. This night was made for you. You go and show everybody just how pretty and sweet you are, do you hear?"

Caroline drew up a chair beside the bed. "Uncle Daniel, I've decided to not go," she said, smoothing out the lines of her gown, now feeling remorseful that it and the time she had spent on her appearance had been wasted. But her uncle still came first. He was the reason that she was in the Carolinas. She mustn't ever forget that.

Daniel shakily lifted his head from his pillows. His eyes were two narrow slits of green. "What do you mean . . . you're . . . not going?" he stormed. He lifted a hand from beneath his blankets and pointed to the door. "Caroline, you leave. This minute. Didn't you say the carriage has arrived? What has changed your mind?"

She couldn't tell him it was because of him, yet she knew that he would know, without her even saying so. "I've just decided that I don't wish to go," she softly argued. "It's as simple as that, Uncle Daniel."

Rosa came into the room, looking meekly from Daniel to Caroline. "The carriage has arrived," she said. "I've told the driver that you will be down in a moment's time, Miss Burton."

Caroline rose from her chair and touch Rosa gently on an arm. "Please go and inform the driver that I won't be going," she half whispered. "It's Uncle Daniel. He just had some sort of spell. I fear leaving him."

"What sort of spell?" Rosa asked, her eyes full of concern.

"He had some sort of trouble breathing," Caroline said, flinching when her uncle began shouting at her.

"What's the whispering about?" he fumed.

"Go ahead, Rosa," Caroline whispered harshly. "Send the carriage away. I have no choice *but* to stay here with my uncle."

"Yes, ma'am," Rosa said, then rushed on away leaving Caroline alone to deal with her uncle.

Straightening her shoulders and emitting a trembling breath, Caroline returned to Daniel's bedside and met his challenging glare. She listened sadly to the carriage wheels rumbling away from Twin Oaks. It was as though her heart was traveling with the carriage. She had looked forward to possibly seeing Gavin at the ball. Yet if she did meet him, it could prove dangerous under the scrutiny of Randolph Jamieson. He could report back to her uncle. But surely he wouldn't. He wouldn't have cause to!

"Caroline, don't treat me as if I'm senile," Daniel said, reaching to take her hand in his. "As you know, I still have my full faculties. Now tell me, what were you and Rosa discussing so quietly?"

"I told her to send the carriage away," Caroline said, watching and waiting for another explosion from her uncle.

"You did that, knowing how I feel about you attending the ball?" Daniel said, dropping his hand away from Caroline, hurt dissolving his anger. He looked away from her, silent.

"Uncle Daniel?" Caroline murmured, leaning over, touching him softly on his withered hand. "Are you all right?" She couldn't believe his reaction. She would rather have him shout at her than have him look like such a wounded puppy. It was quite pitiful.

Caroline lay his hand gently aside and rose to go to the other side of the bed. She took his face in her hands and forced their eyes to meet. "Uncle, I'm sorry," she murmured. "I didn't mean to hurt your feelings. But the carriage has already been sent away. There's nothing I can do about it now."

"It's not too late, Caroline," Daniel said, his voice strained and weak. "Elroy can drive you to Randolph's. Just inform Rosa to tell Elroy to get the buggy ready."

"Elroy?" Caroline paled, remembering the after-

noon at St. Clair Manor much too vividly. The farther
she kept from Elroy the better. She didn't wish to give
him any cause to go to her uncle and reveal the secrets
she wished to keep hidden. Oh, this practice of deceit
was so wearying!

"Yes. Elroy," Daniel said, eyeing her suspiciously.
"Do I sense a dislike for Elroy on your part, Caroline?"

"No. None at all," she quietly said, not wanting to
give her uncle cause to question Elroy.

"Then do as I say. Let Elroy take you to the ball,"
he demanded.

"All right," she murmured, still not relishing the
thought of being with Elroy for any length of time,
especially after the black cloak of night had fallen.
There was much about him that made her greatly
uneasy. Yet she knew that her feelings were unwar-
ranted. He had done nothing except flirt, and that she
was fast growing to expect from Southern gentlemen!

"Leave immediately, Caroline," Daniel grumbled,
quickly becoming his old self. "And have yourself a
good time!"

Caroline gave him a weary look. She wanted to ask
if he truly thought that he would be all right, yet knew
that it would only anger him again should she ask.

She gave him a nervous smile, lowered a soft kiss
onto his cheek, then grabbed her purse and shawl and
hurried from the room to make the necessary prepara-
tions.

After she was in the buggy and driving beneath a
large canopy of live oaks, she was glad again that she
would attend the ball. There was no denying the thrill
that raced through her at the thought of possibly
seeing Gavin.

"So you're mixin' with the most affluent of Charleston tonight, are you?" Elroy asked, interrupting Caroline's deep thoughts. "Needin' to get away from old
Daniel, are you? Or are you needin' the attentions of a
man?"

Elroy looked over his shoulder from the driver's

seat of the buggy. His gaze revealed that he approved of Caroline, sitting so delicately in the spill of the moonlight. "You need look no farther, Caroline. I'm your man." He laughed.

His boisterous laughter and teasing manner quickly unnerved Caroline. She stiffened and ignored him, not wishing to have any sort of discussion with him.

"Too good for Elroy, ain'tcha?" Elroy accused, snapping the reins loudly against the sleek, black horse leading the buggy. "Let me tell you, before the war I got many a lady lookin' my way. Now I don't, 'cause of this damn lame leg. Is that why you look on past me as though I don't exist? 'Cause I'm lame?"

Caroline's face flushed red. "Elroy, please . . ." she scolded. "Just drive? There's no need for this sort of conversation between us. You have a wife and a sweet little girl. Isn't that enough?"

He squinted his eyes as he again looked at Caroline over his shoulder. "Don't know when a body is teasin', do you?" He chuckled. "That's what it was. Just teasin'."

Flustered, Caroline squirmed on the seat, thinking she would never understand this man's complex personality. What he called teasing, she called flirting. And neither amused or suited her! It seemed that most of his words were edged with sarcasm. She had to remind herself that he had cause to be bitter. The war had left many scars emotionally and physically on his person.

The sight of bright lights ahead emanating from a magnificent house with high, white columns and wide verandas, the many reined horses and beautiful, stately carriages, made Caroline scoot to the edge of her seat, quickly forgetting her annoyances with Elroy. At this moment she realized just how much she had needed to get away from Twin Oaks. Her heart hummed with joy, it seemed, and her pulse raced briskly onward!

And as the buggy drew her even closer, she began scanning the other arriving guests. She was watching for a tall man whose dark hair matched his even darker eyes.

And then apprehension washed through her, as she wondered if Gavin were here, would he be in the company of another woman? Just the thought of it ate away at her heart. She prayed that it wouldn't be so. She wanted the opportunity to face him on what could be called neutral territory. Perhaps even dance with him! Of course that wasn't in her *uncle's* plans. But he wasn't here, was he, to guide her every whim and movement?

When she saw a beautiful roan stallion approaching, Caroline's breath was stolen momentarily away. She quickly recognized Gavin. He looked handsomer than ever beneath the mystical glow of the moonlight.

Caroline's gaze moved slowly over him, fully absorbing his presence. She was glad that he was not escorting a lady to the ball. He was dressed expensively in a dark frock coat and matching breeches, the white spill of ruffles at his throat making the darkness of his face even more pronounced. As always, he was hatless, his midnight-black hair slightly wind blown. And as he drew even closer, Caroline could see his straight, aristocratic nose, full, sensual lips, and square jaw.

Then he disappeared from her sight as Elroy crowded the horse and buggy between two others before Gavin had the opportunity to see her.

But she had been lucky enough to see him and to know that he had come alone. Surely, once inside they would meet and perhaps even dance.

Smiling, Caroline let Elroy help her from the buggy. Nodding in thanks to him, she climbed the wide, marble front stairway of Randolph's stately mansion and then was immediately swept into a room of music, dancing, and laughter.

# *Seven*

$A$s she was escorted by Randolph around the room filled with beautifully dressed women in luscious gowns, and handsomely attired gentlemen, some of them even wearing swallow-tailed coats, Caroline searched for Gavin. Disappointment assailed her, as she failed to find him standing at the outer edges of the massive room yet she was relieved not to see him among those crowded in the center of the floor, dancing.

"I had thought you had changed your mind about attending my ball, Caroline," Randolph said, glancing admiringly down at her. "I received word that Daniel had worsened. Does your presence mean that he is better? How did you then arrange transportation here?"

Caroline laughed softly. "Randolph, please," she said. "Just one question at a time. My head is already spinning from the activity all about me. Your ball has drawn so many guests and your house is so very charming."

"I'm glad you approve of my home," he said, smiling. Her loveliness was quite distracting. "It was built in 1800 by my grandfather, with profits made from shipping cotton to England. It just recently became mine, upon the death of my father."

"I didn't know of your recent loss, Randolph," Caroline said, casting him a heavy-lashed look. "Your mother? Does she live here with you?"

"No. She passed away some time ago," he said thickly. "This house is mine. Its emptiness leaves much to be desired."

"You inquired about my uncle's health," she quickly said, sensing this conversation was leading in a direction she wanted to avoid. She did not want to delude him into believing she could fill the emptiness left behind by the death of his parents. "He is not as well as he should be. I fear that I have even made a mistake by coming tonight."

Again, she searched through the crowd for Gavin, yet still did not see him. Had her eyes played tricks on her earlier? Had she not seen Gavin's roan stallion? Had she only wished to see Gavin . . .?

"I'm sure you have no need to worry yourself about Daniel," Randolph encouraged, lifting a forefinger to her chin to get her attention "I'm sure he's much improved or you wouldn't have left his bedside."

Caroline nodded, smiling. "Yes, I hope I used good judgment," she murmured. "It is such a delight to be here. It's been so long since I've allowed myself such entertainment."

Randolph's eyes gleamed into hers. "I gather then it's been awhile since you've danced?" he questioned smoothly.

"It's been forever." Caroline laughed.

"Then you need wait no longer," Randolph said, offering her an arm. "We shall dance now."

Caroline smiled up at him, then let her gaze travel over him. He was dressed for this night's festive occasion in a suit of crisp linen and a white ruffled shirt, worn with a gold brocade vest. His gray-splashed, sandy hair was combed to perfection, and he smelled of an expensive man's cologne. All of this should have made any woman's heart sing, except that for Caroline, he was the wrong man.

But she did wish to dance. She wanted to take part in this evening's excitement. And by dancing she would be able to move about the room and look for Gavin. "Yes, I would love to dance," she said.

Having left her shawl and purse with the butler who had met her arrival into this grand antebellum home, Caroline was free to lift the tail of her skirt with one hand, and to place the other on Randolph's shoulder. She began twirling around the dance floor to the light and airy waltzes being played by a four-stringed quartet at the far end of the room.

She smiled yet couldn't truly enjoy herself until she found Gavin. Even now her eyes searched among the crowd for him. But all that she saw were the gorgeous dresses spinning around her, the brilliance of the hundreds of candles glowing in the many hanging, crystal chandeliers, and the magnificence of the room's decor.

This mansion had its own ballroom. Extravagant gilded plasterwork along the walls depicted musical instruments and cherubs performing and dancing. Bronze busts graced the room. High-ceilinged, it also boasted paintings, sculptures, and long windows hung with luxurious gold velvet draperies.

Impressed, but only vaguely so, since her family had never been one to want for anything, Caroline continued to watch for signs of Gavin.

And then her heart lurched as the dancers were forced to move aside to make room for Gavin. He seemed to have emerged from out of nowhere and was now walking determinedly toward her and Randolph.

His dark pools of eyes made Caroline's blood begin to heat. And as he stepped up to Randolph and tapped on his shoulder, her face flamed with color. She awaited Randolph's reaction.

Drawing Caroline possessively to his side, Randolph smiled up at Gavin. "Well, if it isn't my competition," he said, chuckling.

Caroline's eyes widened and her heart skipped a beat. Competition? Did Randolph already know about Gavin's interest in her . . .?

"And how is business, Gavin?" Randolph added. "Have you argued any new cases lately?"

Caroline gaped at Gavin, then back at Randolph.

*Now* what was Randolph referring to? Was Gavin also . . . a . . . lawyer . . . ?

Gavin's eyes didn't leave Caroline. "I keep busy enough," he said. "And you?"

"I've had my fair share of cases also," Randolph said. He glanced down at Caroline, then looked slowly back up at Gavin, sensing a strain between them. Had they met? "But I've been devoting a lot of my time lately to Daniel Burton. But, of course, you know him. Your properties join."

"Yes. I know Daniel Burton," Gavin said, nodding. "And also his niece."

"Oh? You and Caroline have met?" Randolph said, nervously fidgeting with his cravat. He already knew the answer to his question by just watching the vibrations being exchanged between Caroline and Gavin.

"Yes. We have met," Gavin said throatily. "And it would please me if she would dance with me."

As though in a trance, forgetting everyone and everything but the unspoken passion in Gavin's eyes, Caroline moved easily away from Randolph and into Gavin's arms. She only half heard Randolph's gasp of humiliation. The only thing of which she was fully aware was the pressure of Gavin's fingers at her waist and around one hand and his hypnotic smile as he began gliding her about the floor, skillfully guiding her around the other dancers.

This moment was what dreams were made of. Caroline's head was spinning with delight, and her heart was racing. To her, Gavin was the only man in this room of many. Expensively dressed in his dark frock coat, the white spill of ruffles at his throat causing the darkness of his face and eyes to be more pronounced, he was no longer the man of mystery to her. He was the man she loved.

"You are full of surprises," Gavin said, smiling coyly down at her. "I never know where I'll run into you next. First at my mansion and now Randolph

Jamieson's? What about your ailing uncle? Or doesn't he know you're here either?"

His sudden sarcasm cut through the magic of the moment like a knife. Caroline looked questioningly up at him, then wrenched her way free and began pushing her way through the dancers. She had been wrong to delude herself into believing there could be anything special between her and Gavin. His sarcasm reminded her of her initial feelings about him when they had first met. He was a most unlikable man . . . a man she could do without!

Nothing was as she had planned. She held her chin high and left the room, and just as she raised a hand to summon the butler to bring her shawl and purse so she could return to Twin Oaks, she felt a strong hand grasp her by the wrist. Breathless, she felt herself being forced around.

When she found that it was Gavin, she glowered up at him. She tried to jerk her wrist free from his grip. "Unhand me," she hissed. "Can't you see that I want to leave? I've had enough of your insinuations. How dare you imply *anything* about me. Who do you think you *are*?"

Eyes flaming with anger, she tossed her head haughtily and looked over his shoulder toward the ballroom. "Go back to the ball," she said dryly. "Surely you can find yourself a charming dance partner . . . one who wishes to have you in her company as you see that I don't."

"Before you or I go anywhere, we have to talk," he said, his voice low, yet filled with determination.

"I don't know what about," Caroline hissed, again struggling to set her wrist free, but only succeeding in causing it to pain her. She nodded in the direction of the laughter and music. "Time is wasting, Gavin. Some pretty thing just might slip right through your fingers if you don't hurry back to the ball."

Gavin stepped to her side and locked his arm about her waist. He guided her to the double doors that opened to one of the many verandas. "To hell with anyone but you," he spat. "Caroline, I want some answers and by damn you are going to give them to me."

Caroline squirmed, trying to move away from his side, though his touch was causing her insides to blossom with a sensual warmth. "I don't know what you're talking about," she argued, though softly, trying to keep attention from being drawn their way. "What sort of answers? Gavin, please just let me go."

Gavin led her out onto the veranda and upon finding it fully occupied by other couples, guided her on down a short flight of steps and out into a formal, sunken garden boasting hedges trimmed with all the art of an English country home. The moonlight spilled its softness through a splashing fountain surrounded by roses and azaleas, which gave off an aroma similar to expensive French perfume.

Steel arms enfolded Caroline as Gavin swept her around to totally face him. "I thought you said that you had to stay at Twin Oaks because of your uncle," he said sharply. "And then I find you here, dancing with Randolph Jamieson. Why, Caroline? You refused to accept my invitation to acquaint you with the city of Charleston, yet I find you here with Randolph. What aren't you telling me? Do you find my company so intolerable? I would have to doubt that from the way you returned my kisses."

Caroline's heart soared. Now she fully understood why he had been so sarcastic while dancing with her, and the reason made her almost radiant. He was jealous of Randolph.

She smiled coyly up at him. "A glamorous ball is much better than a tour of a war-torn city," she teased. "Surely you can understand why I would choose the one over the other. Can't you, Gavin?"

"By choosing to attend the ball, you have chosen Randolph Jamieson over me," he argued, his arms tightening, drawing her even closer. "I must see to it that that doesn't happen again. I don't think that he can offer you *this*."

His lips stung hers as he kissed her with a fierce, possessive passion. She was fast becoming consumed by a sweet dizziness that caused her to return the kiss, even lace her arms about his neck. His scent was intoxicating, a manly combination of the outdoors and cologne, and his touch was like a brand, telling her that she was his as he spun his silver web of magic around her.

"Caroline," Gavin whispered. "Now tell me that you prefer Randolph's company over mine."

"Gavin, it wasn't a matter of my choosing you or him," she murmured, melting beneath his heated stare. "It was my Uncle Daniel. *He* wanted me to come. He has worried about my being cooped up at Twin Oaks. He doesn't know that I've wandered on my daily strolls as far as St. Clair Manor."

"And why haven't you confessed this to him?" Gavin growled. "Why would being with me have to be kept such a secret?"

Caroline cast her eyes downward. "It's not you," she softly explained. "It is your uncle. My Uncle Daniel didn't approve of him nor his, shall I say, occupation as an artist who had women coming and going freely from his house."

Her eyes raised, soft and green in the misty moonlight. "He warned me to stay away from St. Clair Manor, so I must at least pretend to have obeyed," she added. "That's the way it must be, Gavin. I can't do anything to upset my uncle."

She let a low smile lift her lips. "I would imagine that my uncle would throw quite a fit should he find out that you and I have more than just become mere speaking acquaintances," she said, giggling. "You see, he surely would think that you were poured from the same mold as your uncle."

Again she lowered her eyes. "And perhaps he would be right," she softly said. "I have seen the roguish side of you, you know."

"And I do believe that I apologized for my behavior that morning at St. Clair Manor," Gavin said hoarsely. "And if I remember correctly, you accepted the apology."

She let herself again become consumed by passion when she chose to let her eyes lock with his. "Yes, I did, but manners so lacking are hard for a lady to forget," she murmured. "But I promise to try harder, Gavin."

He placed a hand on her cheek and let his thumb caress her flesh beneath her delicate line of chin. "I'll tell you what would make me happy," he said huskily.

"And what would that be?" she dared to ask, trembling from troubled passion as he scorched her skin with his touch. Her eyes hazed over as his free hand lowered and took the liberty of cupping her full breast through the sleek material of her dress. She swallowed hard, again melting.

"Leave this place. Now," he said, seeing how the moonlight caught and lit her like a silver flame, enhancing her loveliness. "Come away with me. Let us be alone."

Caroline's breath quickened with a yearning that she had only just recently begun to know, only since having met Gavin. "I mustn't," she whispered, forcing herself to step back from him. "Either I return to the ball or go back to Twin Oaks. If I don't do one or the other, my uncle will surely find out."

She lifted the skirt of her dress away from the dew-laden grass of the garden. The wind sang through the distant pines, whispering against the heated flesh of her face. She rushed away from Gavin, knowing that she had already acted questionably in Randolph Jamieson's presence. How was she to know that he wouldn't complain to her uncle about her behavior. Surely he had seen her escape the crowd with Gavin, and go outside to be alone with him? First she had Elroy to worry about and now Randolph. Surely her uncle would find out . . . !

"Caroline!" Gavin growled, grabbing her by a wrist,

forcing her to stop her flight from him. He urged her
to face him. "I'm not going to let you get away from
me so easily this time. Now I think we can come up
with some sort of plan that could eliminate all your
worries about your uncle. Are you willing to listen to
what I have to say?"

Caroline's eyes wavered. "I don't know, Gavin,"
she softly uttered. "I do want to be with you, but I
think it best if I return to Twin Oaks. If my uncle
should hear that I did anything questionable,
well . . . I just don't want to chance it."

Gavin's eyes darkened in a silent fury. He dropped
his hand away from her as though she were a hot coal.
"Perhaps I've been wrong about you," he growled.
"Are you concerned for your uncle because you are
afraid that he might cut you out of his will? It would
seem so, Caroline."

Caroline was taken aback by this sudden, outland-
ish accusation. She squared her shoulders and doubled her hands into fists. "What a terrible thing to
say," she said. "How can you even think that of me?
Gavin, you're wrong. Wrong."

"If I'm wrong, prove it to me," he dared, placing his
hands on his hips.

"I don't think I care to," she snapped, her eyes
blazing with anger. "Anyhow, I don't even know how
I could. You're as hardheaded as a mule!"

"Touché," he laughed, making a mock bow. His
eyes twinkled now. He was glad to see that he had
been wrong about her. He now understood that she
was only concerned about her uncle's health. That
was understandable. But there were ways around even
that.

"So? What were you going to suggest that I do to
prove my true feelings for my uncle?" Caroline said,
tossing her head. She walked slowly away from him,
knowing that he would follow.

Gavin fell into step beside her. "Come away with
me tonight. Take a stroll in the moonlight by the river.
Then I will return you safely home at a decent hour,"

he said, easing an arm about her tiny waist. "Now doesn't that sound just too good to refuse?"

"Maybe so, but I just can't," she sighed, swirling her skirt and froth of petticoats around to face him. "First I would have Elroy to explain to, and then Randolph."

Gavin's eyes widened. He raked his fingers through his midnight-black hair. "I can understand your problem with Randolph," he said thickly. "But who the hell is Elroy?"

Caroline softly laughed. "Elroy served as my driver tonight," she said. "He brought me to Randolph's at the request of my uncle. Elroy is my uncle's handyman at Twin Oaks. He's usually quite harmless, yet sometimes I wonder. But I do know that he could very easily tell my uncle that I returned home by way other than the family buggy."

Gavin rubbed his chin contemplatively. "When describing Elroy as a handyman, do you mean that he is not what you would call on the wealthy side?" he asked. "That he just might consider accepting a few coins for his silence?"

Caroline's head jerked up with surprise at his suggestion. "Gavin, a *bribe*?" she gasped.

"Yes," he chuckled. "I guess you could call it that. Don't you think your freedom for the rest of the evening is worth that?"

Clasping her hands nervously together, Caroline strolled over to the fountain, shivering when a soft spray of water caressed her face. "I would like that," she murmured, then smiled almost bashfully up at Gavin. "Though agreeing to such a suggestion would make me feel quite wicked, Gavin."

"Wicked is as wicked does," he said hoarsely, drawing her back around into his arms. He reverently breathed her name, then kissed her hungrily.

Caroline found herself falling into an abyss of ecstasy. She twined her arms about his neck and returned his kiss, then they jerked apart when approaching footsteps startled them.

Randolph's eyes caught the reflection of the moon as he squinted and found Caroline and Gavin only inches apart. He stopped and glared from one to the other, then reached a hand to Caroline. "I believe your uncle wanted me to introduce you around, Caroline," he grumbled, taking her by an elbow and whisking her away from Gavin. "I don't see how that is possible if you remain in the garden all night. Come along."

Looking back across her shoulder, Caroline pleaded softly to Gavin with her eyes. When he slowly nodded, urging her to go on with Randolph, she smiled sheepishly and did as he suggested. She knew to expect Gavin to slip a few coins into Elroy's pocket, but what was he to do about Randolph? Whatever, she hoped that he would be quick about it!

Feeling Randolph's eyes on her, she smiled coyly at him. . . .

# *Eight*

*T*he long mahogany dining table, lighted by a massive candelabra, was set with a silver service, the napkin rings carefully crafted silver creatures of rabbits, leprechauns, and deers. The chairs were upholstered in maroon velvet.

Sitting at this table with Randolph and many of his other guests, Caroline tried to attend to what was being said among them, but her thoughts were on Gavin. Her gaze kept moving toward the door which led out into the hallway. He had eaten and then had politely excused himself. Had he had trouble with Elroy? Had Gavin even decided to forget their plan?

Caroline knew that it would be best for her if he chose not to escort her from the ball, for even now she felt uneasy to know that she had so easily agreed.

But she continually found it harder to deny Gavin anything he wished of her and she feared this power he had over her more than fear itself. No other man had caused her to betray her own self, let alone betray her beloved uncle.

But never before had she so loved a man. Her childish love for Harold Hicks had only been a fantasy. Her love for Gavin was real, undeniably true. She only hoped that her emotions would not be wasted. If he were truly a rogue . . . ?

She straightened herself in her chair, trying to concentrate on what was going on around her. Surely Gavin would arrive soon.

Wine flowed freely from dated bottles into long-stemmed crystal glasses at the dining table. Randolph plied his guests not only with fine wines, but also with imported French champagne and dishes prepared by a French chef.

White-gloved houseboys scurried around the table, carrying trays of food from the kitchen in silver serving bowls and platters. Beluga caviar, duck consommé with ginger, and sautéed breast of duck had been served, but Caroline had barely tasted them. Even now she toyed with the food on her plate, forcing a smile as Randolph looked her way from where he sat at her left at the head of the table.

Dabbing his lips with a white damask napkin, Randolph smiled back at Caroline. He leaned closer to her, placing the napkin aside. "You've barely touched your food," he whispered. "You even appear troubled. Is it your uncle? Are you worrying about him?"

He wanted to ask her about Gavin St. Clair and what their relationship was. Somehow he felt that Caroline's silence and moodiness had to do with having been interrupted in the garden. But he couldn't be so bold as to ask her anything about her feelings about another man. Especially Gavin St. Clair, who had been his rival in every sense of the word, from way back. Was it to be the same now? Would Gavin also win when it came to women . . .?

Caroline's eyes wavered beneath his close scrutiny. Randolph had seen enough this evening to raise questions. She was glad that he was being a gentleman by not inquiring about Gavin, and what he meant to her. What could she even say if he did . . . ? She was not skilled in telling falsehoods, though it was becoming more necessary with her each added heartbeat!

"Yes, I'm worried about my uncle," she finally said. "I only hope he hasn't worsened again while I've been gone."

She caught a glimpse of Gavin as he came into view out in the hallway. When he nodded toward her and smiled, she knew that their plans were still intact. A sensual thrill coursed through her veins at the thought.

"In fact, Randolph," she blurted softly, "I feel that I must leave early tonight. Will you understand?"

Randolph's brow furrowed. He lifted a wine glass to his lips and sipped the sparkling red liquid, then placed the glass back down onto the table. "If you leave before the others, I could not personally see to your return home. It would not be polite to my guests," he grumbled. "And, Caroline, I had looked forward to that opportunity. Surely you will change your mind and stay longer."

Fidgeting in her chair and seeing Gavin still patiently waiting in the hallway, Caroline felt a desperation rising inside her. She had to be convincing. Randolph had to be made to believe that she truly needed to return to Twin Oaks. If not now, it would be too late! She did not wish to return to Twin Oaks in the company of Randolph. Surely he would try to make advances to her! What was she to do? Hadn't Gavin thought of a plan that included dealing with Randolph? Or had he left Randolph to her?

The four-stringed quartet resumed playing waltzes in the ballroom, giving Caroline an idea. She smiled coyly over at Randolph. "Randolph, let's not talk further about my leaving," she purred. "Please let's dance?"

A smug look enveloped his face. "Only if you will promise to stay until I am free to return you, personally, to Twin Oaks."

Caroline's smile faded. She cast her eyes downward. "I cannot agree to that, Randolph," she said softly. Her eyes rose and challenged his steady stare. "Please understand. But I will share one more dance with you before I leave. Surely you won't deny me that."

"And how do you plan to return home?" he said thickly. "At least you must agree to let my carriage do the honors."

"Elroy is waiting for me with the buggy," she said with a straight face, yet her hands trembled in her lap, disbelieving how easily the lies slipped from her lips. Surely Gavin had already sent Elroy away! "But thank you anyway, Randolph. You are kind to offer."

Sliding his chair back, Randolph stood up and assisted Caroline from her chair. "Though dancing with you this last time will only hasten your departure, I see that this is what you want," he said quietly. "I only wish there was some way I could change your mind."

"I must do what I must," Caroline murmured, gliding along beside him in her rustling petticoats and dress as they left the elaborate dining room behind and moved down the hallway to the ballroom. She gave Gavin a knowing smile as she passed by him, then fluttered her thick eyelashes up at Randolph as they began making a turn on the dance floor.

Caroline's heart soared as the music played, and her head began to spin lightly as Randolph led her around and through the throng of dancers. And if anyone noticed her glowing, they would think Randolph was the reason. But Gavin was the true cause. And even she found it hard to grasp . . . this feeling for a man who only a short while ago had not been known to her by face, voice, or name!

But it was true. Oh, how it was true!

When the music momentarily stopped and Randolph guided Caroline from the floor toward where her shawl and purse had been left in waiting, she panicked. She now realized that Randolph would adamantly insist on at least escorting her to her waiting buggy. Now what was she to do? Elroy was most surely not the one waiting. . . .

Politely smiling, yet slowly dying inside, Caroline accepted her shawl and purse. Her smile was frozen to her face, she feared the next moments so, but she went through all the motions of letting Randolph place the shawl about her fair shoulders while she eagerly watched for Gavin.

Randolph sensed Caroline's tenseness. He lifted a sandy eyebrow in silent question. Then he shrugged, remembering her anxiousness over her uncle.

"Shall I come to Twin Oaks tomorrow to call on you, Caroline?" he said, dismissing her odd behavior from his mind. "It would be late in the afternoon, after my business hours. I could even come later, let's say, to dine with you? With Daniel being bedfast, I am sure you must grow weary of dining alone."

Caroline only half heard his invitation, troubled by what she would say when finding Elroy gone. Would Gavin be waiting there for Randolph to discover? And how, even, did Gavin propose to deliver her anywhere? She was just remembering how he had arrived to the ball—on his roan stallion! Not by way of buggy! Oh, things seemed to be getting more complicated by the minute.

"Caroline, a reply to my question would be appreciated," Randolph said impatiently, guiding her outside to the porch with a possessive grip on her elbow. "Tomorrow? I assume you are free?"

Seeing Elroy still waiting for her made Caroline stop with a start. Gavin hadn't succeeded in his efforts with Elroy after all! Then why had Gavin looked so cocksure of himself when he had nodded and smiled at her in the dining room? At present, she felt as though she were being drawn in two separate directions. Yet she had no choice but to board her uncle's buggy and worry about Gavin later.

When turning to say her good-bye to Randolph, she was rudely reminded by the sour look on his face that she still owed him an answer for his request to see her again. "Tomorrow?" she said, drawing her shawl more snugly about her shoulders. "No, Randolph, I don't think that would be good. I should spend the evening with Uncle Daniel since I was gone tonight."

Randolph jerked as though having been shot, injured by her refusal. He set his lips into a narrow line and helped her into the buggy, then lifted her hand to his lips and kissed it. "I understand," he said thickly. "But you can expect to see me. Soon."

"Thank you for tonight," Caroline said politely, shivering at the wet coldness that his lips had left on her hand. "I did enjoy it, Randolph. Immensely."

"It was my pleasure," Randolph said, taking a step back from the buggy, clasping his hands tightly behind his back. He nodded to Elroy. "Get her safely home, Elroy. Or you will answer to me."

Elroy glared down at Randolph and mumbled a reply, then snapped the reins and sent the gelding onward. Caroline slumped her shoulders and leaned back against the plush cushion of the seat, confused over the outcome of this evening's end. Where was Gavin? Was he enjoying this little game he was playing with her? At this moment she couldn't loathe him more.

The breeze was brisk and damp, blowing from the direction of Charleston Harbor. Caroline snuggled herself into her shawl, sniffling. She felt empty inside where only moments ago she had been warm with the special glow of knowing she would be with Gavin.

After arriving in Charleston, she watched the houses pass beside her, where not long ago had stood a wilderness of ruin. Many houses had been left with crumbling walls and blackened chimneys after the war. But though Charleston had been bruised and impoverished after the Civil War, it hadn't been abandoned. Charleston had survived bad fires, hurricanes, tornadoes, bombardment by sea and by land, and two enemy occupations, and yet she still stood, a city of old houses glittering by the sea.

The mournful wail of a French harp carried to Caroline's ears from somewhere afar, saddening her. Then she sat suddenly upright, seeing that Elroy wasn't traveling the way he had come from Twin Oaks. He had sent the gelding off onto a side street, toward the shine of the harbor.

"Elroy, where are you taking me?" Caroline

shouted, afraid. "This isn't the way to Twin Oaks. Turn around. *Immediately*."

Elroy sat stiff-backed on the driver's seat of the buggy, ignoring her. He snapped the reins. He shouted to the horse, sending the buggy recklessly onward, jolting over the slick crowns of the cobblestones of the street.

Caroline's hair came loose from its slides and whipped around, into her eyes. She clung desperately to the seat, her heart thudding wildly against her ribs.

And then Elroy reined the gelding to a shuddering halt as a stately carriage with flickering lamps flanking its perch suddenly appeared from another side street, to stop alongside Caroline's buggy. A coachman saluted Elroy, who nodded back. Then he looked over his shoulder and gave Caroline a dark frown just as Gavin stepped from the carriage and extended a hand toward her.

Breathless, Caroline stared openly at Gavin, unable to grasp what was truly happening. Her hand went to her face to brush her loosened hair back from her eyes.

"Caroline, this was the only way I could do this," Gavin said, taking her hand in his. "I knew that Randolph would insist on walking you to your buggy. He had to find Elroy there. Otherwise he would have suspected that I was involved."

"But you should have told me," she said, blinking her eyes nervously. She cast Elroy a questioning look and leaned closer to Gavin. "And Elroy? What can I expect from him? Do you have his *word* that he is to tell no one? Especially my Uncle Daniel?"

"He has been paid well for his silence," Gavin said, scowling at Elroy. "If I find that he has said anything to anyone, I'll have more than his hide."

Caroline shook her head. "I shouldn't have gotten involved in this," she sighed. "None of it is right."

Gavin urged her from the buggy and began walking her to his carriage. "I shall make it well worth your while, darling," he murmured. "Just trust me?"

Laughing softly, Caroline gave him a winsome look.
"I'm not sure if I even know the meaning of that word
anymore," she said. "My Uncle Daniel trusts me and
what do I do? I shamefully go with a man behind his
back. He would call me a wanton hussy. I just know
it."

Glad now to be inside the closed confines of
Gavin's carriage, with its fringed swags decorating the
windows, and comfortable on its plump-cushioned
seat, Caroline gave Gavin a look of wonder. "How did
you arrange all of this? Is that why you were gone so
long after you excused yourself from the dining
table?"

"I couldn't carry you away on my stallion, now
could I?" Gavin chuckled. He slammed the door shut
and drew her into his embrace as the carriage began
ambling down the street.

"I can stay with you for only a short while," she
explained, feeling the heat of his body against her
side. "Just for the length of time that I would normally have been gone for the ball."

"I think that can be arranged," Gavin said, then
threw the carriage door open again when the vehicle
came to another halt. "But I promised you a walk
beside the harbor, did I not? A walk it is, my sweet."

He stepped from the carriage and reached up to lift
her down onto the cobblestones. His lean, muscled
arm held her against him as together they began
walking along the waterfront. The moon was spilling
onto the darkened water, and farther out, Fort Sumter
sat like a Cyclops, dark and brooding, a reminder of
the war that had recently ravaged the city.

"It's so quiet here," Caroline said, shifting her gaze
away from the foreboding sight of the fort. "But I'm
sure that's a blessing. At one time it was anything *but*
quiet. It must have been terrifying for everyone in
Charleston when the first gunfire was sounded over
Fort Sumter. Where were you at the time?"

"I was among those who fired the first shots,"
Gavin said hoarsely. "Caroline, I was a major for the

Confederacy." He gave her a half-glance. "So was Randolph Jamieson. He and I competed for the best commands as we now compete as attorneys. It seems we now even compete for the same woman."

Caroline felt a blush heating her cheeks. "I felt as though there was much unspoken between you two," she murmured. "It is quite obvious that you have no love for one another."

He drew her around and cradled her close. "And what are your true feelings for Randolph?" he asked, his dark eyes heavy-lidded with jealousy.

"I have none whatsoever," she murmured. "He is my uncle's attorney. Nothing more."

"Randolph would like to be more than just a mere acquaintance," Gavin growled. "But of course I don't have to tell you that. You were there tonight, witness to his feelings."

"Gavin, let's not spoil this time together by discussing Randolph," Caroline whispered, curving her lower lip into a seductive pout. "I truly don't have much time." She glanced over at the carriage and saw that the coachman had momentarily departed from it. She now felt safely alone with Gavin. She turned her eyes bashfully back to him, thinking this aloneness sweet.

Her breath quickened when he drew her fully against him, and she felt the warm pressure of his body. She flamed in passion as his lips lowered and his mouth seized hers demandingly. His hands reached beneath her shawl and wandered eagerly down the lines of her back, caressing her all the way; his tongue parted her lips and plunged into the warm moistness of her mouth.

"Come with me to my townhouse," he whispered against her cheek after their kiss ended. "Darling, I must have you. Now."

Feeling a strange, tingling fear, Caroline inched away from him, her eyes wide. Her hair spilled in sultry reds across her shoulders, having become undone in the wild ride of the buggy. "I can't do that," she gasped. "Why, that would be quite improper. Even . . . immoral. Gavin, I don't want to think that . . . that . . . my first assumptions about you were right. Do you only wish for my company for . . . fulfillment of your carnal needs? If so, I am sorry that . . . I ever trusted you."

She drew her shawl snugly about her shoulders and stormed toward the carriage. When he grabbed her by a wrist and swung her around to face him, she saw a deep hurt in his eyes.

"You know better than that," he snapped. "My feelings for you are sincere. They are noble. What we would be sharing would be just that. A sharing of feelings because I know that you feel the same about me. I love you, Caroline. You . . . love . . . me."

Yanking her to him, he kissed her with force. She protested, pushing at his chest of steel, sensing that her surrender could leave a brand. But she was too weak with desire to protest. She shuddered as his tongue probed between her lips and his hand cupped her swelling breast.

Moaning, she returned his kiss and laced her arms about his neck, and when he lifted her up into his arms and began carrying her toward the waiting carriage, she knew that soon she would be introduced into true womanhood. . . .

# *Nine*

$L$arge oil lamps, lit before sunset, swung from posts on every street corner burning through the night. Gavin's two-storied, handsome mansion stood at the northwest corner of Alexander and Chapel streets. Though solidly constructed, the architecturally graceful lines and wrought iron trim gave the house an elegant appearance. Fog was creeping in from Charleston Harbor, silvering the festoons of vines which clung to the walls.

The townhouse loomed almost menacingly over Caroline as Gavin led her through the front gate and up a narrow, flagstone walk that was lined on either side by swaying, purple wisteria. Were this a fantasy dreamed up inside her head, what she was about to do would be more easy for her to accept.

But as it was, it was real and the pressure of Gavin's hand in hers reminded her of that fact.

The cool sea breeze nipped at her rosy cheeks, causing a shiver to ride her spine. When she felt Gavin's eyes imploring her, she gave him a faint smile, wishing she were snugly in her bed at Twin Oaks. If she were, guilt wouldn't be so heavy on her heart, threatening to ruin this time with Gavin, her love.

"Are you all right?" Gavin asked, his breath warming her cooled cheek as he leaned down against it. "You aren't having second thoughts, are you?"

Never one to back down once her mind was made up, Caroline stiffened her back and gave him a more steady smile. "No," she said firmly. "But you have to understand . . . this is not something that I make a habit of doing. I cannot believe that I . . . I am so willing." Her smile faded. "What must you think of me?"

He gathered her closer as he guided her up the marble steps which led onto a wide porch. "I think you're the most beautiful creature to ever have been placed on this earth," he said huskily. "And I think that what we've jointly agreed to is quite proper, Caroline, because of our true feelings for one another."

He slipped his key into its lock, turned the knob, and opened the door, gesturing with an arm for Caroline to step on inside. Tensely silent, she followed alongside him through the foyer and into a drawing room, where a soft fire on the hearth awaited their arrival.

"But if you prefer, we will share only a glass of port this night, Caroline," Gavin suggested. "I would then very honorably return you to Twin Oaks. Never would I ever force a lady. Especially not the lady I love."

His confession of love made Caroline almost swoon with joy. Her doubts were quickly being cast into the wind, yet she still had that same gnawing fear at the pit of her stomach. She would have never thought herself capable of wantonly giving herself to a man without first having a priest's words spoken between them. Yes, a glass of wine, maybe two, would have to be consumed, to give her the courage to be wholly with him.

"A glass of port would be fine," she said, trembling with rapture when his hands brushed against her bare shoulders as he removed her shawl. She avoided his eyes when she smiled up at him, sensing that he took her request to be a ploy to deny him the other pleasure he sought.

"The glass of port is to warm me," she quickly corrected. "The night breeze gave me a chill."

Gavin gently ushered her further into the room, to stand before the fire. "There are many ways to warm you," he chuckled. "And, hopefully, I will show you a number of them before returning you to your uncle's home."

Caroline didn't look his way when she heard his footsteps fading behind her. But when they could no longer be heard and she knew that he had momentarily left her alone, she turned and let herself study the way in which he lived.

In all designs and decor this was a man's house. Kerosene lamps reflected a golden glow onto dark, paneled walls with many rows of bookshelves filled with all assortments of leather-bound books. The old rosewood and mahogany pieces of furniture were mismatched, a lone sofa in a paling velvet, and high-backed chairs covered in dark leather.

The floor was bare of carpet. The high rafters of the room seemed scarcely to have been dusted and the drapes hung limply at the windows.

The room was in negligent disorder. Caroline saw paper cases for filing documents, globes, charts, and potted plants. It was obvious that the room had lacked a woman's touch for some time now, which made a peaceful smile spread across Caroline's face.

And then her smile faded when she saw something protruding from behind a chair in the far corner. Caroline's breath became shallow and her pulse raced at the sight of what appeared to be the corner of a dark oak frame.

Could it be one of the portraits? She had never considered he might have moved the portraits from St. Clair Manor!

Moving gingerly across the room, her heart threatening to drown her in its thundering beats, she went to the chair and slipped behind it. Her eyes grew wide with discovery. Here were the portraits. She dropped to her knees to examine them, then discovered there were only a few. Why had he separated them? Where were the rest?

But knowing that she didn't have much time in which to search for the only one that had intrigued her, she hurried onward. With trembling fingers she looked at one, set it aside, then looked at another. And when only two were left, she heard Gavin's footsteps approaching from the direction of the hallway. She would have to look at the remaining two later! She couldn't let Gavin find her snooping. Again she would be placed in the position of having to tell him more than she felt she should.

Swallowing hard, Caroline placed the portraits back in the order in which she had found them and tiptoed hurriedly back to the fireplace. She smiled up at Gavin as he entered the room, now shed of his frock coat, vest, and cravat, with his shirt half unbuttoned to his waist.

The sight of his tanned, sleekly muscled chest with its dark curls of hair filled Caroline with a hunger she did not understand. Troubled by this, she focused her eyes elsewhere, on the two goblets of wine that he was carrying, one of which he now kindly offered her.

"Has the fire yet warmed you?" he asked, taking her by an elbow and guiding her to the sofa which faced the hearth. "I must say . . . your cheeks are rosier than usual."

Caroline eased onto the soft cushions of the sofa and drew a ragged breath when Gavin sat down beside her and draped his arm about her shoulder. "Yes. I am quite warmed now," she murmured, hoping that he wouldn't see her fingers trembling as she clasped the long stem of the wine glass.

"Rosy cheeks quite become you," Gavin said, his fingers playing along the gentle slope of her shoulder.

"Thank you," she replied, knowing that he must sense her awkwardness. But she wondered how long he would deal in idle chatter. How could she do more than that? Now that she had found those portraits, she could hardly think of anything else. Where were the others? Could one of the two that she hadn't seen even be the one that she had been searching for? When could she have the opportunity to find out?

"My, but aren't we polite?" Gavin chuckled. "Thank you? Is that all you can say? Caroline, I can think of much more to say than that."

She slowly moved her eyes to him, not wanting to let his nearness wholly consume her again. But his dark, penetrating eyes and the sensual fullness of his lips were quickly dashing all wonder about the portraits from her mind. She didn't want to think again of the mysterious side to his nature and the fact that he seemed to know that she wanted to discover the truth about the portrait. She just wanted to enjoy being with him, for all her tomorrows just might deny her this opportunity again.

"And what do you have to say, Gavin?" she purred. "Isn't the wine to your liking? Why, you haven't taken even that first drink from your glass."

She lifted her glass to her lips and slowly tasted the tartness of the wine, already feeling a giddiness invading her senses, yet knowing that one lone sip of wine wasn't the cause. It was Gavin. Totally Gavin. . . .

Gavin set his glass on a table beside the sofa. "Darling, the wine was for *your* benefit," he said huskily. "Not at all for me. I'm already warmed. If I would get any hotter, I would most surely be set on fire."

"Gavin . . ." Caroline gasped, shocked at his boldness. "What a thing to say."

His eyelids heavy with building passion, Gavin eased the glass from between her fingers. "I believe you said that you mustn't stay long," he murmured. "Why are we wasting time talking, when all I want is to have you in my arms?"

As though pulled by unseen puppet strings, she drifted toward him, unresisting. Moving into his embrace, she welcomed his kiss. His lips were sweet and hungry, as though born that way. She was filled with a splendid joy at his touch, desire blossoming inside her, his hands fire upon her flesh as he cupped her swelling breasts.

She drew only a fraction away from him. "We mustn't," she whispered. "The servants . . .?"

"None are here," he said thickly. "Only on occasion do I have a need for servants. I like . . . my privacy."

Caroline smiled lazily and boldly slid searching fingers beneath his shirt to stroke his chest. She could feel his thundering heartbeat against her palms. She could hear him struggling with uneven breaths. And when he reached around and began unsnapping her gown, she felt as though she were floating, her euphoria was so heightened. There were no longer any thoughts about portraits, mysteries left uncovered, or the fact that she was just about to participate in a full, shared seduction with a man. That it was Gavin, was enough.

Even her doubts about the mysterious side of him were going to be placed aside. She loved him. She could never deny that. It was especially impossible to deny him to her throbbing heart. . . .

Slipping her gown down and away from her shoulders, she revealed to Gavin her full, round breasts. His lips lowered and consumed a hardened, dark tip. His loins ached. His hands wandered over her young, sweet body and attempted to push her gown lower. But the encumbrance of petticoats was like a wall, stopping him.

Becoming breathless, his kisses inflaming her, Caroline moaned sensuously. She moved her fingers to the buttons of his shirt and unbuttoned them. Brazenly, she slipped the shirt away from his shoulders and down the muscled length of his arms.

Her eyes were hazed over with desire as she watched him draw away from her to toss his shirt aside. And when he stood and drew her up and then fully into his arms and began carrying her from the room, she did not protest but placed her cheek gently against his chest.

No words were exchanged as he carried her up a stairway which spiraled to the second floor. Nor did they speak as he bore her into a dimly lit bedroom. Beneath the faint light of a candle, Caroline saw that a massive, four-poster, brass bed without a canopy or bedspread awaited, with its goose-feathered pillows plumped. A huge, dark armoire with an aging mirror stood on the far wall, and a highboy dresser and a washstand with a porcelain top supporting a pitcher and a cracked bowl, made up the rest of the drab room's furnishings.

The windows were curtainless, yet close-shuttered, giving them full privacy, which Gavin was quickly taking advantage of. He carried Caroline to the bed and gently placed her there; then, watching her with a soft smile, he continued to undress her.

When she was spread out before him all silken and provocative in her slenderness, he stood before her and removed his own clothes, until he was standing boldly naked before her.

Seeing how his wide shoulders tapered to narrow hips, and how his manly strength stood so brazenly stiff before her eyes, Caroline's cheeks blazed with embarrassment and she turned her eyes quickly away. She now fully understood what she was about to do. She chewed her lower lip in frustration, feeling wickedly wanton. But when she felt the weight of him sinking the mattress beside her, she cared not and turned and fully accepted his steel frame against hers.

"Don't ever forget that I love you," Gavin whispered, trailing his eager hands down the alluring curves of her body. "I do, Caroline. And, God, you're so lovely."

"Love me," Caroline whispered. "Just love me."

"You're sure?" Gavin asked, fearing the answer, yet feeling that it was necessary to ask. The first time with a man was sometimes traumatic for a woman. He only wanted it to be right for Caroline. But how hard it was to hold back! The softness of her breasts against his chest was driving him wild with want. Her leg now lifted over his, causing his manhood to rest against the core of her womanhood and making his heart hammer wildly against his ribs. He swept a hand down across her stomach and with his forefinger began stroking the sensitive nub of flesh between her legs, teasing it until she gave a sensuous tremor and a low moan.

"Please don't question anything. Not now," Caroline said, lifting her head to shake her red tresses across the bed till they lay like a halo of brilliant red roses about her head. She reveled in the exquisite sensations spiraling through her body. She was falling into a helpless abyss of ecstasy.

"I don't want to even be reminded that there should be questions asked at a time like this. I just want you, Gavin. Only you," she said huskily, hardly recognizing her own voice.

"I will be gentle," he whispered, leading her deeper into a world of sensual pleasures. "The pain will only be brief, and then you will experience total pleasure."

Lifting himself up he leaned down over her. His lips claimed hers in a meltingly hot kiss. He eased his hardness against her, and she allowed her thighs to part, an open admission of her need to delve into unknown realms with him.

Slowly he began working his manhood into her tightness. And suddenly, with one hearty thrust, he was inside her. He drowned her cry of pain with another kiss and then began to move his hips against her, thrusting deeply.

The bed became a cradle of pleasure, as a wondrous rapture Caroline had never known existed unfolded inside her. Gavin loved her with wild abandon, plunging her into unfathomed depths, sweeping her away in currents of sensation as torrential as the tides.

Caroline relished this discovery and opened herself wider to him, locking her legs about his waist. Her throat arched backward in a pleasurable sigh. His tongue flicked over one breast and then the other. Again and again he kissed her . . . sweet and long, his tongue parting her lips and seductively entering her eager mouth, inviting her tongue to meet his in a play of passion.

Then he cradled her close, pressing her breasts hard into his chest. They groaned in whispers into one another's ears, hands stroking, hips rising, falling. Gavin buried his face into the delicate line of her neck and stiffened, knowing that his release was near. But he held back, wanting her to fully experience the heights of ecstasy this her first time.

Caroline's body was growing feverish. Desire gripped her. Her heart was racing out of control, her fingers were digging into his shoulders. The burning ache between her thighs grew hotter and then the sudden onslaught of passion fully engulfed her. She moaned softly, she tossed her head, she gripped him hard at his waist as she realized that he was also in the throes of the same fiery explosion of sensations that she was experiencing. She clung to him, meeting his eager thrusts, his kiss of fire. And as the licking flames inside her slowly burned out, she was left limp and breathless against him, yet clinging still.

The heat of his gaze was scorching as he drew away from her and looked down upon her. And then his lips lowered to hers in a series of teasing kisses. The fingers of one hand softly kneaded a breast while the other traveled over her long, tapering calves and silken thighs.

Again, he paused to look down at her. A slow smile lifted his lips when he saw the peace in her eyes. "So you also enjoyed it?" he asked, laughing softly. "Woman, I'll never forget it."

"Nor shall I ever forget it," Caroline whispered, trailing a hand over the square of his jaw to the perfect line of his lips. "Gavin, I would have loved to have it last forever."

"Ah, but it is only a fleeting pleasure, is it not?" He sighed. "But one always worth waiting for."

He drew her into a sitting position on the bed, holding her close. "But I know that it must end for this night," he said sullenly. "I must return you to Twin Oaks."

Caroline joined in the sigh. "Yes, you must," she murmured. "Surely, I am so radiantly happy I am glowing."

"Yes. You are. Even more brilliantly than the moonlight," Gavin teased, his fingers again searching her slim, sensuous body.

Becoming shaken again with desire, Caroline brushed his hand aside. "Please don't," she murmured. "I do believe it's best that I leave. Now. As soon as possible."

"Yes. I know," Gavin said thickly. He climbed from the bed and urged her out of it. He drew her into his arms, fitting her body into the curve of his. "But, darling, we have tomorrow."

Caroline looked wonderingly up at him. "Tomorrow?" she said in a half-whisper.

"I will be at St. Clair Manor. Come to me," he asked, softly pressing his hardness against her thigh.

Her blood quickened with fresh desire and unnerved by his new ability to manipulate her body, Caroline slid from his embrace. Turning her back to him, she began dressing. "I think not, Gavin," she murmured. "I shouldn't have even been with you tonight. Twice surely would be sinful."

"Not if you come to St. Clair Manor for a definite, innocent purpose," he said, slipping into his breeches.

Caroline turned and faced him, her eyes wide, while her fingers worked at snapping her gown. "Oh? And what could that be?" she asked, glad that he had covered the part of him that stirred her to feelings that she had no control over.

"The key to my mansion. Have you used it yet?" he asked, combing his fingers through his midnight black hair, smoothing it down, against his scalp. "Did you find the bolts of material and the catalog of wallpaper samples I purposely placed there for you?"

Caroline wavered, not wanting to tell him that she had already been at his mansion and that, yes, she had found the material and catalog. This could make her appear too eager. And she had yet to know anything about his family other than the little bit Daniel had told her about his uncle. Why would her services be needed when surely he had a mother or sister somewhere who would be glad to do the honors?

Gavin, slipped into his boots, eyeing Caroline questioningly. "Well? Have you used the key? Did you choose any wallpaper for the walls or fabric for drapes?"

"No, I have yet to use your key," Caroline lied, whipping her hair back and across her shoulders, now fully dressed. "Perhaps your mother or even a sister would rather help in the renovations."

She watched a pained expression enter his eyes and his smile fade into a brooding frown. She went to him and placed her arms about his neck. "Did I say something wrong? Did I ask questions that you do not want to answer? If so, I am sorry," she softly apologized.

He locked his arms about her waist. He gazed hauntingly down into her eyes. "My mother and father died many years ago in a fire," he said hoarsely. "In their apartment in New York. I wasn't with them at the time. I was here, in the Carolinas, visiting my uncle." He swallowed hard and lowered his eyes. "I was left in the custody of my uncle."

"How horrible," Caroline said softly, her heart aching for him, having experienced the same sort of loss not all that long ago. "And . . . you . . . were the only child?"

"Yes. And quite a *lonely* child," he said, again imploring her with his eyes. "My uncle tried to console me with material things. He even saw to it that I attended the best schools. He enrolled me in the best law school. I eventually lived totally away from him. Before the war I made my residence here in my uncle's townhouse. I felt that I was my own person, and deserved my privacy. My uncle understood. I stayed on here even after he died, not caring to live in

St. Clair Manor. Its location is undesirable, being so far from the city. That is why the townhouse mansion was acquired by my uncle's parents in the first place. While cotton was not being planted, hoed, or harvested, there was ample opportunity to enjoy the social life of Charleston. The family usually lived in the townhouse during the winter months when the social season was on. When my aunt died, my uncle gave up that practice."

"But you do wish to live at St. Clair Manor now?"

"Perhaps."

"But you *are* planning to renovate it."

"At the time I decided to do this, I thought maybe of selling the mansion. But when I saw you, my thoughts began changing. St. Clair Manor would be an ideal place to raise a family."

Blushing, Caroline laughed. "I think this is not the time to talk about *that*," she said. "I *must* be going, Gavin. Please? I fear that I have already lingered too long."

She cast her eyes downward. "In fact, I know I have lingered too long," she softly said. "I shouldn't even be here. You know that."

He swept his arm about her waist and began guiding her to the door. "Now let's hear no more talk like that," he said. "What we did was right. Beautiful. Never regret it, Caroline."

"I don't wish to," she said. "I, too, thought it beautiful."

They walked, arm in arm, down the stairs. Gavin placed her shawl about her shoulders, handed her her purse, and then escorted her out to his waiting carriage. Once inside, he cradled her close. They exchanged sweet kisses and passion-filled whispers until the carriage reached the drive leading to Twin Oaks.

Caroline placed a hand on Gavin's cheek. "I must go the rest of the way alone," she said, her eyes devouring him in the pale light of the moonlight in the small carriage window. "Should my uncle hear another carriage . . ."

"I understand," Gavin said. He crushed her to him and gave her a heady kiss, then released her, opened the carriage door, and helped her outside. "Tomorrow, Caroline?"

"Give me a full day with my uncle, Gavin. I feel I've been neglecting him. But I can meet you at St. Clair Manor the next day," she said. "But only if you promise to behave while I'm there," she teased.

"I'll be there and I'll behave," he promised, laughing.

He kissed her hard and long. She then turned and began running down the dark drive. The carriage waited until she got safely to the house. When she did and she heard it ambling on away, she stopped, breathless, watching it until it slowly shrank to a speck of black.

Swinging around, she began to climb the stairs that led up to the porch, catapulted back into the real world. The past hours surely were only a pleasant, sensual dream.

But suddenly the dream faded, for she felt eyes upon her. Turning with a start on the top step, she searched the darkness around her. Her gaze fell upon a group of bushes near the corner of the house. In the night, they were a series of black, secret shapes. But among these shapes was the outline of a man. Someone was watching her. Panic-stricken, Caroline froze as this furtive, stealthy figure then moved away in the darkness.

Her heart beating nervously and her knees weakening from building fear, Caroline edged backward toward the door. When she reached it, she turned and hurried inside the house, stopping to get her breath as she leaned against the closed door.

# *Ten*

*R*emembering the man in the shadows the previous night, Caroline went cautiously to the parlor window and slowly drew a drape aside to look toward the bushes where she had seen him. Why had he been there watching her? Who would want to spy on her? Who disliked her this much?

She smoothed the drape back in place, not wanting to worry herself further. Not this morning. Her night had been free of nightmares, instead filled with wondrous dreams of how it had felt to find passion's fulfillment in Gavin's arms. Her face flamed with color, even now tingling with the thought of what she had shared with Gavin at his townhouse.

But guilt kept plaguing her in momentary flashes, for she knew how her uncle trusted and respected her. If he found out how wanton she was, how would he then feel about her?

Her thoughts went to Aunt Amelia. Had she been drawn into being unfaithful to her husband by feeling for Gavin's uncle the same way Caroline now felt for Gavin?

The sound of voices in the hallway and footsteps drawing close drew Caroline's thoughts to the present. She tensed when she recognized Randolph Jamieson's voice. In Caroline's distant state of mind she hadn't heard the arrival of his buggy. And why was he here? Caroline had made a special effort to discourage his coming today. She *had* felt the need to share many hours with her uncle. Sitting by her uncle's bedside, watching over him all day, would be a way to make amends for her undutiful behavior of late. But now it seemed that Randolph had taken it upon himself to be her replacement again.

Or had he come for other reasons? Had he come because of *her*? Now that he had witnessed the tender scene between her and Gavin in the garden, would he pursue her affections even more heartily? Gavin and Randolph had both mentioned being competitive. Would she also become a prize to be fought over between them?

Caroline squared her shoulders as Randolph entered the dining room. As always, he was impeccably dressed in expensive, tailored clothes and not a lock of his hair was out of place. Caroline could see approval in his eyes as they danced over her, taking in her delicate, pale green cotton dress with lace at its low-swept bodice and at the fully-gathered waist. Her hair was swept back from her face and held in place on each side by slides, and her green eyes held within them a secret sparkle, caused by her moments of passion with Gavin.

"Caroline. How good it is to see you again so soon," Randolph said, taking her hand and politely kissing it. "I hope you don't mind that I came. A client cancelled an appointment at the last minute. I felt this gave me the opportunity to come and report to your uncle."

Caroline eased her hand from his. She locked her fingers together behind her back. "Report?" she said softly, forking an eyebrow. "What do you mean?"

"Why, last night's activities, of course," Randolph said, tucking his thumbs in his vest pockets, dangling his fingers. "What else?"

Caroline paled. Her throat felt momentarily constricted. "Last night?" she murmured. "What about . . . last night?"

Randolph detected her uneasiness. This confirmed his earlier suspicions. She *was* involved with Gavin

St. Clair. He had seen Gavin leaving Twin Oaks's premises one morning several days ago, though neither Gavin nor Caroline had seen him watching from his hidden buggy. And he had found them in his garden only last night. Of course Caroline would pale at the thought of Daniel's finding out. Daniel Burton and George St. Clair had never liked each other, though Randolph had never known why.

But Randolph did know that Daniel would not wish his niece to become involved with a St. Clair!

"About my ball and how everyone was smitten by your loveliness, Caroline," Randolph said smugly. "What else would I have to report?" He laughed. "You seem a bit unnerved. Was it something I said?"

Caroline laughed nervously. "You're imagining things, Randolph," she lied, knowing very well that he was implying more than he was saying. "I feel quite relaxed. Why wouldn't I be? I'm in the company of a friend, am I not?"

Randolph chuckled and his eyes gleamed. "I would hope to be more than that," he said. He took a step closer to her, dropping his hands to his sides. "You're quite beautiful this morning, Caroline. There seems to be some sort of radiance enveloping you. Were I the cause . . ."

"Randolph, I think your trip to Twin Oaks was for naught this morning," Caroline said, interrupting him. She took a step backward, lodging herself against the back of a chair as Randolph again moved toward her. "I only moments ago checked on my uncle and he was sound asleep. Perhaps it's best you leave and come back later."

"Mr. Jamieson . . .?" Rosa said, suddenly entering the parlor. "Daniel is now awake. He is anxious to see you. Please do go on up."

Caroline sighed with relief, glad to be rescued, yet truly dreading for Randolph to speak with her uncle. But for now, the latter was much preferred if it meant being spared being alone with Randolph herself.

Randolph swung around. "Thank you, Rosa," he

said hoarsely. He slowly turned to face Caroline again. "I will talk to you after I visit Daniel for awhile."

Caroline placed a hand on her brow. "No. I don't think so," she murmured. "You see, I have a sudden headache. Please excuse me, Randolph. I must go to my room to lie down." She fluttered her lashes. "And please let yourself out when you are ready to leave. I plan to be napping."

Holding her breath, she brushed on past him. She felt Rosa's eyes on her, following her up the stairs. And when she finally reached her room, she closed the door behind her and leaned against it, breathless.

She tensed as she heard Randolph's footsteps pass outside her door and then fade away as he went on to Uncle Daniel's room. And then she began pacing. She could hardly bear the suspense of not knowing what was being said in her uncle's room! Having to wait out Randolph's leave made her feel trapped. She must get away. She would go to St. Clair Manor . . . busy herself in the mystery of the missing portrait. She would even choose fabrics for Gavin's windows. She would do anything but stay at Twin Oaks while Randolph was "reporting" to her Uncle Daniel!

Taking Gavin's key from hiding and securing it in the pocket of her dress, Caroline crept noiselessly from the house. Being in a dazed sort of state, wondering about so many things, she failed to notice Elroy. When she saw movement out of the corner of her eye, she jumped, startled.

"Where are you off to this mornin'?" Elroy asked, bending to hammer a nail into a loose board of a porch step, leaning his full weight against the porch. "Bet your uncle don't know you're out feistying around."

Caroline glared down at Elroy. "What I do and when I do it is none of your business," she snapped. "And, Elroy, I would appreciate it if you would remember that."

Then she became quite shaken when he paused his

hammer in midair and gave her a knowing look with
his squinted, dead-gray eyes, a snarl lifting his lips
into a dangerous sort of smile. She knew that he was
thinking about how he had been paid the previous
night, and why. Would he tell? Or would he just
torment her because of his knowing? He had already
threatened her more than once!

"How *is* ol' Daniel this mornin'?" he asked, chuckling low. "But it's too early to tell, ain't it? You
wanted to sneak over to the ol' St. Clair place again, to
meet Gavin, before your uncle would even know.
Ain't I right, Caroline?"

Her face flaming, Caroline gave him an angered
look, then spun around on a heel and began stomping
away from him.

"Cat got your tongue this mornin' also?" Elroy
shouted after her. "Or don't ladies from the North
have manners?"

His laughter followed Caroline as she hurried onward, knowing that he was only playing a game with
her. Surely the sort of life he led was boring. She was
just something different in his life, something he
could toy with. She had to believe that he was
harmless. He was just an egotistical bore whose life
had been changed by the horrors of war. She could
sympathize with him, having been affected by the
war, herself.

As Caroline moved on past the flower garden, her
eyes caught the shine of golden hair amid the lively
colors of the proliferation of assorted flowers. Caroline met Sally's approach with outstretched arms.
"Why, what have we here?" She softly laughed. "A
flower among flowers?"

Sally offered Caroline a daisy, yet didn't speak a
word. And Caroline would have thought the gift of
flower was enough, but the glassiness in Sally's eyes
took her aback and made her own smile fade.

Stooping before Sally, Caroline accepted the flower.
"Thank you," she murmured, closely studying Sally's
eyes. Then she laid the daisy aside and held Sally at

arm's length. "Honey, are you all right? You . . . you don't look as though you are."

Again Sally didn't speak. She just slowly nodded her head up and down in a silent response.

Caroline frowned. She dropped her hands away from Sally and picked up the daisy, then straightened her back into another standing position. She knew that she wasn't going to receive any answers from this small child, who looked like an angel this morning dressed in her freshly-starched blue cotton dress, with her golden hair streaming across her frail shoulders. Caroline knew that Rosa was aware of something amiss about her daughter. It was Rosa's place, not Caroline's, to delve into the reason for this strangeness.

"Well, Sally, I must be on my way," Caroline said, smiling down at the silent little girl. She nodded toward the flower garden. "And you be careful of the bees while picking flowers. Their stingers inflict quite a bit of pain."

Sally turned and began walking slowly away from Caroline in a lethargic manner instead of her usual brisk, lively way. Caroline shook her head woefully, sighed, then turned and began making her way around the bleakness of the lagoon, welcoming her uncle's collie at her side. . . .

Randolph drew a chair up beside Daniel's bed. He stifled a cough with the palm of his right hand, the medicinal smell of the room much worse this morning.

Daniel peered up at Randolph with his snappish green eyes. "It's good of you to come," he said. "Tell me all about your ball. Does Caroline dance as skillfully as she is pretty?" He chuckled low and winked at Randolph. "Did you by chance even sneak a kiss, Randolph?"

Randolph crossed his legs and drummed his fingers on the leather of his shoe. "The ball was quite profitable for the poor," he said matter-of-factly, ignoring the reference made to a stolen kiss. It seemed that Gavin had probably already beat him to that.

"And for yourself?" Daniel persisted, groaning as he twisted his neck while trying to raise it further up onto his pillow. "Tell me about your evening with Caroline, damn it."

A tickle in Randolph's throat caused him to cough again. He looked across the bleak room toward the closed drapes which hid the closed windows and shutters. He ran a finger about the cravat which felt so chokingly tight at his throat and looked back at Daniel. "Daniel, I think I need some air," he said hoarsely. "If I could open a window just a crack . . .?"

"I never open my windows," Daniel growled. "Lets in too much of the outside world. I prefer them closed."

"Then my visit will have to be cut short," Randolph said, rising from the chair. "I need some air, Daniel. My throat is scratchy."

Frustrated, not wanting Randolph to leave, Daniel flailed a hand in the air. "Then open a damn window," he shouted. His voice lowered as did his hand. "But only a crack, mind you."

"Thanks, Daniel," Randolph said, going to the window. "Just a bit of air and I'll be as good as new."

Dust flew as Randolph pushed the drapes aside on their rods. And as he shoved a window open and then the shutters and he looked outside, his eyes widened and his heart skipped a beat.

His gaze followed Caroline as she fled away from Twin Oaks toward St. Clair Manor. He watched her until she became hidden behind the tall fence outlined with creeping vines.

Angry from the discovery, he turned on a heel and walked heavily back to Daniel's bed and stood there, staring down at him.

Daniel sensed anger in his silence and stared back at Randolph, then looked toward the window. "Did you see something that upset you?" he softly questioned.

"It's Caroline," Randolph said, easing back down onto the chair. He leaned forward, resting his elbows on his knees. "Did you know that she and Gavin St. Clair have become acquainted?"

Daniel's head jerked. He began wheezing, then finally caught his breath. "No. She has said nothing about Gavin St. Clair," he said weakly, remembrances of past heated words with another St. Clair flashing through his consciousness. "How do you know this, Randolph? Surely you are wrong."

"No. This was made evident to me last night. She and Gavin danced. They even went to my garden, alone. She's going to St. Clair Manor even *now*," Randolph said guardedly, seeing the alarm in Daniel's eyes.

"What . . .?" Daniel gasped, rasping. "Why . . . would . . . she . . .?"

"To see Gavin." Randolph shrugged. "Why else?" He hated to upset Daniel, yet felt that he must get the old man on his side if he was to win this new victory over Gavin St. Clair. This was the only way. Daniel had to know. He would order Caroline not to see Gavin again.

Daniel lifted a bony hand and grabbed Randolph by a wrist. "You must stop her," he demanded. "The St. Clairs are a worthless lot. The manor—it's . . . not . . . a safe place to be."

Randolph was surprised by the strength in Daniel's hand. Daniel's fingers were even cutting hard into the flesh of Randolph's wrist. "What are you saying?" he asked, easing Daniel's hand away from him. "Did something happen at the St. Clair place that I don't know about?"

"It happened a long time ago. There was never any proof," Daniel said weakly, turning his eyes away from Randolph. "But there was much speculation."

"What speculation?" Randolph persisted.

Daniel moved his head slowly around. His eyes locked with Randolph's. "Disappearances. Murders," he growled.

Randolph's body jerked. "Murders?" he gasped. "What murders?"

"Like I said, there wasn't any proof," Daniel said dryly. "And speculation wasn't enough for the authorities. They refused to even question George St. Clair about the missin' women. They were too tangled up in worries of secedin' from the Union. Things like that."

"Women?" Randolph said, eyes wide. "What women?"

"Like I said, there wasn't proof," Daniel sighed. "But my Amelia did strangely disappear."

"You're speaking of your wife? You think she was *murdered*?"

Daniel's voice was weak, his eyes hazy with tears. He reached for Randolph's hand and clutched onto it. "Get Caroline away from that St. Clair place," he said, his head bobbing as he attempted to raise it from his pillow. "Keep her from Gavin St. Clair. Marry her, Randolph. Marry her, damn it. . . ."

# *Eleven*

$S$t. Clair Manor loomed over Caroline, casting its shadows all about her. The morning sun wasn't strong enough yet to illuminate the house into something more acceptable.

A chill traveled through Caroline as her gaze moved up to the tower windows. They seemed to be alive, like wide, gaping eyes, forever watching her! If it wasn't for Gavin and the mystery of the missing portrait, she would turn and flee, never to return again.

But as it was, she was compelled to go on inside, regardless of how the house affected her.

As though willed to, her gaze traveled to the stable behind the house. Again the boarded-up doors conjured up images inside her head, images only brought to her consciousness by her nightmares.

Shaking off her dread, she hurried into the house. Moving lightly across the bare floor, making barely a sound, she went to the library. In the dark shadows she looked around and found the branch of candles that she had left there the last time she had been at St. Clair Manor. She groaned, seeing that the candles had burned down to only stubs of melted wax with hardly a wick left to light.

But still she tried. The flames sputtered and then began glowing golden in the room, which was dark and austere from its grimy windows and tall shelves of books smelling musty on all sides of her.

To lighten her mood, and to surprise Gavin, Caroline decided to choose a bolt of cloth for drapes and wallpaper for the walls. Then she would search for the portrait. . . .

Carrying the branch of candles before her, she walked toward the desk where she had left the fabrics and catalog. But she could already see they were no longer there. Her eyes swept from one end of the massive desk to the other. When she reached it, she stooped to even look behind and beside it but still she couldn't find them.

Confused, she took a step backward and let her gaze move slowly about the room, still searching.

Then anger flamed inside her. Gavin was surely playing games with her. Why else had the fabric and catalog been moved? Did he or didn't he want her suggestions? Why had he even given her the key? To play games?

She stormed from the room, in the mood for anything but games. She had a mystery to solve and she wouldn't let anyone's foolishness stand in the way. She would use Gavin's key for a purpose . . . her purpose. She would find the portrait and then throw the key in Gavin's face!

Determination and anger spurring her onward, Caroline chose to start her search from the top of this dreadful mansion and work her way downward. She would first examine the tower room. It seemed a likely enough place in which to hide things. Perhaps she would even find the bolts of fabric and catalog!

Caroline's anger soon fused with fear as she looked up the dark staircase. Her uneasiness was heightened by the eerie quiet of the house. It was as though someone was there, hardly daring to breathe, waiting to pounce on her. Hadn't her Cousin Todd done this to her many times in Aunt Meg's big old house? Caroline hadn't seen or heard him until he had jumped out and grabbed her by the wrists, laughing hysterically into her face grown ashen with fright.

But that was long ago, in a different house, under

different circumstances. This was now and she knew she was alone. The only other person known to have a key to St. Clair Manor besides herself was Gavin, and he certainly wasn't there. She was free to do as she pleased and she must be done with it quickly. Randolph Jamieson didn't usually stay long at Twin Oaks. She must return to see to her uncle . . .

Yet Caroline's throat was still tight as she climbed the lonesome staircase. Her eyes kept turning upward, watching for any sudden ghostly movements. And when she reached the second floor and saw how it was so dark, quiet, and closed up, going farther became even harder. But she had no other choice if she was to ever find the portrait. That had been her objective from the beginning, not helping Gavin renovate this ghostly manor!

Audibly sighing, she finally began her ascent up the stairs that led to the tower. The stairs creaked and gave slightly beneath her weight. She was anxiously glad when she finally reached the door. But her hopes faltered when she found the door securely locked.

Frustrated, she turned and worked the doorknob, then shook her head in disgust and stormed back down the stairs, again wondering about Gavin. First he hides the fabrics and catalog from her and now he denies her access to this room? Why would he, when he had heartily welcomed her into his other rooms?

Her face darkened with a frown. The portraits were probably there. But she wouldn't let that stop her from looking in the other rooms. She just might be wrong.

Relieved to find no other doors locked, Caroline began going from room to room, finding each one dusky behind its grimy windows. All the upstairs rooms were bedrooms, as she had earlier surmised, with massive, four-poster beds and empty, musty wardrobes.

And then Caroline entered another bedroom that seemed to have been used for another purpose. She looked about her with interest. This bedroom had evidently been used for the storage of odds and ends. There were several pieces of broken furniture crowded together, rolls of carpet, and bundles of faded curtains.

She began exploring. An overturned box contained old rags. Another was filled with books with crumbling, yellowed pages. Others were filled with lacy things, feather boas, plumes from hats, and tarnished jewelry of no value. There were bundles of letters tied with lavender ribbon, a large Bible with a gilt clasp, buttoned boots, and an assortment of different-colored parasols.

And then Caroline found bolts of fabric, but not the ones she had previously seen. These were much older, lying among debris on the bed.

Placing her branch of candles on a table, she went to the bed and lifted a heavy bolt of fabric into her arms. Blowing dust from it, she found this length of fabric to be of rose satin, with gold braid decoration. She placed it back on the bed and let her fingers smooth over other bolts of material, some of silk, others of brocade.

"We have here the beginnings of drapes," she said, laughing softly, practicing what she would say to Gavin the next time they would be in St. Clair Manor together. Who needed the bolts now hidden from her! She would show Gavin!

And feeling as though she had taken enough time away from her uncle, she left the bedroom and again traveled the darkness of the stairs to the first floor. She looked wistfully about her, wondering if she would ever find the portrait. But it had been hidden from her for a reason and she would never give up until she found it, *and* the reason why it had been kept from her.

Blowing the candles out and placing the holder on a table, she left the house. She securely locked the door, then fled down the steps and across the lawn. As she took the turn from the gate, her breath was stolen from her when she almost ran into a buggy.

Her eyes widened in disbelief when she found
Randolph sitting in the buggy, looking smugly down
at her.

"Your headache? Is it better?" Randolph said sarcastically, resting the buggy reins on his lap. "And, my
dear, is this where you take your naps when you feel
the need to ward off a headache? I think it unwise,
whatever your reason for being at St. Clair Manor."

Caroline gathered her wits and cast aside her initial
shock of finding Randolph Jamieson there. Her eyes
sparkled with rage. Her cheeks grew hot. "Are you
spying on me?" she hissed.

Randolph shrugged. "Not exactly," he mused. "I
just happened along when I saw you leaving St. Clair
Manor." He leaned into her face. "I must confess I am
intrigued as to why you are here. Or do I even have to
ask?" He straightened his back and looked toward St.
Clair Manor. "Where is he, Caroline? Surely you've
come to be with Gavin St. Clair."

"How dare you even suggest . . ." Caroline said
icily, but quite aware of her pounding heart upon
having been discovered at St. Clair Manor by yet
another man. First Gavin, then Elroy. Now Randolph! Surely her uncle would be the next to know!

Again Randolph shrugged. "I've suggested nothing," he said, a smile lifting his lips. "I have only seen
and wondered." Again he leaned into Caroline's face.
"As would your uncle, should he find out."

"And you're the one to tell him? Is that what you're
saying, Randolph?" Caroline cried, doubling her fingers into tight fists.

"He wouldn't be happy knowing," Randolph said.
"If he did, he would demand that you never see Gavin
St. Clair again."

"And that's what you want, isn't it, Randolph?"
Caroline said, placing her hands on her hips. "To
what length would you go to win a victory over Gavin
St. Clair?"

Randolph's smile faded. He ran a finger nervously
about his collar. "Victory?" he said, paling.

"Gavin told me how you two have always competed against each other," Caroline spat. "And *you* called Gavin your competition at the ball. Randolph? Am I a prize you wish to win? Would you go to my uncle and tell him about my being at St. Clair Manor to help your cause along? If so, you will be wasting your time, sir. I would never choose you over any man for any reason."

With a swish of skirt and flip of hair, Caroline hurried away from him.

"Caroline, couldn't you accuse Gavin of the same?" Randolph shouted from behind her. "He, too, loves a challenge!"

Caroline's footsteps faltered as Randolph's words hit her like a slap in the face. Had Gavin known all along that Randolph was her uncle's lawyer? Had she been the pawn in another competition between him and Randolph?

But then she remembered that *she* had made the first move. He had found her on his property. It was at that moment, before he even knew who she was, that their eyes had met and held, and passion had even then begun to weave between them. . . .

Totally ignoring Randolph's suggestion, Caroline continued her flight, glad when she was safely inside Twin Oaks, yet somewhat fearful of facing her uncle.

"Miss Burton? Your uncle is asking for you," Rosa said in the hallway. "You'd best go on up. He seems bothered by something."

"Randolph. Randolph Jamieson," Caroline said, kneading her brow. "He's surely the cause. I'm beginning to believe his visits are a hindrance instead of a help to my uncle. He's not at all like I at first thought. He's not to be trusted. Rosa, I might suggest you even deny him entrance into my uncle's room any time soon."

"But your uncle looks forward—"

"I've got to believe he will be better off, Rosa. Please do as I suggest."

Caroline whipped around and hurried to her uncle's room. Brushing the door open, she stopped and stared in disbelief at the opened drapes, window, and shutters. Her uncle had never let her open these for sunshine and fresh air. And he most certainly wouldn't have let Rosa. Rosa had complained of his refusal to do so many times. Then it could have only been Randolph. He knew ways to twist her uncle around his little finger!

Caroline glanced over at her uncle. He was dozing, his snores breaking the silence of the room. She then tiptoed to the window and an iciness filled her veins when she saw how the window had a direct view of St. Clair Manor. Randolph must have seen her go there. He hadn't just happened by. He had gone there purposely!

"So there you are," Daniel grumbled. "Caroline, will you close the damn window? I don't even know why I agreed to let Randolph open it. The breeze is giving me a chill."

With trembling fingers, Caroline did as he asked. Then she went to sit beside him, fearing even more the questions he would now most surely ask her.

"How are you this morning, Uncle Daniel?" she asked in a weaker than usual voice.

"Fine. Just fine," Daniel said, studying her. "And you?"

"Oh, quite well, thank you," Caroline said, laughing softly. She was aware of his strained politeness, which had to mean that Randolph had told him something of her recent behavior. But what?

"And did you enjoy Randolph's spiffy function last night?" Daniel asked, reaching to pat her hand. "He said that it went quite well. But I'd like to hear your comments."

Caroline hoped that her uncle wouldn't feel the cold clamminess of her hand as he wrapped his bony fingers around it. He had to be observing her uneasiness under his close scrutiny. His green eyes were almost devouring her!

"It was a lovely ball," she said quickly. "He has a lovely house."

Daniel's eyes squinted and his jaw tightened. "I imagine his garden is lovely also?" he slyly questioned.

Caroline's pulse quickened. She fluttered her lashes nervously. "Garden . . . ?" she murmured.

"Did you or did you not take a stroll in Randolph's garden?" he asked with an edge of sarcasm in his voice.

Caroline grew suddenly angry, now realizing that at least one incident had been reported to her uncle by Randolph. He had told him of finding her in his garden with Gavin. Why else would her uncle question her so closely?

"Does it matter so much what I think of Randolph's garden?" she asked, ready to defend herself instead of recoiling from her uncle's accusing stare.

"No. But it matters to me who you were with while you were *in* the garden," Daniel growled. He pulled his hand from Caroline's and pointed a shaking finger at her. "You stay away from Gavin St. Clair. Do you hear? He's from a no-good family. I told you what I thought about George St. Clair. His nephew surely is no better. I want more for you, Caroline. Randolph Jamieson is more to my liking."

Caroline saw his flushed cheeks and the wildness in his eyes. He was much too upset. She must do anything to settle him down. Even if she must add to her list of lies, she had to make sure that he didn't have further cause to be upset, though she so wanted to question him more about the St. Clairs. Surely he hadn't told her everything . . .

Rising from her chair and almost toppling it backward in her anxiousness to console her uncle, Caroline leaned over him and placed her hands on his cheeks. She bent to kiss his brow.

"Uncle Daniel, it seems Randolph has needlessly worried you," she murmured. "Yes, I did go to the

garden with Gavin St. Clair. It was quite crowded and
warm in Randolph's house. I needed a breath of air.
Mr. St. Clair was kind enough to escort me to the
garden. You wouldn't have wanted me to go alone.
Now wouldn't I have looked like a wallflower?"

"You could have asked Randolph to escort you to
the garden," he said sullenly.

"Randolph was mingling with other guests," she
lied, hating herself for having to do it. Damn that
Randolph for placing her in this position!

"Randolph saw you going toward St. Clair Manor
from the open window only a short while ago, Caroline," Daniel grumbled. "Were you going there to
meet Gavin St. Clair?"

Caroline paled. Randolph had told everything, it
seemed. "No. Certainly not," she gasped. "I was
taking my morning stroll. Even you suggested I do
so."

"I told you to stay away from that St. Clair place,"
he said weakly.

Lowering her eyes, Caroline nodded. "I know," she
murmured.

"Don't go there again, Caroline," Daniel said, his
voice fading.

Caroline's eyes slowly lifted. She was spared another lie, for her uncle had thankfully drifted off into a
sudden sleep. How could she have told him that she
would never go to St. Clair Manor again when in truth
she would be going tomorrow? Though Gavin had
played games with the bolts of fabric and catalog of
wallpaper samples, Caroline would still go to meet
him at St. Clair Manor.

But she must tell him that this would be the last
time. Even if she didn't find the portrait, she had to
do what was best for her uncle. Even if she couldn't
see Gavin again. . . .

# *Twelve*

*D*efying her uncle's wishes and feeling guilty for doing so, Caroline fled from Twin Oaks to meet with Gavin. She truly had no choice but to go. If she didn't arrive at St. Clair Manor as she had promised Gavin, there was a chance he would come to Twin Oaks, asking why. She had to prevent that at all costs. Her uncle's dislike of the St. Clairs had been proven to Caroline more than once. Did he suspect Aunt Amelia's infidelity? Had she *been* unfaithful?

This question gnawed at Caroline's insides. She was not the sort to let a question go unanswered. And she so wanted to try to find these answers from Gavin. But should she be wrong about her aunt, Caroline would look not only foolish but also as though she were a busybody.

The sun was hazed over by clouds, cooling Caroline. Though she knew she had to fight the low limbs of the gnarled live oaks and the briars of the weeds, she had chosen to not wear a drab skirt and blouse this day. Instead, she had dressed in a low-cut gingham dress with tiny rosebud designs on the foreground. Its gaily puffed sleeves and fully-gathered skirt accentuated her tininess.

Her hair, hanging loose and scarlet across her pale shoulders, emphasized the gentle oval shape of her face and the crisp green of her eyes. Her tiny tapered ankles and small black slippers flashed beneath her skirt as she began stepping widely around the marshy

mud and headed more into the thicket than she
desired.

Her heart beat erratically showing just how nervous
she was because of her anxiousness to see Gavin and
her frustrations over how her uncle would feel about
what she was doing. But she would make this visit to
St. Clair Manor brief. She would explain in the best
way she could that she must never return to the
ghostly manor again. But when Gavin asked her why,
what could she say? And *could* she refrain from going
there again? The portrait would always be in her
mind, haunting her. . . .

Gavin suddenly came into view, riding up behind
St. Clair Manor on his beautiful stallion. Caroline felt
her heartbeat thunder like horse's hooves inside her,
seeing him again, loving him so.

Yet he seemed to carry with him the same sort of
mysterious air she had seen that first time she had
watched him from her bedroom window at Twin
Oaks. And feeling this added to Caroline's apprehension over meeting him this day, though the fact that
she was hopelessly in love with him made her cast all
doubts aside. Breathless, she began running toward
him. . . .

She and Gavin arrived at the front of the house at
the same time. Gavin dismounted his steed while
Caroline took the horse's reins and secured them at a
hitching post. And then drawn as the tide is by the
moon, they moved into each other's arms, undaunted
by being in the open for anyone to see.

"I'm so glad you came," Gavin whispered, his
breath hot against her silken cheek.

Her lips sought his. Caroline unashamedly coiled
her arms about Gavin's neck, feeling the press of his
hard, muscled body against hers, ignoring the partial
intrusion of the holstered pistol at his waist.

And then they parted and walked hand-in-hand up
the front steps and on into the manor where gloomy
shadows lay heavy all about them.

"Gavin, there's something about this place that

always gives me the shivers," Caroline whispered, unable to suppress a shudder. "Do you truly think you can ever make it altogether livable? I, myself, doubt that."

"I must give it a wholehearted try," Gavin said, stepping away from her. "I just can't sit idly by any longer and see it go to waste. I've neglected it long enough. I feel I must restore it as payment to my uncle who took me in when I was left orphaned. That is what he would want."

He gazed about him, his dark eyes heavy with an unspoken sadness. "Ghostly?" he said, rubbing his chin. "Yes, I guess you could call it that. I sometimes feel that my uncle is close by, watching. His personality was such an enigmatic one, quite overpowering, to say the least. If anyone's soul could linger, it would be his."

Caroline hugged herself with her arms, shivering even more at the way in which Gavin was speaking about his uncle. "Gavin, please don't talk like that," she murmured. "This house is foreboding enough without having to hear about ghosts lingering, spying souls."

Gavin laughed throatily. He took a silver candleholder from a table and lit its half-burned candle. He held it close to Caroline, and lifted his lips into an amused, teasing smile. "Why, darling, do you believe in ghosts?"

"Only if they walk and talk," she tried to tease back, not believing for one second that she was convincing in her forced, lighthearted manner.

Taking Caroline by an elbow, Gavin led her into the dark hallway. He smiled down at her. "I can guarantee that the ghosts who dwell in St. Clair Manor neither talk nor walk," he continued to tease. "Does that make you feel better, darling?"

"Should it?" She softly laughed. "I think not."

The candle's glow was a nervous gold shimmer, casting its soft light on Gavin, revealing his neat ruffled white shirt buttoned to the collar, and the tightness of his fawn breeches tucked into black riding boots.

His midnight black hair shone as though waxed and only a slight wave had fallen onto his sleekly tanned brow. His proud, straight nose and enticing eyes caused the usual flutter in Caroline's heart.

Gavin led her toward the library. "Well? Did you choose a wallpaper to your liking?" he asked, smiling down at her. "And did you even find a bolt of material to your liking?" He laughed softly. "Though many of each truly must be chosen. This house has many neglected windows and walls."

While worrying over her uncle and having to tell Gavin that she could no longer come to St. Clair Manor, Caroline had forgotten about the missing objects of which Gavin now spoke. She swirled away from him, to face him. "Why, Gavin, I loved them all," she tested, her eyes gleaming. "In fact, so much that I can't wait to show them to you."

"Good," Gavin said. "I'm glad. Let's go into the library. Show me which ones you have chosen."

Caroline forked an eyebrow, looking in awe at Gavin. He knew the bolts of material and the wallpaper samples were no longer in the library, yet he continued to play a game with her!

Well, she could play it as well as he.

"I'd love to," she said, smiling wickedly up at him. She walked on ahead of him into the library. She gave him another smile across her shoulder as she walked to the desk. And when she turned and found the fabrics and the wallpaper samples there again, she paled and took an awkward step backward.

Gavin was quickly at her side, staring down at her questioningly. "What is it, Caroline?" he asked softly. "You look as though you've seen a ghost."

Anger flashed in her eyes. She placed her hands on her hips. "Why are you doing this?" she fumed.

Gavin was taken aback. His eyes widened. "Doing what?" he asked.

"Playing games," Caroline said dryly. "I don't find it amusing, Gavin."

"I don't know what you're talking about," Gavin said, nervously raking his fingers through his hair.

"You moved them and now they're back," she accused. "Why, Gavin? Don't act as though you don't know."

"I don't."

"And now you even lie?"

"I'm not lying. What the hell's going on, Caroline?"

"You tell me, Gavin."

"How can I, when I don't know."

Caroline frowned, seeing so much in his eyes and hearing so much in his voice. He seemed genuinely confused, as though he didn't know what she was talking about. "You didn't hide the fabrics and wall-paper samples from me and then return them to the desk?" she asked in an almost whisper.

"What?" he gasped.

"You didn't did you, Gavin?" Caroline asked, a shiver racing across her flesh, believing him and knowing that someone else had.

"Hell, no," he growled.

Caroline looked slowly about her, feeling a ghostly presence as she had at other times. "Someone did," she murmured. "My eyes do not play tricks on me, Gavin."

Gavin circled an arm about her waist and drew her to him. "Honey, surely you are imagining things," he chuckled. "Who would do that? Why? And how would anyone get in here to do it?"

"Gavin, I saw . . ."

"Well, it's nothing to get so fretful over," he said, chuckling, yet in wonder himself as he looked to Caroline and then the desk. He then swept her from the library and she didn't even question him when he began leading her up the nebulous gloom of the staircase, quite aware of the heat of his touch as he held her possessively by the arm. . . .

"As I said earlier, I'm glad you came," Gavin said thickly. "I had thought that after the other night, you would have second thoughts. I could understand your apprehensions, should you have them. But I see that you have accepted that which has begun between us. And I'm glad."

Not wishing to speak of such sensual matters for she knew where such talk could lead, Caroline flipped the satin of her hair from across her shoulders and down her back and led the conversation into a different, much safer direction.

"And what have you already planned for St. Clair Manor's rooms?" she said softly, not wanting to tell him so quickly that this was her last time to be there. She would prolong the agony of telling him just a little longer. She so wanted to be with him, forever. . . .

"Which rooms are you going to renovate first?" she added. "The bedrooms? That does seem to be your focus this morning."

The mere mention of bedrooms caused her cheeks to flame in color, and she wished that she had chosen her words more carefully . . . more wisely. . . .

"You have already seen the one bedroom," Gavin mused. "Do you think it needs fresh wallpaper? Fresh paint at the window casings? Or did you find it exactly to your liking?"

Caroline tensed. "I would suggest looking into ideas for other bedrooms," she said softly, edging from his side to take a quick step upward away from him. "Surely you plan to renovate all of the rooms, do you not?"

Gavin chuckled low. He again stepped to her side just as they together reached the second floor landing. He took her by a hand and began leading her to the master bedroom. "Ah, come on, now," he teased. "Let us first begin with the room already somewhat familiar to us. You know that it could be easier to renovate."

"Gavin, I don't wish . . ." Caroline said, but already found herself being guided into the room where the huge mirror opposite the magnificent bed already showed her reflection back to her.

She turned and looked up at Gavin, seeing that he had already placed the candle on a table. "Gavin . . ." she said, but he clasped onto her shoulders and yanked her fiercely to him, causing her words to fade. His lips met hers in a wild passion, his fingers were digging into the flesh of her shoulders.

Caroline was fast becoming mindless and found herself returning his kiss in a silent surrender. Even when she found herself being led backward toward the bed she couldn't find the will power to fight against what she knew must not happen again.

Yet his embrace was so torrid and ecstatic, heated waves of rapture were already splashing through her.

Now fully spread out on the bed, with him leaning over her, Caroline softly moaned when his hands unbuttoned her dress and eased it from her shoulders, and then fully cupped her breasts. She tossed her head, her eyes misting over with tears of passion's torment.

"Gavin, please . . . don't . . ." she murmured, then chewed her lower lip in ecstasy as his tongue spiraled around the peak of a breast, urging it to stiffness.

"Darling, just relax," Gavin urged. "Let me love you again. One night could never be enough for either of us. You know that."

"I just don't want to *want* you in this way," Caroline whispered, now feverish as she watched him pull her dress and petticoats away from her, and then remove her shoes. "I shouldn't, Gavin. I know that it's wrong." She crossed her arms over her breasts and began sliding away from him. "I must leave. I must go back to Twin Oaks now. I had only come to tell you that I could never come to St. Clair Manor again. My uncle . . ."

Gavin seemed not to have heard her. He removed his holstered pistol and laid it aside. He then began unbuttoning his shirt, revealing his wide, muscular shoulders and dark chest hairs that led downward to where Caroline could see his hardened man's strength as he dropped his breeches.

And as she reached for her dress, he was there holding her wrists to the bed. He again leaned over her, spreading her legs with a bold sweep of his knee. "You don't believe any of that nonsense that you are saying," he said huskily. "You know that I love you. I told you that I did. Darling, I was awake all night, waiting for the moment to be wholly with you again. Don't you want me as much? You did the other night."

Shaking her head, trying to avoid his lips which were now searching for hers, she softly cried, "Yes, I wanted you," she said. "I do want you. But not like this. I don't want to meet you in a cheap rendezvous. And my uncle—I can no longer betray him. He trusts me so. Gavin, please understand."

"All I understand right now is that you are fighting against something that shared again could be so beautiful," he argued softly. "Caroline, just let it happen. You and I are the only witnesses. Your uncle need never know. Love me, Caroline. Love me."

His hands, taunting her, smoothing seductively over her body, made Caroline squirm. Drugged by pleasure, she shook her head. "Yes, yes," she whispered.

Her mouth flowered open as his lips met hers in a blaze of urgency. His tongue moved into her mouth, tasting the sweetness that she now willingly offered him. Her hands swept wildly over the expanse of his sleekly muscled chest and then locked together behind his neck and drew his mouth even harder into hers as he entered her from below.

A thick, husky groan filled the room as Gavin began his even thrusts. He gripped her soft buttocks and lifted her higher, smiling to himself when he found her willingly hot and wet as her hips worked against him to meet each of his thrusts inside her.

Caroline opened her eyes and looked toward the mirror, flaming even more inside when she saw how she and Gavin were locked so sensually together. And when he turned his eyes and also looked in the mirror's reflection, it was then that their explosion of love shook them both in rapture. The sight of their matched loveplay drugged them into completion.

Still clinging and breathless, Gavin's fingers twined through Caroline's hair. He led her lips to his and pressed hot kisses into them. Her hands, trailing over his body down to where he had pleasured her, caused him to feel strength rising in his manhood again. He began soft strokes inside her. She opened herself fully to him, feeling that her hunger for him would never be fully fed.

Gavin's eyes branded her as he looked down at her. His hands kneaded her breasts, his body moved, stroking, softly stroking.

"I've never wanted a woman more than you," he whispered. "I shall never want another woman again."

His mouth was scalding as he again kissed her, causing a scorching flame to shoot through Caroline. She clung about his neck; she locked her legs about his thighs. Her senses reeled in drunken pleasure. As she felt the curl of this familiar heat growing in her lower body, she knew that again she was about to experience the ultimate of pleasure shared with a man, and was filled with wonder of herself and him. . . .

And then again the world melted away, their naked bodies fusing into one. . . .

Gavin buried his face in Caroline's cleavage, drinking in the sweet scent of her. Exhausted from his labors, he panted. His hands would not keep still, but kept wandering over the sweet plane of her body. He chuckled softly.

"Darling, what do you suggest for this room? You never did tell me," he teased. "Do you think the mirror should remain? Or do you think it is too effective?"

Caroline swept a stray hair back from her brow. His breath was so sweet and hot against her breasts.

"Effective? What do you mean, Gavin?" she asked, though innocent she was not. She had understood only too well just moments ago the true purpose of the mirror. She had to wonder just how many bodies it had magnified and teased throughout the years.

Even now were there some reflections captured there for eternity? Some neither she nor Gavin could even see? Had her Aunt Amelia been reflected in the mirror? The thought gave Caroline a fearful feeling, reminding her of the haunting effects of this ghostly house and of her reasons for being there this day. She must find the courage to tell Gavin.

Gavin slipped away from Caroline, and rolled onto his side, facing her. He caressed her skin lightly with his fingertips. "Ah, but aren't you an innocent one," he chuckled. "You know damn well what I meant. The mirror was placed opposite the bed for only one purpose and you know as well as I that its purpose *was* quite effective this morning."

"Morning . . . ?" Caroline whispered, then bolted from the bed. She grabbed her clothes and hurried into them. "It *is* morning. I hadn't planned to be gone this long. I must be at my uncle's bedside when he awakens. He expects me to be there. And he must never know I was here. He was so adamant about my *not* coming."

Gavin rose up on an elbow. "He knows you've been here?" he asked guardedly.

"Not exactly . . ." Caroline murmured, combing her fingers through her hair.

"Then *what* . . . ?"

Caroline didn't wish to bring Randolph's name into the conversation, though he was the cause of this strain now present in her life.

"I just mustn't come to St. Clair Manor again," she said, edging toward the door. "Please understand, Gavin. And please don't come to Twin Oaks. My uncle's health has worsened."

"God, Caroline, are you saying you won't see me again?" Gavin asked, rushing to his feet.

Frustrated, Caroline shook her head. "I don't know. But I *do* know I must go see to my uncle." Her heart ached as she ran from the room and down the stairs. And once outside she didn't dare look back or she just might change her mind and return to Gavin.

And then she suddenly remembered that she had forgotten to bring his key to give it back to him. She would have an opportunity to meet with him again, but when and where . . . ?

Tears threatening to blind her, Caroline began running, her gaze directed to Twin Oaks and at Rosa who was waving frantically from the wide porch.

Caroline's pulse quickened and a queasiness entered her stomach. There could only be one reason for Rosa to be so upset. It had to be about Uncle Daniel. . . .

# *Thirteen*

$T$he carriage wheels sounded hollow as they ambled up the drive which led to Twin Oaks. Caroline sat shrouded in a black veil and cape, feeling lost and empty, for she had just buried her Uncle Daniel. Though Caroline had known all along that her uncle's death had been imminent, she hadn't expected it to happen so quickly. She now wished that she had been more attentive to him, yet knew there truly hadn't been that much more that she could have done. And now . . . ? She had many responsibilities facing her.

Randolph Jamieson sat beside her in the carriage. Nervously drumming his fingers on the rim of his top hat, he cast Caroline a sideways glance. "And what are your plans now that your uncle is gone?" he asked, trying to hide the strain in his voice. "You do plan to stay on at Twin Oaks, don't you?"

Caroline stiffened, having guessed that he wouldn't wait that long to begin his interferences. Oh, how had she been so wrong about him in the beginning? Her first impressions were becoming untrustworthy, it seemed.

"I haven't thought much one way or the other about my future plans," she said quietly, her eyes still burning from scalding tears, having watched her uncle's casket being lowered into the dark abyss of the ground only moments ago.

Randolph thumped his walking stick on the carriage floorboard. "You have just become quite a wealthy young lady," he said, watching her, wishing he could see more clearly through the veil. "Your uncle was a wise investor and he cleverly made sure that what monies he had on hand at the onset of the war were transferred to New York banks."

"I know that," Caroline sighed. "But the fact that I've inherited my uncle's wealth doesn't make my loss less. I shall forever miss my uncle." She gave Twin Oaks a shadowy glance as the carriage drew to a halt before it. It had been lonely before; what would it be *now*?

Randolph reached across Caroline and opened the carriage door. "Let me see you into your house. Perhaps you would like me to disclose the full terms of the will now. I have no other appointments at this time. It would honor me if you would take me completely into your confidence, as your uncle did."

Caroline glared over at Randolph. "This is not the time for a gentleman's company even if the gentleman thinks he is to be my lawyer," she said icily. "I want to be alone. Totally. But I would expect that you will return in a few days so that we can clear up any questions you and I both might have concerning the will—and you, whom I plan to replace for another lawyer who will be more to my liking."

She lifted her veil and let him see the coldness in her eyes. "Do you understand, Randolph?" she added. "You are going to quickly know that though I am quite young *and* a woman, I can handle my own affairs without your assistance."

Paling, Randolph reached for Caroline. "What are you saying . . . ?" he gasped.

His words were cut short as Caroline lifted the tail of her black cape and dress and helped herself out of the carriage. She was, at this moment, being assailed by many emotions, one of which was pride for having put Randolph in his place. She would forever remember how he had unduly worried her uncle, most surely into an earlier grave!

But most prominent of her emotions was her complete sadness. She already missed her uncle. She didn't want to let guilt plague her. But knowing that she had been with Gavin at the very moment that her uncle had expired tormented her with guilt. Had she been more dutiful to her uncle, then perhaps she would have been at her uncle's bedside comforting him during his last moments on earth.

But it had been Gavin to whom she had been giving her time, not her uncle. . . .

Even now she hungered for Gavin's arms about her. It was she who now needed comforting.

Rushing from the carriage into the house, she was greeted by Rosa, who stood humbly twisting the tail of her apron around her fingers.

"Is it over?" Rosa asked softly. "Is your Uncle Daniel . . . buried?"

Slipping her veil from her head and then the cape from around her shoulders, Caroline nodded. "Yes," she murmured. "It is done."

She looked about her. The hallway seemed thick with black shadows. The silence was oppressive, the loneliness almost overwhelming.

"Ma'am, what are your plans?" Rosa asked, visibly shaken by all that had transpired. "Will you be stayin' on?"

Placing her cape and veil across the banister of the staircase, Caroline shook her head. "I've been asked that same question twice in only a matter of minutes," she murmured. She walked into the parlor. The room was bleak, darkened by the half-drawn drapes at the windows. She heard Rosa following along behind her, her heavy feet creating a muffled rustle along the uncarpeted floor.

Caroline swung around and placed a hand gently on Rosa's arm. "But I understand why you are asking," she said quietly. "You are fearing the future. You fear being suddenly unemployed. Am I right?"

With wide, dark, and anxious eyes, Rosa pleaded. "Yes, ma'am," she said. "My family depends on being employed at Twin Oaks. My husband . . . he . . . ain't fit for much more than what he does around here. It's because of the war, understand."

Caroline patted Rosa's arm. She smiled warmly. "Yes. I understand," she murmured. "And, Rosa, as far as I can gather, I will be staying on. If I should change my mind, you will be the first to know. But please don't worry. My uncle wanted me to look after Twin Oaks. I feel that I must."

A heavy sigh shuddered through Rosa. Her face relaxed. "Thank the Lord," she said, dropping the corner of her apron to lay it in gentle folds over her simple cotton dress.

"I must now be left alone to think, Rosa," Caroline explained. "Please go and brew me a cup of tea. I need its warmth. I feel so . . . so empty and cold."

"Yes, ma'am," Rosa nodded. "I'll get the tea for you. Right away."

Caroline started to slump down into a chair but stopped and again spoke to Rosa. "How is Sally?" she asked. "On my last two outings I haven't seen her. She's usually with Elroy, or close by."

"She's not at all well," Rosa murmured. "But I don't know the cause."

"Have you consulted a doctor, Rosa?"

"No. I felt that the expense would be too much."

"I will pay the expense. See to it that Elroy takes her to the doctor. Right away."

Rosa's eyes brightened. "How nice you are, Miss Burton," she said, clasping her hands together before her. "I'll tell Elroy. Tonight. Oh, thank you, ma'am. Thank you."

Rosa left the room in a flurry of skirts, leaving Caroline alone with her thoughts. She settled down into a chair, staring off into space, seeing nothing, only feeling. Her fingers went to her hair and wove through its thickness, arranging it above her ears and away from her brow.

"What *am* I to do?" she whispered, feeling desperation rising inside her. She hadn't fully realized the responsibility that would come with her uncle's death.

She had been too preoccupied by Gavin . . . and the portrait.

Her eyes became wide, green pools. The portrait! Her uncle's death had caused her to forget that she still had the key to St. Clair Manor!

The sound of horse's hooves outside Twin Oaks made Caroline tense. Who would be coming to call so soon after her uncle's burial? Randolph had just left so it wouldn't be he. Who else but Gavin had she seen on horseback in these almost isolated parts of the country?

Her hands went to her cheeks, feeling their heat as a quick blush rose into them. "Gavin!" she whispered harshly.

With shaking legs, she rose from the chair, went to the window, and meekly drew the drapes aside, giving her a better look. And when she saw Gavin dismounting his proud steed, her heart began a crazy beating, yet she felt ashamed for reacting to him at a time when mourning for her uncle should be the most prominent thought on her mind.

The pounding of the knocker on the door drew her from the window to stand behind a chair, where she clasped her fingers tightly onto its back, waiting. She listened to the quiet exchange of words between Rosa and Gavin. Her heart followed his footsteps down the hallway and on into the room where she stood, transfixed in place and torn by both wanting him and hating her desire.

Gavin was dressed handsomely in a white linen coat, fawn breeches, and matching cravat, yet the holstered pistol at his waist tended to detract from his otherwise utterly wholesome appearance. His hair was only slightly mussed from the romp on his horse; his eyes were filled with sincere sympathy as he went to Caroline and drew her away from the chair and against his steel frame.

"I only just heard about your uncle's death," he said thickly, weaving his hands through her hair as they stood cheek to cheek. "I hope you don't mind that I've come. I couldn't let you bear the burden of sadness alone once I knew. I would have come even sooner but I was called out of town by a client."

Relieved that he wasn't angry with her for having fled from him the last time they had been together, and comforted to know that he had not purposely ignored her during her time of loss, Caroline crept her arms up and about his neck.

She leaned back and let her eyes drink in his nearness, tears warm and moist at the corners of her eyes. "I'm glad you did come. I had thought you just didn't care," she said, stifling a sob.

He placed a hand softly across her lips, shushing her. "I'll always care," he murmured. "I'll always love you."

Caroline forced herself to brush aside the guilt of his being there in what was, until this day, her uncle's house, just wanting to be with him to accept the comfort and love that he was offering. "I'm so glad," she whispered, tears sparkling in her eyes. "Hold me, darling. Hold me."

Gavin's lips pressed hers in a soft kiss, and his hands caressed the slim lines of her back. And then he drew away from her, yet still held her hand. "I can't stay long now, Caroline," he mumbled. "I just did arrive back in Charleston and I have much to do to straighten a mess up that one of my clients is in. I may even have to be gone a couple of days again. One can never tell about these things. Do you understand?"

His hands, warm in hers, gave her the courage to shake her head yes, though she wanted to have the right to deny him his leaving her again so soon.

"Yes," she said, almost choking on the words. "I understand. But please return when you can, Gavin. I've so much on my mind. I'm not even sure where to begin now that . . . that . . . I own all of my uncle's properties. My uncle didn't instruct me about his business matters, so I have much to learn."

She wanted to say that her uncle had purposely avoided teaching her because he had wanted her to

count on Randolph Jamieson to do her the honors!
But she didn't want to think of Randolph Jamieson,
much less speak his name!

Again Gavin drew her into his arms and hugged
her. "I'll help in whatever way I can," he said huskily.
"There aren't too many times that I will be too tied up
with clients to help you. But are you sure you even
want me to? You know how your uncle felt about your
associating with me, a St. Clair."

Caroline's lashes lowered, shielding her eyes.
"Please don't speak of that now," she said. "I don't
want to be reminded of how I behaved behind my
uncle's back."

"Nonsense," Gavin growled. He framed her face
between his hands and forced her eyes to meet his.
"We are two people in love. Never regret what love led
us into."

Their lips met in a tender kiss and then Gavin
swept from her arms and began walking toward the
door, holding her hand, urging her along beside him.
"I really must go, Caroline," he said, giving her a
heavy-lidded sideways glance. "You need your rest
now anyway."

His gaze traveled over her and then their eyes met
and locked. "You're even lovely in black," he said. He
leaned down to kiss the tip of her nose and then
walked to the door. "I'll return as soon as I can."

Caroline walked him outside and watched him
mount his horse. He waved heartily to her as he
galloped away. She returned the wave, then went back
inside the silence of Twin Oaks and stared from a
window toward St. Clair Manor. It seemed to be
beckoning to her, making her realize that the mystery
of the portrait was yet to be solved.

A shiver coursed through her and a coldness engulfed her as she remembered her uncle's warnings.
Surely there was more at St. Clair Manor besides the
portrait that had caused her uncle to demand she not
go there. How could she place the mystery behind
her? She felt that finding out the truth was even more

important now that her uncle was dead. She owed him the truth, even in death. He had never uncovered the mystery of his wife's death. What if Caroline could?

Determined, she headed for the stairs to get the key to the ghostly manor from her bedroom. She would go to St. Clair Manor, but for a much different reason than surveying the ghostly manor for redecorations. The portrait! That was her sole purpose for returning to the house that caused a sense of foreboding to cling to her every step whenever she was alone in it. . . .

Only a few footsteps up the stairs, Caroline stopped with a start. She turned and looked toward the door, having heard a muffled gunshot from somewhere outside.

"Who could be shooting? And at what?" she whispered to herself. Then, shrugging, she moved on up the staircase, her thoughts too filled with other things to wonder about a lone gunshot. . . .

Back again inside St. Clair Manor, Caroline carried a candle down the dark hallway. Her gaze settled on a closed door, one of which she had yet to explore behind. Quietly tiptoeing, she went to the door and opened it.

Holding the candle high, she found herself in another parlor, handsome in its decor. Her gaze traveled around the many gilt chairs and solid oak tables. At the far end of the room the blackened mouth of a fireplace seemed to be staring at her, and sitting before this was a huge divan with its back to her.

Edging her way further into the room, she placed the candle on a table. She would search every inch of the room for the portrait. She looked behind chairs and drapes and stepped to the front of the divan, then saw something so horrifying, her breath felt as if it had been knocked out of her.

Physical revulsion swept over her, her knees went weak, and a slow panic began rising in her throat. She found herself looking transfixed at the lifeless body of her uncle's collie, Lucky, stretched out on the divan, blood spattered on his gorgeous, silken coat of fur and dripping from his mouth.

Caroline heard someone screaming and suddenly realized that it was her own screams bouncing off the walls and back to her. She covered her mouth with a hand and turned and ran from the room, half stumbling through the hallway, and then on outside. Sobbing, she lifted her skirt high past her ankles and began to run. Half-blinded with tears, she struggled through the low overhang of live oak limbs and then on past the lagoon.

Panting and sobbing, she ran toward Twin Oaks, wanting to find refuge behind a locked door, full of wonder as to who would do such a terrible thing as kill her dog? The gunshot that she had heard! Now she knew why the shot had been fired. Someone had shot Lucky! And the dog had seemed planted at St. Clair Manor. Was it a warning? Had someone placed Lucky in St. Clair Manor for her to find? But who? Why?

Her insides grew cold as she remembered Randolph and how she only moments ago had told him that he would no longer be her lawyer. Then she remembered the pistol that Gavin always wore holstered at his hip.

"No!" she softly cried, placing a knuckle to her lips, bearing her teeth down upon it. "Gavin couldn't. Gavin wouldn't."

Her feelings of horror and remorse overwhelmed her. She wiped at her eyes, to clear them of tears, and while doing so blinded herself momentarily. Her heart lurched when she collided with someone along the path which led up to the front porch of Twin Oaks. She slung her hands away from her face and looked up into eyes the color of steel, cool in their assessment of her.

"You're runnin' like a scared rabbit," Elroy grumbled, steadying her with his free hand, while leaning on his cane with the other. "Want to tell me why, Miss Burton?"

Caroline quickly composed herself and eased away from him. She looked over her shoulder toward St. Clair Manor, then back at Elroy. "It's Lucky," she said in an almost whisper, finding it hard to speak. She pointed toward St. Clair Manor. "He's there, Elroy. Someone . . . someone shot him. Someone placed him in a parlor at St. Clair Manor! Why . . . why would anyone do that, Elroy? Why?"

Again, tears flooded her eyes. She looked away from Elroy, sobbing.

"Lucky? Shot? And he's at St. Clair Manor?" Elroy gasped. "Good God, Miss Burton, that's the work of a fiend." He paused, then placed a finger beneath her chin, pulling her face back around to meet his steady gaze. "It had to be Gavin St. Clair. Being the owner, only he has a key." Then his eyebrows forked. "Yet if I remember correctly, you have a key, don't you?"

Elroy's accusation against Gavin pierced Caroline's heart. Even Elroy thought it must be Gavin. Oh, Lord, she didn't want to believe it. She couldn't believe it. He was not the type. There surely wasn't a sinister bone in Gavin's body. To keep her sanity she had to keep thinking it must have been Randolph. Yet how would Randolph have gotten into St. Clair Manor . . . ?

Caroline slipped her hand into her pocket and removed the key. She held it in the palm of her hand and showed it to Elroy. "You know I have a key," she murmured. "You know I plan to help Gavin renovate St. Clair Manor. That's why I was there now. But what does that have to do with this?"

"Takin' on more responsibilities than you can handle, ain't you?" Elroy growled. "I'd think that Twin Oaks would be more than enough to keep your mind occupied."

Caroline squared her shoulders angrily. "Elroy, how I plan to spend my time now or in the future is none of your business," she snapped. Then her eyes wavered, again remembering Lucky's fate. She cast her eyes downward. "I'm sorry to be so snappish," she apologized. "I've just gone through a traumatic experience."

She implored him with her eyes. "Elroy, I must ask a favor of you," she murmured, swallowing hard.

"I thought you wanted no interferences from me," he grumbled, his thin line of lips set in an angry, straight line. "Now you've changed your mind?"

"I would appreciate it if you could go and remove Lucky from St. Clair Manor and bring him home and bury him," she said in a rush of words. "I left the house unlocked. You can go on in without any problem."

She handed the key to Elroy, sullen. "Will you do that for me, Elroy? I just . . . just . . . can't," she quickly added. "And please securely lock St. Clair Manor when you leave?"

"I guess I don't have much choice," he snarled, taking the key, "bein' you're now my boss."

Caroline stood, numbed by this all, and watched him limp away from her in the direction of St. Clair Manor. With speculations stinging her mind, she turned and hurried into Twin Oaks. She was torn with grief and wonder about Gavin. Could he truly have shot Lucky? Was he trying to frighten her away from St. Clair Manor? First he asked her there—even gave her his key—and then she felt as though he didn't want her there. Was it all because of her interest in the portrait? Yet how would he even know of it? She had never mentioned it to him.

Or was she totally wrong about accusing him? Something in her heart kept hoping, insistently, in spite of the evidence pointing to him. . . .

# *Fourteen*

$C$aroline was semi-awake. She knew that she was swinging her arms wildly about in the air above her head. She knew that she was lying on a sweat-soaked sheet and she knew that this sweat was hers.

But she couldn't put a halt to the dream. She was running. Oh, how the calves of her legs ached. It was getting harder to place one foot in front of the other. But she had to. She was being chased through a dense fog. She couldn't make out the face of the assailant, but she could see a knife glistening back at her through the damp grayness.

She continued to run, panting, the sweat pouring profusely down her face as though she was running in the rain. Then she tripped and found herself falling . . . falling . . . then landing against boarded-up double doors.

Full of desperation, she began to claw at the boards, pulling, tugging . . . her fingers becoming raw . . . aching.

When one board became loosened and fell away she began to scream, feeling the coldness of the knife against the throbbing vein in her throat. . . .

"Miss Burton! Wake up!"

Caroline heard a voice shouting her name. She could feel soft hands on her shoulders, shaking her. Her eyes snapped open and she could see the dark, wild eyes of Rosa peering down at her, fear deeply imbedded in them.

"You were having a nightmare," Rosa said, now removing her hands. "I could hear your screams clear down in the parlor. What is it? Is it because of your uncle's death? Is there anything I can do to help you?"

Caroline's breath was coming in short snatches. She slowly rose into a sitting position, her muscles taut, her hands still damp with perspiration. "Lord," she moaned. "It was the same nightmare. Only this time, it was . . . it came so much more clearly than before. Each time, it gets clearer."

Rosa began fidgeting with the rumpled blanket at the foot of Caroline's bed. "What nightmare?" she softly questioned. "You've had it before?"

"Many times . . ." Caroline mumbled, combing her damp hair back from her eyes with her fingers. She thankfully felt her trembling begin to die away and her racing heart begin to slow its beat. "When will it stop?"

She flinched when a shutter began to bang rhythmically against the house, every gust of wind outside her window bringing whistles and moans. "What sort of day is it, Rosa?" she asked, slipping her legs over the side of the bed. She smiled in thanks as Rosa eased a silk robe around her shoulders.

"The sky is steel gray," Rosa said, now going to shove the drapes open. "We'll be seein' rain before the day's out. I just know it. Poor Sally won't be able to play outside. And she so badly needs the sun to put color into her pale cheeks."

"Is she doing better, Rosa?" Caroline asked, rising from the bed. She slipped her feet into slippers and her arms into her robe, tying it securely in front. "I've been too preoccupied to notice."

Rosa blew out a flickering candle beside the bed. "It's hard to tell." She sighed. "And Elroy refuses to take her to a doctor. He says she's all right. Nothin' to worry about. And he should know. He takes care of her more than I."

Rosa's eyes wavered as she looked over at Caroline. "I was meanin' to ask, Caroline," she said.

"Can I have some time off this mornin' to check on Sally myself? Maybe Elroy is doin' somethin' he shouldn't. A mama is more alert than a papa where a daughter is concerned."

"Go whenever you wish, Rosa," Caroline said. She stood before her mirror, seeing how pale and drawn she was. "I think I'll spend some time in the study, going over Uncle Daniel's ledgers."

Halfheartedly she began drawing a brush through her hair. "I don't even think I'll dress," she murmured. "Not until after lunch. I just don't have the energy. So much keeps draining me of ambition. I still can't get over Lucky's death and how he died."

She frowned back at her reflection in the mirror. "And those damn nightmares . . ." she worried aloud. "When will they end?"

"Do you want breakfast, Miss Burton?"

"Only tea. Just take a pot into the study. I'll drink it at my leisure."

Rosa left Caroline alone with her thoughts. After tying her hair with a ribbon, so that it fell in a long tumble of curls down her back, Caroline glanced only briefly toward the window. She cared little to see gray skies or the foreboding St. Clair Manor which always seemed to fill her with a strange, eerie uneasiness. She doubted that she could ever enter the manor again and this saddened her. She would never be able to know the truth about the portrait, nor would she ever be able to see Gavin again. Filled with so many doubts about him, how could she ever let him touch her again . . . ?

She would bury herself in work. She would work on the ledgers. She had to learn everything there was to know about Twin Oaks, though she sometimes thought it would be easier to just sell the estate. But the thought of her uncle and his pride in Twin Oaks always made her realize what she must do. She would keep Twin Oaks.

She looked about her, nodding. Yes. She would renovate a house all right. Hers.

Determined to get herself out of the doldrums, and trying to forget Lucky and the mysterious way in which he had died, she left her bedroom and went to the study. A pile of ledgers awaited her undivided attention on the grand, old oak desk. They had yet to be explained to her by Randolph. The one night he had come to meet with her, Caroline had instructed Rosa to send him away. Even now she dreaded the next time he would arrive at Twin Oaks, for she knew that she must meet with him. He was the only one who could explain to her the details of the will and the way in which her uncle had managed Twin Oaks.

Sighing resolutely, Caroline slipped into the leather chair behind the desk, singled out a ledger, and lifted it from the pile. She placed it on the desk and opened it, frowning when she saw the many scribbles of figures and entries on the pages inside.

Drumming the fingers of one hand on the arm of the chair, she began studying one page after another. She smiled as Rosa brought in a steaming pot of tea and a cup and placed it on the desk. "Thanks, Rosa," she murmured. "I think I need that. I may be here all day. I'll inform you when I want lunch."

Rosa was twisting the tail of her apron around a forefinger. "Since you're going to be occupied, do you think it's all right if I go and check on Sally now?" she asked, smiling awkwardly. "I'd like enough time to bathe her."

"You take as much time as you wish," Caroline said, pouring herself a cup of tea. "I will be busy. I'd rather not be disturbed at all until I inform you that I am through with what I am doing here."

She paused to slide the filled teacup closer to her. "Just you go on. Take your time. Enjoy being with Sally. I know how you've been so concerned about her."

Rosa began edging toward the door, backward. "Thank you, Miss Burton," she said in a rush of words. "Thank you."

And then Rosa turned and fled, her footsteps echoing and then fading down the hallway. Caroline settled herself comfortably in the chair, retying the belt at her waist more securely, then lifted the tea to her lips and sipped. She let herself become completely immersed in studying the figures listed in the ledger. She pushed the teacup aside and let her mind become fully engrossed in her findings and when she heard footsteps enter the room, she jumped as though shot.

Her gaze jerked upward, and she jumped. Gavin was standing in the doorway, silently studying her. "Gavin?" she gasped, pushing her chair back, half stumbling from it. "How did . . . you . . . get in here? Why are you even here?"

"I knocked and no one came, so I just let myself in," he said matter-of-factly, walking into the room. He wore a plain, unruffled white shirt that lay half-buttoned to his waist, revealing his feathering of chest hair beneath it. His pistol, holstered at his waist, was a rude reminder of Lucky and how he had been shot.

"You had no right just coming on in," Caroline said icily, stiffening her spine. "Didn't it ever occur to you that you might be trespassing?"

Gavin tossed his head in a low laugh. "You're one to talk," he said. "Caroline, just how many times did you go into St. Clair Manor without my knowing?"

Placing her hands on her hips, she glared at him. "Are you saying that you didn't want me there?" she dared. "As I recall, you gave me a key."

"You didn't have the key at first," he teased, stepping before her, sensually tracing her lips with a forefinger. "But you do have the key now."

Slapping his hand away, Caroline swallowed back the urge to scream at him. How could he come in here and act as though nothing had happened? Lucky was dead. He had been killed and found in St. Clair Manor!

Then she looked at Gavin in a different light. She hadn't ever truly thought him responsible for such a ghastly deed. And she knew that he wouldn't be here now, acting so casual, so free of guilt, if he had actually pulled the trigger on the gun that had killed Lucky. But who? Why? It had been done purposely, to frighten her, or maybe him. . . .

Yet, she couldn't find the courage to ask, or tell him about it. Talking about it would somehow make it more real, and right now she wanted to forget about it. One day soon she would talk about it. But not now. It was too soon after the fact. The wounds to her heart were still too painfully fresh. When she was ready to talk about it, they would find the guilty party, together!

"Caroline, why are you acting so strangely?" Gavin asked, catching her by the shoulders. "When we were last together, you weren't acting like this. Has something happened? If so, I believe you owe it to me to tell me."

Still, Caroline couldn't relax with him. She eased from his hold and moved away from him. She hugged herself, suddenly aware of how she was dressed and that she had only barely brushed her hair. She was anything but presentable enough for a caller, especially Gavin.

"I don't owe you anything," she murmured. "I don't know why you even think that I do."

She turned on a heel and again glared at him. "But you owe me my privacy," she said accusingly. "You shouldn't have let yourself in like this. Please go."

Gavin rubbed his chin, frustration showing in the depth of his dark eyes. "I only came on into Twin Oaks because I was worried about you," he grumbled. "When there was no answer at the door, I had to come on in, to see if you were all right. You weren't at St. Clair Manor, so I gathered you had to be here."

"You've been inside St. Clair Manor?" Caroline asked in an almost whisper. "What were you doing there?"

Gavin laughed loosely. "God, woman, I own the place. Why else would I be there?" he said, chuckling. "What's the mystery? What's changed you since the last time we were together?"

"Just tell me, Gavin," she softly persisted. "What rooms were you in at St. Clair Manor? Did you find . . . uh . . . anything strange while you were there?"

She was wondering if he had seen the blood that most surely had been left on the divan after Lucky's removal. Yet she still couldn't say the words. Should he have seen, surely he would have already questioned her about it. She had been the last one there, except for Elroy, who had removed Lucky for burial.

Shaking his head, Gavin went to Caroline and framed her delicate face between his hands. "No one room in particular," he said hoarsely. "I was just there for only a moment, hoping you would be there." His eyes darkened in color. "What sort of strange thing should I have seen?"

Swallowing back a fearful knot in her throat, Caroline lifted wavering eyes to meet his wondering gaze. She so wanted to blurt out the truth to him, yet still she couldn't say the words! She didn't want him to know that though only briefly, she had suspected him of being the one responsible for Lucky's death. Such a lack of trust was not something that she wished to reveal to the man whose eyes spoke so lovingly back at her. Though he carried with him an air of mystery, she loved him and had to admit to herself that at this moment, he was fast becoming a tonic to her raw nerves. His touch was magic, now burning away her robe as his fingers slipped down from her cheeks to cup the throbbing swells of her breasts.

Sucking in a breath of rapture, Caroline closed her eyes and let him now draw her fully into his embrace. "Oh, Gavin," she cried. "Please don't ask me any more questions. Just hold me. Let me breathe in the nearness of you."

Lifting her lips to his, she accepted his long and sweet kiss. It was hard for her to recall any cause to distrust or doubt him. All she wanted to know was his touch . . . his kiss . . . his passion. And when he swept her up into his arms and began walking toward the door, even then she didn't protest. She laid her cheek on his chest and closed her eyes, feeling the anxious beat of his heart against her flesh. She needed him. As never before, she needed him. . . .

Climbing the staircase, Gavin let his hand slip inside her robe to stroke her through the silk gown, "Which room is your bedroom?" he asked huskily, letting his fingers run along the sensual curve of her thighs.

"If you will remove my houseshoes, I shall point a toe towards my room once we are upstairs," she giggled, hardly recognizing her own voice, and understanding even less how she had let herself fall so quickly under his magnetic spell. But the giddiness was welcomed. For too many days she had let herself sink lower and lower into despair. Gavin was like a rope, lifting her higher and higher from her dark well of remorse and self-pity. . . .

"The deed is as good as done," he said, slipping off first one houseshoe, and then the other. He casually dropped them on the stairs.

"I take it we're alone," he said, "or you wouldn't for even one minute agree to what I am about."

"Rosa has asked to take leave for awhile," Caroline softly explained, going almost mindless as he slipped a hand inside her nightgown. "She surely will be gone for some time. She wanted to be with her daughter, Sally. The poor child . . . she's been ailing."

Gavin took the final step to the second floor. He laughed amusedly when Caroline looked coyly up at him as she pointed with a toe. "The loveliest toe I've ever seen," he said, walking toward the open bedroom door. "And I must remember to thank it properly for having led me to our soon-to-be lovenest."

Caroline's lethargy changed into a momentary tenseness when she saw her bed, and remembered the chilling nightmare she had experienced not that long ago. Though Rosa had changed the bedding, Caroline could not forget how she had awakened to a bed soaked in her own perspiration, and why. And there was always the memory of her uncle. He always seemed present, as though he hadn't even yet died. . . .

Sensing the change in Caroline, Gavin frowned at her as he set her feet on the floor. "What is it, darling?" he murmured, tilting her chin up with a forefinger. "Have you changed your mind? Do you want me to leave?"

Licking her lips that had become dry with remembrances, she implored him with shimmering green eyes. "It's the strangest thing," she murmured. "I keep having these nightmares. I wake up so . . . so . . . frightened. I just wish I could understand why I'm having them."

"Want to tell me about them? Maybe I could help."

How could she tell him that it was his house that seemed to have caused her nightmares? It was the boarded-up doors like those of his stable that kept entering her nightmares. How could he understand any of this, when she didn't?

She lowered her eyes. "No. I'd rather not," she said in a near whisper. "I would just like to forget them. It was just seeing the bed so soon after. . . ."

"Would you rather we didn't . . . ?" he asked, yet his hands had already slipped her robe from her shoulders, letting it tumble in a soft heap about her ankles.

"I would rather we did," she said, her voice a silken purr. She twined her arms about his neck and drew his lips to hers. "I've never needed you as much as now. Even if I have to seduce you, I shall."

Gavin laughed softly, delighted by her choice of words. He took her mouth savagely with his and fit his steel frame against her softly pliant limbs. His arms locked her in a hard embrace. His hands stroked the gentle curve of her back, then slid lower, to cup her soft buttocks. He pressed her up closer to where he so unmercifully ached, his breeches becoming taut over his hot pulsing desire. And when he felt her softly part her legs to welcome the gyrations that he had just begun, he was keenly aware of the soft moan that trembled from between her lips.

Then, unable to wait any longer, Gavin swept her up into his arms and carried her to the bed. As she clung to his neck, he grabbed the bedspread and tossed it aside, then laid her gently on the mattress. "Do you want me to undress you the rest of the way, or shall you do it yourself, while I take my clothes off?" he asked, one knee on the bed, his hands holding him up on each side of her.

"Whichever way you wish, darling. Either way will eventually lead us to paradise."

Leaning up on an elbow, feverish from her dazzled senses, she seductively slipped one strap of her nightgown down over a shoulder, and then the other. Smiling up at him, she nodded. "Now it's your turn," she whispered. "Piece by piece you shall match mine."

"My lady is a gambler, eh?" he chuckled. "If it's strip poker you wish, my darling, strip poker you shall have."

She smiled wickedly up at his lean, bronzed face. He slipped his shirt off, revealing his massive chest. She hungered to place her hands on his chest and absorb the feel of him, but she knew that now it was her turn to finish removing her gown. Straps were not the same as a full article of clothing. She had been lucky that he hadn't called her a cheater!

While he watched her with fire in his eyes, she sensuously squirmed as she slipped the silken garment past her waist, her thighs, and then down past her tiny ankles. With a nudge of her feet she sent her gown on down to the bottom of the bed and lay satiny nude for Gavin's perusal.

Feeling the storm building within, she watched as he finished disrobing, drinking in the magnificence of his body. When he came to her, their bodies tangled in a blaze of urgency that stole Caroline's breath momentarily away from her.

Then she felt the planes and corded muscles of his

sleek back while his tongue seductively eased her lips apart. Ecstatic waves washed through her as he devoured her with a torrid kiss. Her fingers caressed the sinewy sleekness of his chest and shoulders, and ruffled his tousled hair. She trembled with ecstasy as he returned her caresses, his hand stroking down her leg and then moving back up along the delicate, sensitive inside of her thigh.

And when his fingers sought out the core of her womanhood and stroked her more ardently there, Caroline emitted a nearly soundless moan and opened herself to him in helpless surrender.

Feeling the warm pressure of her body straining upward, and seeing her long, drifting hair spread about her head like a red flame, Gavin experienced the same throbbing urgency in his loins that she always awakened in him. He lowered his lips to one of her budding breasts and drew the nipple between his teeth and softly nipped at it, while one finger probed, slowly probed up inside her, where she felt so wet and sweet.

"Gavin, please. . . ." Caroline whispered. Her face felt hot, as did her eyes. Her heart was racing out of control. And when she felt him thrust himself inside her, she sighed, intoxicated by the hot, possessive touch of his body.

A thick, husky groan filled the air as Gavin buried himself deeper inside her, moving slowly at first, then faster, with quick, sure movements. His hands swept down her silken thighs, then slid back up again to knead her breasts. Again he kissed her, hungrily, demanding. He reverently breathed her name as he twined his fingers through her hair and drew her lips even more closely into his.

Caroline flamed in passion. Her breath quickened, and she gasped at his touch. Her hands splayed across his chest, her head tossed from side to side, as his lips payed homage to first one breast and then the other.

And then Caroline felt Gavin slow his strokes, to get his own breath. He gazed down upon her, his eyes dark pools of passion. "Never have I loved as I love you," he said, touching her softly on a cheek. He kissed her gently, again resuming his thrusts inside her, feeling the pleasure build until he stiffened, then let joy flood his senses as he was spiraled into another world that only spoke of utter fulfillment. . . .

Caroline felt the warm knot of rapture grow and tighten unbearably inside her. She clung to Gavin, locking her legs about his hips. And then the knot sprang loose and the rush of ecstasy splashed throughout her, leaving her spent and weak, yet glad to know that he had shared the same sort of joy as she.

As his palms moved soothingly over her, a tremor went through her. His mouth was soft and passionate as again he kissed her and then he eased himself up and away from her, to flop, breathless on his back beside her.

"Heaven," Gavin said, raking his fingers through his hair. "Pure heaven, Caroline. I guess you know that you've become a habit I cannot break."

Caroline rolled over on her stomach and leaned her chin on her hands, drinking in his nearness. How could she have ever thought that she could deny him anything? The love she felt for him could never be denied, no matter what the reason. And at times like this, she knew that he truly loved her. Why then could she be filled with doubts so quickly? Was that what love was all about? Doubts? Pain?

"As you have become so important, also, to me," she said, her cheeks flushed scarlet from her moments of sheer joy with him.

He turned on his side and leaned into one hand, questioning her with his eyes. "Then why did I get the distinct impression upon my first arrival here today that you wanted anyone but me here with you?" he said thickly. "At that moment, I felt as though if you were strong enough, you would have booted me right back out of Twin Oaks."

He placed a forefinger to her lips and traced their

fullness. "Am I right? Or was I imagining things, Caroline?" he added.

Very well aware of what he meant, Caroline's eyes wavered. What could she say? It would be hard to deny the snappish words that she had said to him. "It's just been hard since my uncle's death," she said, telling a half falsehood. She still couldn't speak of Lucky's death. "I hadn't expected to miss him so much. And I have so many responsibilities staring me in the face, I don't know whether I'm coming or going."

"Are you saying that you won't have time to give me suggestions for renovating St. Clair Manor?" he asked softly with a tinge of sadness.

Caroline felt a slow desperation rising inside her. She knew that she shouldn't go to St. Clair Manor again, yet there was the portrait! She still hadn't had the opportunity to find it. And the more she thought of it, the more stubbornly she thought that she must return to St. Clair Manor. If she didn't solve the mystery of the portraits, she knew that she would never forgive herself for having given up. She wouldn't let the killing of Lucky frighten her away. She just couldn't!

"No, I didn't say that," she said quickly, her old energies building inside her again. "In fact, I shall go to St. Clair Manor tomorrow."

"Good!" Gavin exclaimed, moving to a sitting position. "But I doubt if I will be able to be at my house tomorrow. I still have much to do in Charleston. Clients, you know. But you go ahead. Feel free to do as you please, Caroline. I'm so glad that you still feel that you have time for this. A woman's touch is what St. Clair Manor needs."

She smiled awkwardly up at him as he placed his hands on her waist and eased her around on her back to face him. "Yes," she murmured. "A . . . woman's . . . touch . . ."

His lips took hers by storm, his hands molded her

breasts. She lifted her hips and accepted him inside her again, once more being filled with a sweet, sexual excitement.

"Love me forever, Caroline?" Gavin asked huskily.

"Forever. . . ." she whispered, threads of passion again weaving through her heart. There was only now. All tomorrows would take care of themselves. . . .

# *Fifteen*

W eary of studying the ledgers for several days
now, Caroline went to the study window and peered
toward St. Clair Manor. Though she had told Gavin
she would return there to choose fabric for draperies,
she still hadn't gotten the courage to do so. Whenever she thought of entering the manor again, her
mind's eye would see the way she had found Lucky. If
she only knew who . . . and why! What might this
deranged person do next? She now only felt safe while
inside the protective walls of Twin Oaks. But she had
often wondered . . . was she even safe there?

Hugging herself, Caroline tore herself away from
the window. Though the sun was brilliantly bright
and the air was filled with the songs of birds, St. Clair
Manor still remained as a threat to her sanity.

But still she must return. She would take just one
more look through the rooms. Then if she didn't find
the portrait she could be sure that it was either in the
tower room or at Gavin's townhouse.

She set her jaw determinedly, her eyes flashing.
Even if she had to come right out and ask Gavin, she
would. But still, she must think of Uncle Daniel and
what he would want. The shame of an unfaithful wife
was not something that he would want anyone to
know about. But Caroline must know. She *would*
know. Somehow . . .

Having already had her morning tea and knowing
that Rosa was busy with her chores, Caroline decided

this was the best time to go to St. Clair Manor and to get it over with. Grabbing a shawl to guard against the chill that always seized her at St. Clair Manor, she hurried out of Twin Oaks and across the richly grassed lawn. Baubles of dew still clung to the tips of the grass, sparkling like diamonds in the sunshine. The smell of early morning was distinctly fresh, the touch of the breeze on Caroline's face invigorating.

Her hair took on a velvet cast like petals of a red rose in the sunshine. Her simple cotton dress with its high collar and long sleeves clung to her and wrapped clumsily about her legs as she moved swiftly onward.

During the days and nights spent in her uncle's study, she had felt like a prisoner at times. Though she was headed for the dreaded manor, she at least was enjoying being outdoors. She knew what followed after that. More time spent in the study, and this time, with Randolph Jamieson. He had sent a messenger boy to inform her of his arrival later this morning. She hoped to finally get all that he had to say behind her, to never have to see him again!

The sun soaked on through her shawl, warming her too much, so Caroline let her shawl drape more loosely about her shoulders. She let her gaze move about her, absorbing the loveliness of the garden. The flowers were a patchwork quilt of colors. She squinted her eyes and looked for signs of Sally playing, yet did not see her. Even Princess, with her sleek black fur, was nowhere to be seen. Elroy wasn't in sight either.

A shiver raced across Caroline's flesh; she felt strangely alone. Picking up speed, she passed beneath the gray beards of Spanish moss and stepped gingerly around the muddy slopes of the lagoon and on through the gate of St. Clair Manor.

Before moving on to the house, her attention was again drawn to the boarded-up stable, which reminded her of the fretful nightmare. She could almost feel the touch of the cold blade of the knife against her throat and the pain in her fingers after her attempt to tear off the boards in her nightmare.

Beads of perspiration rose on her brow and her fingers trembled. She looked upward at the looming tower that shadowed her in muted grays.

Trying to shake off the paralyzing dread that had seized her she stepped quickly onto the porch, slipped the key into the lock, and rushed inside, panting.

Leaning against the closed door, she tried to catch her breath before beginning her search. Her gaze was drawn to the open door of the parlor where she had found Lucky dead. She swallowed hard, not wanting to go there ever again, yet knowing that she must. But she would look there last. She knew that Lucky's blood must surely be on the divan, a constant reminder of the horrors of this house. And she knew that she was no safer than Lucky had been.

Why was she so driven to find the portrait? She surely was foolish to ever believe that she would uncover the mystery of her aunt's disappearance. Hadn't the authorities spent days, even weeks, looking for her? Why would she think for one minute that she could have the ability to uncover what they hadn't?

But she was sure they hadn't seen the portrait. Well, she had. And she must find it again.

A gust of wind rattled a window at Caroline's side, startling her. She lurched away from the door and began moving from room to room, finding the windows uncurtained and uncleaned—gray, open gaps on walls covered with faded, peeling wallpaper. Dampness oozed in at some of the windows, running desultorily down the glass like tears. Caroline looked behind sagging chairs, stepped softly over worn carpets, and searched inside cabinets and wardrobes. But still she found no portraits!

It was as though Gavin had hidden them for a definite reason. She plopped down onto a chair to rest before venturing on into the parlor, her last place to search this day. She hadn't been able to search the tower room because its door was locked. Surely that room held within it many mysteries of the past lives of those who had lived at St. Clair Manor. And possibly even those who hadn't . . . ?

Slowly rising from the chair, she drew her shawl more securely about her shoulders, stricken with a fit of chills at the thought of going to the parlor. But she had yet to search it as carefully as she wished. She would have to avoid the divan and its ugly stains of death.

But could she? That day and her findings were etched onto her brain as a leaf fossilized in stone. It would be almost impossible not to relive the horror of that day by even just entering the parlor. The fact that the divan would be there would truly only be secondary . . .

She broke out in a cold sweat of fear as she entered the parlor. She willed her eyes to not stray to the divan, but something out of the corner of her eye drew her attention and when she saw the bloody black bundle of fur stretched out lifeless on the divan on the exact spot where she had found Lucky, she paled immediately. Her eyes went wild; she stifled a scream as she covered her mouth with a hand, and she had to force her knees to not buckle as fear gripped her, icy cold and stabbing.

"No!" she cried, throwing her hand away from her mouth. It just couldn't be. Not Princess too! Who could be so cruel? So heartless?

She turned away, tears stinging her eyes. She edged backward, knowing that she must leave. She knew that the cat had been planted there, as Lucky had, and she had to believe it was meant to frighten her.

But, again she wondered who would hate her so much? She knew that it wasn't Gavin. There was too much love in his kiss, his touch, his words. It was somebody with a motive, but what? Could the motive be her? Would Randolph Jamieson want to win her from Gavin so badly?

But surely he was not the type. Surely her uncle couldn't have been such a poor judge of character!

Yet, hadn't he misjudged his very own wife if she, indeed, had been guilty of infidelities?

Finally out in the hallway, Caroline turned to run. The initial shock and fear of finding Princess dead made Caroline realize that she had had enough of the search for her aunt's portrait. Two killings were enough to make her know the danger she was in. She might be the next victim! She must escape now, while she could.

She hurried outside, not looking back as she began running toward Twin Oaks. Panting, her face flaming from fatigue, she followed the shores of the lagoon to the garden, not stopping until she was safe inside Twin Oaks.

Breathing hard, she went into her own parlor, so safe and free of death, and eased down into a chair. Disappointment assailed her. She had so wanted to find the portrait! It was hard for her to believe that she had given up the search. She had to wonder if the happenings at St. Clair Manor might have anything to do with her Aunt Amelia's disappearance. Yet her aunt had disappeared ten long years ago. Many things had happened during those long years. There had been a war. There had been many deaths in both the St. Clair and Burton families. And St. Clair Manor had changed hands, from one family member to another. Caroline had to put St. Clair Manor and the need to find the portrait out of her mind!

But the cat. The dog. The poor, innocent animals. . . .

The sound of the knocker against the solid oak door sent Caroline suddenly to her feet. She dropped her shawl in the chair and went into the hallway, meeting Rosa. "Rosa, I'll get the door," she said. "I'm sure it's only Randolph Jamieson. He's supposed to be here sometime this morning. Let me see to him, to get it over with and get him gone again."

"Yes, ma'am," Rosa said, turning to walk away.

"Rosa, I forgot to ask," Caroline quickly added. "How's Sally?"

"About the same," Rosa said, shrugging. She lowered her eyes and hurried on down the hall, away from Caroline.

The persistent knocking on the door drew Caroline back around. Sighing, she went to the door and swung it open, awestruck to find Gavin, instead of Randolph, outside.

"Gavin?" she gasped.

Gavin chuckled. "Is finding me at your doorstep so incredible?" he said, resting his hand on his holstered pistol. He looked around her, his dark eyes twinkling. "Might I think that I will soon have an invitation into your house? Or do I have to take it upon myself to step on in, unasked, as I did the last time I arrived here?"

Still in a state of shock over having discovered Princess in St. Clair Manor, and at this moment not even sure whom she could trust, she stood her ground. And wasn't Gavin part of St. Clair Manor and didn't St. Clair Manor mean death?

"Gavin, this isn't the time," she murmured, clasping her hands together behind her.

Gavin's eyebrows forked. "Oh?" he said, looking on past her. "Am I to gather that you have other company?" Then his eyes searched for a waiting carriage, or a reined horse, seeing neither.

"Gavin, just leave?" Caroline said, her eyes snapping. "I've much on my mind today. I really don't wish to explain it to you. Please understand."

"Understand?" he growled, raking his fingers nervously through his hair. "God, woman, you run hot and cold. I never know which way I'll find you next. And damn it, you never have explanations as to why."

"I've explained before that I now have responsibilities," she said. "That should be enough."

"So you've changed your mind again about St. Clair Manor?" he grumbled, his eyes charged with anger. "First you say you'll assist me and then you say you won't. Why do you change your mind so often, Caroline?"

"I truly wish to have no more part of St. Clair Manor," she said in a rush of words, her cheeks flaming in color. "There. I've said it. Do I make myself clear enough?"

"Why, Caroline?" Gavin asked, grabbing her hard by her shoulders.

"Ouch!" Caroline said, squirming. "You're hurting me, Gavin. Unhand me. This minute."

"So you won't tell me?" he asked, dropping his hands away from her.

"There's nothing to tell," she lied, fearing that if she told him anything, she would have to tell him all. And still she knew that she didn't want to have to explain about the mystery of the portrait! And wouldn't he soon discover the cat himself . . . ?

"If there's nothing to tell as to your reason for not wanting to go to St. Clair Manor again, then I guess you're just saying that you don't want anything to do with me," Gavin snarled.

The sarcasm in his voice stung Caroline. She started to reach for him, to apologize, knowing that she never wanted to hurt him as she was obviously doing. But as she lifted her hand, he turned on a heel, mounted his steed, and rode away.

"Gavin . . ." Caroline whispered, placing her hands to her throat.

A wild desperation seized her. She knew that she couldn't lose Gavin. She had to go to him and explain. But seeing him now drawing so close to St. Clair Manor, her insides froze. If she were to follow him, she would have to enter St. Clair Manor again! Could she? She had vowed to herself to never put herself in such a position again! Yet for him, she must! And while she was with him, surely nothing could happen.

Lifting the skirt of her dress up and away from her ankles, she fled down the steps. When she saw Randolph Jamieson's carriage approaching down the drive, she stopped running, suddenly feeling torn. She wanted to get her business with Randolph behind her, and she wanted to go after Gavin to apologize for being so unduly cold to him.

Gavin won in her heart. She saw the look of confusion on Randolph's face as he drew the carriage to a halt beside her. "Randolph, you'll have to come back another time!" she shouted, running on past him. "Come tomorrow! I promise to be an obedient listener tomorrow to all that you have to say!"

Randolph gaped openly at Caroline as she ran in the opposite direction. "Caroline, stop! Wait!" he shouted, waving. "Damn it, Caroline, wait!"

Paying no heed, she ran on, breathless and filled with worry that Gavin wouldn't listen, let alone accept her apology. But she must try! She must try!

Fully winded, she half stumbled up the front steps that led inside St. Clair Manor. Finding the front door ajar, she went inside, then fear again gripped her as she recalled, oh, so much!

She drew an audible breath of relief upon seeing Gavin walking toward her down the dark expanse of the hallway.

"What do you want here?" he said, stopping before her. He dared her with threatening darkness in his eyes and with his hands on his hips. His legs were widespread, causing his fawn-colored breeches to draw tightly against his muscled thighs and the strength of him at his crotch.

"I've . . . come to . . . apologize," Caroline said, breathing hard. "I'm sorry, Gavin. But so much has happened. I think it's time that I explain."

She knew that she would only tell him part of her wonder about—and fears of—St. Clair Manor, but she did know that it was time to tell him about Lucky and Princess. It was apparent that he still didn't know about them. He probably hadn't yet had a need to enter the parlor, to discover the cat. Hadn't he even yet seen the blood left by the shooting of Lucky?

"Yes, I think that would be a good idea," he grumbled.

Caroline bit her lower lip in frustration. She brushed a lock of hair back from her brow. "I don't know where to begin," she murmured, glancing toward the opened door that led into the parlor. "But perhaps it would be easier to just show you."

His gaze followed hers. "Show me *what*?" he said thickly. "Why are you staring at the parlor like that? Has something happened that you're not telling me?"

Caroline nodded. She stepped around Gavin and found herself tiptoeing. Feeling foolish, she caught herself and hurried her steps, glad that he was now beside her. "Come with me, Gavin," she said softly. "I have something to show you."

Gavin followed her into the parlor. When she pointed to the soiled divan, the color drained from his face. "My God," he gasped. He looked from the blood stain, to Caroline, then back to the blood stain again. "Whose?" he said thickly. "And why do you know it's here when I don't?"

The color drained from Caroline's face and her knees grew rubbery as she saw that the lifeless body of Princess had been removed. Someone had entered St. Clair Manor after her and had removed the dead cat! It had to be the same person who had moved the bolts of fabric and wallpaper samples about. It was being done to disorient her and make her feel unbalanced . . . insane. . . .

"Princess!" she gasped. "She's *gone.*"

"Princess? Your uncle's cat?" Gavin asked.

Caroline's finger trembled as she pointed to the divan. "I found her there a short while ago," she softly cried. "She was dead. And now she's gone."

"God. . . ." Gavin gasped, his eyes narrowing.

"I found my uncle's collie, Lucky, there also," Caroline said in an almost whisper. "He'd been shot."

Gavin swung around and took her hands in his. "Are you saying that you also found the dog dead?" he gasped.

"Yes. I found Lucky another time," Caroline

choked. "I'm scared, Gavin." She openly shivered. "Something evil is going on here. Who would kill Lucky and Princess and bring them here to your house? Why? I'm frightened, Gavin. I'm scared to death."

Gavin took Caroline by the elbow and led her from the parlor, closing the door behind him. "How would anyone even get in?" he asked puzzled. He began leading her up the stairs. "Why didn't you tell me about the dog when it happened, Caroline?"

"I never wanted to talk about it," she said, not wanting him to know that she had even wondered if he had killed the dog himself. She shuddered. "It was too horrible. I didn't even want to think about it. I tried to bury myself in my work."

"And now even the cat," Gavin said. "Do you have an enemy, Caroline? I can't think of anyone who would do this to frighten me. I thought I had left my enemies on the battlefield long ago."

Caroline tensed, realizing where he was leading her. "Gavin, I don't think this is the time for going to your bedroom," she softly argued. "I think I'd rather go home. I just came to apologize."

"It's all right, Caroline," he said thickly. "We'll go to the master bedroom because it's the one room we can relax in. And I'll go and get a bottle of wine from the cellar. That should calm you down."

"But I don't even want to be in this house at all," she argued, trying to break free of his hold, but not succeeding. "Gavin, let go. I can't stay here. I must return to Twin Oaks. Please understand."

"It will be all right. Trust me," he said thickly, guiding her up the stairs, drawing her around and into his arms as they stepped into the sun-splashed master bedroom. "It's important to me that you not let these things build a wall between us. It can't be allowed to happen, Caroline. What we have is special. You mustn't let anything cause you to turn your back on what we have found to be so beautiful."

"But what about the parlor and what's happened there? What about the person who did those horrible things?" she said, her heart spinning as his lips were paying homage to hers, softly, playfully. . . .

"For now, we'll pretend it didn't happen," Gavin said huskily. "Just concentrate on being with me. Later? We'll just have to watch for anyone who acts suspicious. Sooner or later we'll find the guilty party."

"But until then, what if something else happens?" she said in a half whine.

"I think it's best that you don't come over here again unless you know I'm here."

"I hadn't planned to."

"Then that's enough worrying about it for now."

His mouth seared hers with a passionate kiss. The euphoria that filled her in his embrace was almost more than she could bear. Yet the thought of making love in his wretched house caused her to pull away.

"No, Gavin," she murmured. His finely chiseled face was a mask of passion as he heatedly gazed down at her. "Not here. Not in this place. There's been too much. . . ."

He placed a hand softly over her mouth, silencing her protest. "Darling, the house is not the cause," he explained. "It is the person who has chosen to do horrid things in it who is making it appear to be so. St. Clair Manor was once a fascinating showcase. Age has been unkind to it, but let's not be unkind as well, making it out to be something monstrous."

"Gavin, surely you don't feel its evil vibrations as I do," Caroline murmured, looking cautiously about her. She jumped when she saw her reflection in the large mirror on the far side of the room and looked quickly away from it and up into Gavin's eyes. "Gavin, you said something about wine?"

"Surely later, Caroline," he said huskily. He drew her next to him. "Later, darling?" he whispered against her cheek, sending a thrill throughout her as the warmth of his breath teased her ear.

She shuddered with desire as he began loosening her dress from behind. She felt the feverish pitch building inside her, knowing that she was no longer troubled by anything but his touch. . . .

He eased her dress down and away from her shoulders and then removed her underthings. Her breath was momentarily stolen when he lowered his head and his lips and tongue began skillfully teasing her taut breasts. She squirmed out of the rest of her clothes, then stepped away from him and eased down onto the bed.

Stretching out on the bed, she watched him undress, feeling wicked, yet marvelously so. As he stepped out of his final piece of clothing, his muscles corded down the length of his lean, tanned body, tantalizing Caroline into near mindlessness. And when he joined her on the bed, she was beyond coherent thought as he wasted no time in joining her wholly to him.

As he excited her even more with his hands and mouth, she moaned softly and began to move against him. A delicious pressure built up inside her. She lifted her hips to meet his sweet strokes as he filled her, moving rhythmically within her. His long, hot kiss enflamed her even more; her hands were wild along his taut back and his sleek buttocks.

Her face and neck throbbed with his kisses. Her breasts swelled and felt as though melting when he flicked his tongue around their rosy peaks.

"Darling . . . ," Gavin said, framing her face between his hands. He kissed her sweetly, his tongue licking her lower lip. And then he groaned as his insides exploded with pleasure just as the exquisite feelings inside Caroline dissolved into a delicious, tingling blaze of heat, spreading, glowing like the evening sunset in its fiery, final good-bye. . . .

And then they lay relaxed against each other, their lips joined together, their kisses soft, Caroline's breasts pulsing warmly as his muscled chest pressed down onto them.

"I love you," Gavin whispered against her lips. "Marry me, Caroline."

Caroline's heart soared to heights never attained before. She drew away from him, staring lovingly back up at him. "You're proposing?" she whispered, radiant.

"Don't act so surprised," he chuckled. "You knew that I had purposely chosen you to renovate St. Clair Manor. You were the woman I was doing it for. I thought I told you that."

"So much that you have said has been lost in the confusion of other things," Caroline softly admitted. Her smile faded and a coldness splashed through her. "I could never live here, Gavin. Never," she said suddenly.

"In time, I think you could change your mind," he said, leaning up and away from her. He stepped from the bed and drew on his breeches. "We'll get to the bottom of who's trying to frighten you."

Then he frowned down at her. "Or me," he said thickly. "Whoever is doing this, probably wanted to scare us both. Anyone who has been observing St. Clair Manor lately has to know that we both spend time inside the house. So wouldn't one assume that we both are the target of this sick prank?"

"I had thought the same," Caroline said, stepping gingerly to the floor, hurriedly slipping into her petticoat. "But no matter, Gavin. I know that I could never live here."

"We'll see," he said, drawing her into his embrace. "The main thing is, do you agree to marry me, Caroline?"

Trembling from ecstasy, Caroline smiled up at him. "Yes," she murmured. "Oh, yes. . . ."

His kiss was tender, his hands sweet as they cupped and kneaded a breast. "When?" he said, drawing his lips from hers. "When, darling?"

"Let me get things in order at Twin Oaks first," she murmured. "And we can even talk of the possibilities of our living there, Gavin. Can't we?"

"Perhaps," he said. "Perhaps . . ."

Again he kissed her. Caroline was thrilling inside, and she knew that now even her hopes of eventually finding the portrait would be realized. If she married Gavin, she would be the joint owner of all he possessed. The thought pleased her in every way possible. . . .

# *Sixteen*

*T*hat should finalize things, shouldn't it?" Caroline asked smoothly, sorting through the legal documents that gave her full control of her uncle's possessions and the freedom to choose a new attorney. She stood behind her desk, proud and beautiful in her pale green, low-swept, flowing dress. Her hair was drawn up into a loose swirl atop her head, with tiny ringlets of curls framing her oval face. She had dressed to look her loveliest for Gavin, who was to arrive momentarily.

Randolph angrily slammed his briefcase shut, glowering at Caroline. "Daniel wouldn't approve of how you've chosen to handle things," he argued. "It has always been his wish that I continue to handle the Burton estate, even after his death."

"For reasons I will not go into, it's best that Gavin St. Clair now act as my attorney," she said icily, placing the documents in a neat stack on her desk. She wanted to question Randolph about his recent pastimes. Had they taken him to St. Clair Manor?

"I should have known," Randolph said, his thin, angular face paling. "Now I fully understand everything. Gavin has won everything, it seems. He is a wily one."

"I don't care to hear any more of such talk," Caroline said, walking around the desk to boldly face him. "Gavin doesn't do anything deviously. He's a sincere, honest man. And he most certainly doesn't

185

do anything with you in mind. Why would he? He doesn't have to. He proved himself to be the best between you two long ago."

With a flip of the skirt of her dress, Caroline went to the door. She gestured with a sweep of her hand. "Please leave now, Randolph," she said dryly. "I consider all of our business transactions over."

Gathering his briefcase beneath an arm and picking up his walking stick from where he had left it leaning against, a chair, Randolph walked toward Caroline, frowning. "Yes. I guess it's time I get back to Charleston," he said. "But if you should change your mind?"

"Never," she said flatly, escorting him toward the front door. She hadn't expected him to give up so easily. She had thought she would have to argue with him for at least awhile longer, and had even feared that Gavin might arrive before Randolph left.

But as it was, Randolph even seemed eager to get away from Twin Oaks. She knew that she should be glad, yet something gnawed at her insides, making her suspicious of his too easy manner. Perhaps he had been the one who had tried to frighten her. Or had he tried to frighten Gavin? Didn't Randolph have a motive? Did he even have something more planned? Was this the reason behind his sudden casual manner?

"Caroline, my hat?" Randolph said, leaning down to look her squarely in the eye. "Caroline, where have your thoughts taken you? I'd like my hat."

Caroline jumped, startled from her reverie. She found herself closely studying Randolph, again wondering if he could be responsible for the deaths of Lucky and Princess. Her gaze dropped to his waist. His frock coat didn't bulge where a holstered pistol would be belted. And recalling the other times that she had been with him, she realized she hadn't seen him wearing a gun. So surely she was wrong to silently accuse him of such ghastly deeds!

"Your hat . . . ?" she said. She laughed softly. "Oh, yes. I must get it for you. I momentarily forgot that

Rosa hasn't yet arrived this morning, though I must admit I'm wondering why."

She retrieved his top hat from the hallway closet where she had placed it upon his arrival. Handing it to him, she again found herself studying him. Though he was a scoundrel in other ways, he didn't seem to be the type to kill an innocent dog and cat. But who . . . ? Would she ever know?

Randolph put on his hat. His face darkened with a frown. "Caroline, I get the idea that I'm being closely scrutinized for some reason," he grumbled. "Do you want to tell me why?"

Not wanting to have to apologize to him for her rudeness, she smiled up at him and locked her arm through his, guiding him to the porch. She forced a laugh. "Why you're imagining things, Randolph," she said. "I was just preoccupied by thoughts of Rosa. I'm concerned about her. I must go and check on her, to see if anything is wrong. This isn't like her. She should have been here long ago."

Randolph lifted his thin shoulders into a shrug. "She is only a servant," he stated flatly. "Why waste your time worrying about her? There are many in Charleston who would gladly take her place at Twin Oaks. Don't forget the plight of those who lost everything because of the war. You could pick and choose, Caroline, and have any servants that you personally wished."

He frowned again as he glared down at her. "Since you're changing so many other things that Daniel chose, surely you wouldn't hesitate at also ridding yourself of a mere servant," he growled.

And with that, he stomped from the porch and climbed into his buggy. Yet he politely tipped his hat before he drove away from her. Caroline shook her head, wondering about his complexities, yet glad to finally be rid of him.

The skirt of her dress blew gently in the breeze, lifting to reveal the preponderance of lace that edged her petticoat. The sun was warm on her face, and the air was heavy with the perfumed scent rising from funnel-shaped blossoms of the azaleas that lined the drive.

Caroline soaked up the smell of the flowers, the warmth of the sun, feeling free now that she had just succeeded in getting rid of Randolph for good. She hugged herself, smiling. But her smile faded when she looked toward the drab, weather-beaten slave's cabin at the far end of the estate. There were no signs of life. And Rosa! Where was she?

Determined to find out, Caroline lifted the skirt of her dress and descended the steps. She hurried across the green carpet of grass, past the garden, to the door of the cabin. Before knocking she leaned her ear close, listening for voices. But when hearing none, she knocked on the door and waited, dreading the certainty of being face to face with Elroy at any moment.

But when Rosa slowly opened the door and peeked out with tear-swollen eyes, Caroline hurriedly cast all thoughts of Elroy aside. Her gaze traveled over Rosa's sleep-crushed dress and her uncombed hair.

"Rosa?" Caroline said softly. "What's happened? Why are you crying?"

Then Caroline's insides twisted as she suddenly remembered Sally. "Oh, Lord," she said, placing a hand to her throat. "It's not Sally, is it? Is she worse?"

Not wanting Caroline to see the bleak interior of her dwelling, Rosa slipped outside, blinking as the sun burned into her reddened eyes. "It's Elroy *and* Sally," she sobbed, wiping a new flood of tears from her cheeks.

Trying to look past Rosa into the cabin, Caroline became anxious. "What about Sally and Elroy?" she blurted. "Are they both ill?"

Rosa shook her head sadly. "I don't know," she murmured, her eyes wavering.

Frustrated, Caroline grasped Rosa by the shoulders. "What do you mean, you don't know?" she asked thickly. "Lord, Rosa, why don't you?"

A wounded look fell over Rosa's face. "They're both gone," she stammered. "They've been gone all night. I don't know where. When I came to the cabin last night after leaving Twin Oaks, they were gone then."

"Has this ever happened before?" Caroline asked, dropping her hands away from Rosa. She didn't know what to think, whether to be worried or suspicious of Elroy. Why had he left with his daughter without a word? Yet she scoffed at herself, knowing how she had suddenly begun to suspect everyone about everything. But she had reasons for her distrust, hadn't she?

"Well, not exactly," Rosa said, wiping her nose with the back of a hand. "Elroy's been gone overnight at times, but never with Sally. Why would he take Sally with him to . . . to . . . find his pleasures with another woman? I just know that's where he's gone. Doesn't he know that young girls are impressionable?"

"Rosa, please just calm down," Caroline said, patting Rosa on the arm. "Surely there's more to this than what you are thinking. Perhaps Elroy went to Charleston to pick up supplies and the buggy broke down. Please don't think the worst. You must continue to believe that Elroy wouldn't let any harm come to your daughter. Just you wait and see. Elroy will come riding home at any time and tell you that the buggy broke down and he wasn't able to get the parts until this morning."

Rosa's eyes grew wide with hope. "Do you truly believe that?" she asked anxiously.

Caroline forced a smile, trying to reassure Rosa. "Yes, Rosa," she murmured. "I truly believe that Elroy will arrive home all full of apologies. Why don't you try to busy yourself to get your mind off your worries?" Her eyes traveled over Rosa again, taking in her unkempt appearance. "Refresh yourself, then come to Twin Oaks. I'm expecting Gavin at any moment now. It would be nice to have a fresh pot of tea awaiting his arrival."

"Yes, ma'am," Rosa said, nodding her head. "And

thank you for understanding why I didn't come to Twin Oaks earlier. I . . . I . . . wanted to wait here until Elroy arrived home."

"If you still feel you must, do as you wish," Caroline said, smiling warmly. "But I, personally, think you should busy yourself."

"Yes. I think you're right," Rosa said, blinking tears from her lashes. "I've almost made myself ill from crying. I'd best get hold of myself."

"Then I can expect you at Twin Oaks soon?" Caroline queried, glancing up the drive and seeing the faint outline of an approaching horseman in the far distance. Her heart pounded out the moments until she would again be in Gavin's arms. They had plans to make. Soon she would become Mrs. Gavin St. Clair!

The name St. Clair was the only cause for her to feel uneasy. She had to find a way to stop connecting Gavin with the deaths at St. Clair Manor, and the morbid thoughts that came when she looked at the foreboding house, that always reminded her of her nightmares.

And she had to convince Gavin they would have to make their residence, when married, in Twin Oaks. Once renovated, surely St. Clair Manor would be easy to sell.

"Yes, ma'am. I will be there as soon as I make myself presentable," Rosa said, also seeing the approaching horseman. "I hope it won't be an inconvenience for you that the tea won't be ready upon Mr. St. Clair's arrival." She shielded her eyes with a cupped hand. "That *is* him comin' up the drive, isn't it?"

Caroline frowned. She had just realized that the horse was not Gavin's beautiful roan stallion and that the rider was not as tall and lean as Gavin. It was someone else approaching.

"No," she said, wonder filling her. "It isn't."

Rosa emitted a sharp cry. "Oh, Lordy be, what if it's someone comin' to give me bad news of Elroy and Sally?"

With the skirt of her dress flying, Rosa began running across the lawn and toward the lane. Stunned, Caroline ran after her. They stopped, standing together, panting, as the rider, a young man with a thick shock of red hair, drew rein before them.

"What is it?" Caroline asked, wringing her hands. "What do you want, young man?"

"I have a message for a Caroline Burton," the man said, slipping a small envelope from his shirt pocket. He looked from Rosa to Caroline. "Is one of you Caroline Burton?"

Caroline thrust her hand out toward him. "Yes, I'm Caroline Burton," she said. "From whom is this message?"

"Gavin St. Clair," he said, handing Caroline an envelope. He then gave a mocking half salute. "Good day, ladies."

"Thank you," Caroline shouted after him as he wheeled his horse around and began galloping back down the drive.

Her fingers trembled as she tore the envelope open. Unfolding the paper she hurriedly read the words written there which ended with the neat inscription of Gavin's name.

"Is everything all right?" Rosa asked, relieved that the message hadn't been bad news of her husband and daughter. At least for the moment, Rosa felt that she could still hope. And she could tell by the soft glow in Caroline's eyes that the news brought to her hadn't been bad for her either.

Rosa was glad. Miss Burton needed no more burdens to weigh her down. And Gavin St. Clair's pursuit of her could be what Caroline needed to place all her grief behind her. Yet Rosa knew of Miss Burton's dislike of Gavin's house and how this could create problems that could hardly be avoided. . . .

"It's Gavin," Caroline murmured, placing the note back inside the envelope. "He's been detained. He's asked that I come on into the city and meet with him at his townhouse."

"But Elroy isn't here to take you," Rosa openly worried.

"Rosa, I don't need Elroy to take me to Charleston," Caroline said, laughing softly. "I am quite capable of taking myself."

Then her smile faded. She placed a hand on Rosa's arm. "But should I leave? Will you be all right?" she asked. "If you would rather I stay until Elroy returns, I shall."

Rosa shook her head. "No, Miss Burton," she said, tears again sparkling at the corners of her eyes. "There ain't no reason for your day bein' messed up just because Elroy is out gallavanting around." She nodded toward the drive. "Please go on. You don't want to disappoint your betrothed. That ain't a way to begin a lasting relationship."

"If you truly don't think you'll need me," Caroline said, her heart anxious to leave.

"I'll do as you suggested earlier," Rosa said solemnly. "I'll just busy myself."

"I do think that's best," Caroline said, now walking alongside Rosa toward the house. She nodded toward Rosa's cabin. "You go on and get yourself presentable. You come to Twin Oaks whenever you feel you are ready."

"Yes, ma'am," Rosa said, then began walking briskly away, leaving Caroline to hurry up the steps and into the house. And after Caroline had secured her straw bonnet by tying its green satin bow beneath her chin, and draped her lace-trimmed shawl across her shoulders, she grabbed her purse and fled on out to the carriage house.

The sight of two buggies inside gave her a start. She knew that one was normally used by Elroy, the other by her. Smiling, she assumed that Elroy had finally returned home and that everything was all right. She felt that she could leave now without worrying, knowing that it was between Elroy and Rosa to work out their troubles in private.

Anxious to get on her way, she prepared her own horse and buggy and soon found herself riding down the streets of Charleston, admiring the city. Its streets were narrow, oleander-lined lanes, its public buildings small, and reminiscent of Greek or Roman temples. The houses were white, and embellished with fretwork and great verandas that the Charlestonians called *piazzas*.

Caroline had questioned her uncle about why so many of the houses were built with one end, rather than the front, facing the street, and why what appeared to be porches or verandas were called *piazzas*. She knew that *piazza*, after all, was an Italian word meaning a square or open space.

"Piazza?" her uncle had said. "When the English architect Inigo Jones came back to London from Italy, he designed Covent Garden, putting in a piazza and a colonnade. But the English thought the colonnade, not the open space, was the piazza, and they began to call any covered walk a piazza. Well, that usage eventually got here."

He had gone on to tell her about the Charleston single houses, so called because they were only one room wide.

"I think Charleston single houses evolved from long and narrow row houses. There had been a series of fires, and it became necessary to get away from row houses, to provide firebreaks," he said. "So they began to build a house, then leave an open space, then build a house, and so on. The single house and the row house have many common features: the chimney set inside the wall, the blank or almost blank back wall."

Caroline looked at the houses. Indeed, it did appear as if a block of row houses had been pulled apart, and lovely gardens inserted between the houses.

"Now, because the street door of these houses usually led into a merchant's shop," her uncle had continued, "a door was opened farther back for a family entrance, another for a slave entrance. The path to these doors was then provided with a covered walkway . . . a piazza."

Seeing Gavin's mansion come into view in the distance, Caroline slapped the reins, commanding her horse onward. She sat daintily on the padded black leather seat of the two-seated buggy which rode like a breeze above its elliptic springs. Yet she found herself occasionally wobbling as the wheels of the buggy slipped and slid over the rounded cobblestones of the street.

The incessant accompanying clip-clop of her horse's hooves and rattling buggy wheels blended in with the clatter of other vehicles in the crowded streets, which were filled with carriages, buggies, and mule-drawn wagons creaking under the weight of cabbages, carrots, lettuce, and red, shiny tomatoes, heading for the market.

Ornamental planters sat on the doorsteps of houses and businesses alike, displaying roses, ferns, and little trees covered with blood-red peppers. At an open-stalled market, fish hung on hooks and were piled in baskets, and vendors shouted about the sea-gray shrimp they had for sale.

Along the sidewalks women were scarce, but occasionally one or two would be seen, their parasols opened above their heads, shading them from the warming rays of the sun. The gentlemen escorting them were dressed expensively in white linen coats and breeches.

But the city seemed busy mostly with merchants from ships and workers who were still busy renovating it from the ravages of the war. Charleston, with its many wharves along East Bay Street, had become a busy commercial seaport. Ships of all styles and shapes, laden with raw materials, even now lay anchored at the harbor.

Drawing her buggy to a halt beside the white picket fence which enclosed Gavin's private lawn, Caroline waited to catch her breath before going on up to his townhouse. She didn't see his horse, so assumed that he still was being detained.

"But surely he left the door unlocked so I can go on inside," she worried to herself. She remembered how he had said that he had only occasional servants, so she knew she might be on her own until he returned.

A broad smile brightened her face. "The portraits!" she murmured to herself. At last she would be able to see those that she had missed the last time she was there.

Anxious, she alighted from the buggy and tied the horse's reins through a bronze loop at the hitching post. Her heart thundered against her ribs as she pushed the gate of the fence open, discovery possibly only moments away.

"I hope it's here," she whispered. She wanted to finally be able to put this mystery behind her, to concentrate on more beautiful things, like her upcoming marriage to the man she loved. . . .

She went to the door and knocked. When there was no answer, she slowly turned the knob and sighed with relief when the door creaked open. Stepping inside, she drew a deep breath and tiptoed toward the drawing room . . .

# Seventeen

$O$nly the faint light of a kerosene lamp and the soft glow of a simmering fire on the hearth emanated from Gavin's drawing room. She could just make out the dark paneled walls, the bookcases filled with odds and ends of books, and the mismatched chairs and tables as she crept into the room. The drapes were drawn closed at the windows, the bare floor echoed her footsteps. And as her eyes adjusted to the dim light, her gaze was drawn immediately to the chair behind which she had last seen the portraits. To her chagrin, they were no longer there.

Gavin had moved them again! Keenly disappointed, she slowly searched about the room, but found no signs of them.

She should have known he wouldn't hand them to her on a silver platter. But how could he even know she wanted to see them? She hadn't mentioned her interest in them.

She set her jaw firmly. And she still wouldn't tell him. This was a mystery to be solved by herself alone. It involved only her and her Aunt Amelia.

Untying her bonnet, she glanced over at the clock on the fireplace mantel. Its tiny pendulum swung lazily back and forth, its golden hands now pointing out the hour of eleven. But knowing the time didn't help Caroline. Gavin hadn't said when he would arrive at his townhouse. He had only asked that she meet him there.

Perhaps she would have time to look around. She laid her bonnet, purse, and shawl on a table.

Her cheeks grew warm, and her green eyes took on the slant of a cat's as she stepped, breathless, back out into the narrow hallway which led to many other rooms as well as the staircase to the second floor. Not wanting to feel the intruder she in truth was, she worked her way down the hallway, choosing which room to explore first. But if Gavin should find her. . . .

With trembling fingers, she placed her hand on a doorknob and turned. Her eyes grew wide with discovery. Finally luck was with her. She had found a storage closet, deep and wide and filled to capacity with all sorts of what appeared to be memorabilia. She narrowed her eyes, trying to make out individual items, but it was too dark to see.

Well, she knew how to take care of that. She swirled around and walked determinedly back to the drawing room, where she found a brass candleholder supporting a half-burned candle. She lowered it down into the fire of the kerosene lamp. And when flames sputtered and caught the wick, Caroline smiled victoriously.

With her head high she carried the candle back out **to the** hallway and held it inside the closet. Slowly she let her gaze move from item to item. And then her heart fluttered wildly. Her search was over. From behind a stack of fat ledgers the corner of a portrait peeked back at her.

With an anxious heartbeat, she set the candle on the floor and began lifting the ledgers aside, slowly revealing more and more of the portraits. But when she reached for them and lifted one out, and then another, she was again disappointed. None were of the lady with the special cameo necklace. Her search had all been in vain.

Shaking her head despairingly, she began to wonder if she had ever really seen the portrait at all. Had it been a figment of her imagination? She had only been afforded a brief glance. If only Gavin had not arrived at that very moment of discovery that day! She would have fully seen the portrait and this would have been done with long ago!

Well, that was that, she thought, replacing the last ledger, trying to hide all signs of her snooping.

She closed the closet door, lifted the candle, and began making her way back to the drawing room, just as the front door swung suddenly open and Gavin entered, looking at her, perplexed.

"Darling, why the candle . . . ?" he asked, closing the door behind him. "Where have you been? Did you not find the drawing room adequately comfortable while awaiting my arrival?"

Caroline paled. She knew that guilt had to be written all over her face. And the thought that he had almost discovered her again invading his privacy caused her knees to become suddenly weak. She must think up a convincing answer, quickly. First he found her snooping in St. Clair Manor, and now in his *townhouse*! Surely he would demand to know what warranted her continuing strange behavior.

"Gavin, darling," she purred, rushing toward him. "I just *had* to see the rest of your townhouse. Surely you don't mind that I did. Anything that is a part of you sorely intrigues me. Surely you understand."

She placed the candle on a table, and then snuggled into his arms. "Tell me that you understand?" she asked, imploring him with her wide, green eyes. "I was getting bored waiting."

"I think I could understand," he grumbled, arching a dark eyebrow, "except that you have such a damn guilty look on your face. It's as though you've been up to more than looking. Why is that, darling?"

Her heart racing, she slid her hands beneath his expensive brown tweed frock coat and splayed her fingers across his hard, powerful chest. As she inhaled his manly fragrance and gazed up at his handsome features, she felt herself melting beneath the heat that seemed to radiate from his moody, dark eyes.

His hair shone in its neatly coiffured midnight

black curls. The hardness in his loins pressed against her, making her unable to concentrate on the moment at hand and the web in which she was again slowly becoming ensnared.

"Gavin, please quit toying with me," she purred, pretending to be innocent of what his voice and eyes accused her of. "You asked to meet with me today because you said that you had something to show me. What is it? Please tell me now."

She gently laid her hand on his cheek. A sweet current of warmth swept through her at the mere touch. "It must be very important or you wouldn't have sent word for me to come ahead to your townhouse to meet you when you found that you were going to be delayed by business," she went on. "Were you that anxious, darling, that you didn't want to have to wait until you rode, yourself, to Twin Oaks?"

Ah, such a vision of loveliness she was, Gavin thought as he reached for her hand and softly kissed its palm. "So your anxiousness tends to get you into mischief?" He chuckled. "You couldn't sit still? You had to wander through my house?"

Caroline's thick lashes lowered over her eyes, and her cheeks colored. "And does it truly matter that I wish to see how my future husband lives?" she murmured, her pulse racing, fearing that Gavin was not going to back away from questioning her until she was forced to blurt out the truth. But this time she wouldn't allow it to happen. She was wise to how he drew words from inside her that she did not ever think to speak.

"And? Do you approve of the way in which I choose to live?" Gavin said thickly. He lifted her chin with his finger. "Or do you still agree that my life needs a woman?"

Relief washed over Caroline as she realized that her choice of words had worked. She smiled coyly up at him. "Yes, quite lacking," she murmured. "And do you still intend to let me remedy that?"

"You know damn well the answer to that question,"

he said huskily. His gaze raked over her. The fullness of her breasts was temptingly exposed where her dress dipped low at the bodice, and her creamy, bare shoulders seemed to invite a kiss. Her cheeks were rosy, her lips like wine, and her tantalizing green eyes almost drove him mad with desire.

"Darling, I am yours, wholly," Caroline whispered, watching his lips lower to hers. His mouth burned over hers, evoking a hungry response in her. Locking her arms about his neck, she returned the kiss, wildly . . . wantonly.

His hands crept between them and fully cupped her breasts through the silk of her dress, teasing her nipples into taut buds. And when his hands slid around to the back of her dress and he began unfastening it, Caroline felt herself swept away by her pounding heartbeat.

A sensuous tremor rocked her as Gavin's lips drifted lower, kissing the gentle curve of her throat, and then trailed down to where her breasts lay openly waiting, her dress and petticoats now billowing in a silken heap about her ankles.

A low moan rose from deep inside Caroline when she felt Gavin's kisses burn a path even lower on her body. She arched her throat backward, closed her eyes, and stiffened her arms at her sides as she felt his lips on her lower abdomen, down to where her womanhood throbbed to be touched. And when she felt the sweet, warm wetness of his tongue even there, she was at first thrown into an euphoric state. Then it suddenly came to her exactly what he was about.

Opening her eyes wildly she looked down and saw him stooped to one knee before her, his fingers splayed along her flat stomach, his lips still paying homage where none had ever been before.

Gasping, she stepped quickly back away from him, suddenly shy in her nudity. She tried to cover her lower body with her hands, fearing the delicious quivering that his tongue and kisses had aroused between her thighs. Nothing about what he was doing

seemed right. It surely was wicked! How could it not
be . . . ?

"Gavin, please," she whispered. "What must you
take me for, that you feel you . . . you can take
such . . . devilish liberties?"

Gavin rose to a full standing position. He took her
hands away from her body, his eyes dark with heated
passion. "My darling," he said huskily, "you've much
to learn in the ways of making love. What I was
doing? It's beautiful. It's a way a man can prove his
full love to a woman, fully unselfish in the act of
making love."

Holding her wrists, he drew her to him. "You are
soon to be my wife," he murmured. "Everything we
now choose to do is right. You shouldn't feel ashamed
to let me love you . . . wholly love you."

He showered her face with kisses. "Let me love you,
darling," he whispered.

Trembling, Caroline reveled in the touch of his lips.
"But, Gavin, I didn't come here today, to . . . to make
love," she softly argued, knowing her voice sounded
weak and passion-filled. "You asked me here for
another reason. Surely you weren't only jesting, asking me here for just another romp in your bed."

"Romp in bed?" Gavin said, chuckling. He drew
away from her. "Well, I must say, that's not a bad
idea. Shall we do it now? Or later?"

Caroline's jaw squared and her lips formed an
angry, straight line. She jerked away from him, reaching for her clothes. "I knew that I shouldn't have
come," she hissed. She turned and faced him, her
arms now filled with her petticoats. "But I think I've
heard myself say that before. Why must I whenever I
am with you, Gavin? Why do you always put me in
the position of having to say it? Will you always
behave so . . . so . . . impossibly after we are married?"

Gavin's eyes twinkled and a playful smile lifted his
lips. He reached inside his waistcoat pocket and
withdrew a tiny, velvet-covered box. "My reason for

wanting to see you today is this," he said, offering her the box. "It's yours, darling, if you'll have it."

When she refused to accept it, remaining angrily poised, the lace of the petticoat blending with the delicate paleness of her skin, Gavin took one of her hands and very politely placed the box inside it.

"I said this is yours," he said, his eyes twinkling. "Open it now, or open it later, Caroline. I guess it doesn't really matter."

He turned on a heel and walked away, leaving her staring blankly down at the crimson velvet of the tiny box. Her heart thundered against her ribs, her eyes became misty with tears. She knew what must be inside the box. Oh, how foolishly she had just behaved. But he stirred her to such frustrated anger by his shenanigans! Sometimes it was just too much to bear or understand!

Caroline caressed the softness of the box with her fingers, wanting badly to open it. But she knew the moment of discovery should be shared with Gavin. It was surely the ring that would seal their love forever.

Running, almost stumbling over the tail end of her petticoats which hung loosely from her arms, she began to search the rooms for Gavin. And when the search took her upstairs, she found herself in his bedroom. She was taken aback to see him lying nonchalantly nude on his bed, his legs crossed at his ankles, his head resting on his upstretched arms. A cigar lay in the corner of his mouth, soft smoke spiraling from its tip.

A slow anger began to rise again inside Caroline. He had known that she would follow him and he had made sure that he was ready in the way in which he wanted her to find him. He would have his moment in bed this day, or die trying, it seemed!

Well, she would have none of it. She saw nothing whatsoever romantic in the way he was handling this special day. Stomping to the bed, she threw the velvet box at him. But where it landed, caused him to wince in pain and elecited a giggle from Caroline that turned into a full gale of helpless laughter. She doubled over in hysteria. Had she aimed, she could have never made such a direct hit! His manhood had jerked quite comically as the box had made contact! And she wished she could have framed the look on his face!

"Damn . . ." Gavin said, chuckling low. "Where'd you learn to throw like that?"

Wiping the tears of laughter from the corners of her eyes, Caroline met Gavin's amused smile with one of her own. "I truly didn't mean to," she said, giggling. "Lord, Gavin, if you had seen the look on your face." She let her gaze move lower. "If you had seen how your . . . your . . ."

She covered her mouth with her hands, laughing hard again. Like a streak of lightning, he rushed from the bed and grabbed her. He thrust his cigar into an ashtray with one hand while holding her immobile with the other.

"So it's games you wish to play today, huh?" he teased, working her down onto the bed. He brushed her petticoats aside and crushed his mouth hard against hers, his hands stroking her silken flesh, caressing the gentle curve of her hips, and then the tender inside of her thighs.

"I need you," he whispered. "Darling, I need you now. Don't deny me. . . ."

"I need you, too," she whispered back. "Please love me, Gavin. Love me now. I'm so sorry for becoming angry with you. It's just that I love you so much I don't ever want you to think me cheap."

"How could I?" he said, his loins aching as he felt her hands on his body.

He trailed fiery kisses from breast to breast, his hands lifting her higher, to be more accessible to his lips. And then as he again let his lips move lower, to where she was now so open to him, she closed her eyes and let herself experience the rapture. His hands kneaded her breasts, his lips sent spirals of delicious warmth upward from her pulsing womanhood to her brain, dizzying her.

And then he mounted her and pressed his taut, muscular body against hers, filling her with his hard strength. She welcomed his lips with her own as he kissed her with a lazy warmth that left her weak.

She clung to him, floating on waves of pleasure. Her hips rose upward, meeting his sure, but easy strokes. She could feel the familiar feverish rapture rising inside her until it reached an almost unbearable pitch, her body turning into a strange, warm liquid, melting . . . melting. . . .

Their bodies rocked together. Their breaths mingled, their tongues danced against each other as again they became lost in passion's kiss. Gavin's fingers bit into her shoulders, his breathing became heavy. And as he was sent into the world of momentary pleasure, he pulled her along with him, feeling her passions cresting to match his.

Then, passions spent, bodies still entwined, Gavin and Caroline lay quietly together, enjoying the afterglow of lovemaking.

"I love you, darling," Gavin whispered against Caroline's dampened cheek. "I never want to be without you. Tell me again. Say that you are mine."

His lips teased hers with feathery kisses as he smiled down at her, awaiting an answer. She was intoxicated by his lips, his eyes, and the magic of his hands. Even his voice seduced her into loving him even more.

"I am yours," she whispered, returning his kiss, running her tongue seductively over his lower lip. "Always, Gavin. Always . . . always."

"Words to store inside my heart," he said, now slipping his lips over the stiffened peak of her breast. Then he rose up and away from her, his eyes searching around him on the bed.

"Where *is* that thing?" he grumbled, running his hands all around him.

"What are you looking for, Gavin?" Caroline asked, leaning up on an elbow. Her hair had fallen from its fancy swirl and now hung in satin streams across her pale shoulders. Her eyes were glowing from excitement, her cheeks never rosier.

"How can you forget?" Gavin asked incredulously, giving her a perplexed look. "My gift. The velvet box? The weapon you nearly emasculated me with."

Caroline's eyes widened. She sat upright, unable to suppress a giggle.

Gavin's eyes now twinkled, his lips rose into a mellow grin. "So you think that's funny?" he teased. Then he spied the box partially hidden beneath a pillow.

"Ah *hah,*" he chuckled, reaching for it. "I do believe the search is over."

Caroline fell into an anxious silence. She locked her arms about her knees and watched as he placed the box before her. She could hardly stand the strain of waiting, having already waited too long. And when he raised the lid and the sparkle of a king-sized diamond flashed back at her from where it lay on a red velvet cushion, she could do nothing but utter a deep sigh and stare down at it.

Gavin withdrew the diamond ring from its bed of velvet. Solemnly, he took Caroline's hands away from her knees and slid the ring onto her tiny finger.

"It fits perfectly," he said thickly. "I was afraid that I was choosing one too small for you. But I should have known how delicately small your fingers were. God, it's beautiful on your finger. On our wedding day it shall be yours to wear forever."

Caroline held her finger up and let the light from the window play onto it. "It will be mine?" she murmured. "Truly mine, Gavin?"

"Yes. And that's just the beginning," he said, lowering a sweet kiss to her brow. "On our wedding night I shall give you something else quite special."

"Oh, what . . . ?" she asked, her heart pounding, her insides a soft glowing.

"If I told you now, the surprise would be spoiled," he chuckled. "But I will tell you that it is also something that you will wear."

"Jewelry?" she prodded. "Gavin, you mustn't keep me in suspense."

He rose from the bed and slipped his breeches on. "Oh, all right. If I must tell you, I must," he boisterously teased, smiling down at her. "That something of which I speak is *me.*"

Caroline's lips parted in a surprised gasp. "You . . . ?" she whispered. "You were speaking of yourself as my special gift?"

Gavin chuckled low. "Where's your sense of humor?" he said. "Aren't I enough? Or did you expect a fancy necklace, one engraved with my love on its back?"

"A necklace?" Caroline said in a near whisper, now suddenly remembering another necklace, another wedding night, and thinking it strange that Gavin should make mention of the same.

She was again reminded of the portrait and the necklace that the model who had posed for it had worn. It had been a cameo necklace, exactly like the one her Aunt Amelia had worn . . . the necklace that her aunt's husband had given her on their wedding night. The memory somehow lessened the sweetness of this moment with Gavin. Oh, why did she have to remember, at such a time?

Why had he felt the need to tease? Why did he need to mention a necklace? Why couldn't she place the portrait and her aunt from her mind?

But she knew that she would never forget until she had positive proof that she was either wrong or right about the portrait!

Gavin sank down on the bed beside Caroline. He took her hands in his. "Caroline, what is it?" he said. "What did I say? You suddenly look as though you've seen a ghost. Do my teasings upset you that much, darling?"

Caroline smiled weakly up at him. She blinked her eyes nervously. "It's nothing," she murmured. "I don't know what got into me. Am I forgiven for worrying you?"

"Only if I know that it wasn't something that I did or said that bothered you," he grumbled.

"No. Positively not," she said, swallowing hard. "And, darling, might I have a glass of wine before I leave for Twin Oaks? I believe this day calls for a celebration, don't you?"

"Anything my lady wants, my lady gets," Gavin said, kissing the tip of her nose.

She slid the ring off and watched meditatively as Gavin placed it back into its box. She was glad when he slipped his arms about her and completely stole her breath away with a torrid kiss and again they locked together in a full lover's embrace.

But too soon it was over and she knew that she must return home. It wasn't proper to be alone with Gavin at his townhouse. She had already been there too long. . . .

Gavin rose from the bed with her and hurried into his clothes, yet his smile wasn't as wholehearted as before, for he still saw a trace of sadness in Caroline's eyes, and wondered why. What was she hiding from him? He always seemed to feel she was keeping something from him. It had begun the first time they had met. He believed it might have something to do with St. Clair Manor, and what had first drawn her there. In time, surely in time he would know. . . .

But did he even want to? He felt as though knowing might be a threat to their happiness. . . .

# *Eighteen*

$S$till filled with the afterglow of having been with Gavin, Caroline arrived back at Twin Oaks. While unfastening her horse from her buggy she glanced over at the other buggy in the carriage house and began wondering about Elroy and Rosa. Had they reconciled their differences upon his return home? Had he been detained for honorable reasons . . . or had it been because of a woman, as Rosa had feared? Had Sally been affected in any way by whatever reason Elroy had chosen to stay away for a full night?

"The poor dear," Caroline sighed, then went on to Twin Oaks and stopped short upon finding Rosa inside, still beside herself with worry.

"Rosa, what is it?" Caroline asked, flinging her shawl aside. She went and took Rosa's hands in hers. "Is it Sally?"

Tears burst forth from Rosa's eyes. "Neither Elroy nor Sally has yet to return home," she whimpered. "Elroy has never stayed away this long with Sally."

Caroline raised her eyebrows in surprise. "But, Rosa," she said, "Elroy's buggy is here. I thought he had returned home."

Rosa eased her hands from Caroline, growing pale. "The buggy . . . is . . . here?" she murmured. "Then Elroy is home." She rushed away from Caroline.

Caroline reached a hand to her. "But, Rosa," she tried to explain, "the buggy . . ."

But Rosa was already outside, headed toward her cabin.

Rosa hadn't waited to hear Caroline say that the buggy had been there even before she had left for Charleston. Caroline thought hard. Had Elroy arrived home between the time that she had gone inside Twin Oaks to get her things and when she'd gone to get the buggy. Had he just gone on inside his cabin with Sally without having informed Rosa of his return? Had Rosa failed to return to the cabin to see if he had arrived the whole time Caroline had been gone?

Caroline had to believe that Rosa had stood vigil beside a window all of this time, watching for the buggy's arrival, not ever having thought to guess that Elroy had already arrived without her having noticed.

But it no longer mattered. Now Rosa would know that he was home. It was too bad that she hadn't checked her cabin earlier. It could have saved her much worry.

Caroline was full of wonder. If Elroy had arrived back home with Sally, why hadn't he gone to Twin Oaks and let Rosa know that he was home? Or had he feared her wrath for having stayed away all night?

Regardless, Caroline believed it would all work out for the best. She was already involved in other thoughts as she stared from a window toward St. Clair Manor. She knew that she had a battle to win of her own. She had to resolve her fears of Gavin's house once and for all. And there was no time to do that like the present!

She knew that nothing would please Gavin more than her telling him that she no longer feared his house nor the ghosts that seemed to be lurking there. She would return there *now* and conquer the fear that haunted her.

And, perhaps she could also find the portraits. She would check the rooms at St. Clair Manor once again, though she was sure that the key to the mystery lay behind the locked doors of the tower room. Since she

soon would become Mrs. Gavin St. Clair, she wasn't
about to deface the lock that secured the door to the
tower. If she had to, she would wait until the keys
became legally hers to search that particular place.

Wasting no more time thinking about it, Caroline
readied herself for going to St. Clair Manor. She
removed her bonnet, placed her purse aside, and
without thought of the fact that she was still dressed
in one of her finest silk dresses, she hurried outside.

Her hair was still loose from her passion-filled
moments with Gavin, yet brushed to wave lustrously
long down her back. Her heart was still filled with
rapture, oh, so loving Gavin St. Clair! Her lighthearted mood helped her dismiss the foreboding that
usually accompanied her approach to St. Clair
Manor. Instead, she fully enjoyed the beauty of the
day.

Lifting her eyes to the sky, she watched the sun's
descent behind the magnificent live oaks and pines,
the orange-tinted rays reflecting from bases of puffy
clouds onto the powerfully stroking wings of an
osprey overhead.

An avoc, a water-oriented bird resembling a hawk,
raced across the sky, lugging a fish to its hungry
youngsters, who waited, impatiently, lined up dangerously near the edge of their massive, woven-stick nest
at the apex of a dead tree trunk, only footsteps from
where Caroline now was walking.

Smiling, Caroline ran softly on, listening to the
raucous squawks of water birds scuffling over choice
roosting places around the end of the lagoon where it
reached into dense, swamplike undergrowth.

And then Caroline tensed, hearing the intermittent
spooky hoots and ghostlike cackles of great owls,
which warned her of just how soon it would be dark.

But not dissuaded by sounds of nightfall or the
setting of the sun, Caroline hurried on and soon
found herself standing in the gloomy, gray abyss of St.
Clair Manor. Though she fought it, she was again
seized by that same strange, eerie feeling which always

crept over her when entering the manor. She couldn't suppress a slight shiver. She felt dispirited, uneasy.

Determined to fight these feelings, she went into the parlor and searched until she found a candleholder, glad to find a fresh, unburned candle just waiting to be used. After lighting it, she set it in its brass holder, carried it to the hallway, and again began her search, moving through the rooms like a ghost.

As she had suspected, she found nothing on the lower level of the house. She began her ascent up the dark staircase, jumping nervously each time the stairway creaked. A shadow being reflected on the wall beside her gave her a sudden fright, but she laughed softly when realizing that it was her own.

She doubted if she would ever be able to prove she was anything but uneasy of this place. She was afraid she would have to disappoint Gavin. Would he think less of her for fearing this house? Oh, what should she do?

At the second floor, Caroline lifted the candle and halfheartedly tried to choose a room to search. She let her gaze move from door to door. Then remembering the bolts of material and the other assortments of things stored in the one bedroom, she felt that should be the room to tackle first. Surely beneath all of those relics she would find something. Though she had already looked beneath the furniture and its dustcovers, she knew that one more look was required to set her mind at ease.

With quiet footsteps she went to the door of the room and slowly opened it. Inside, the sunset was splashing its orange streaks onto the walls, making them appear freshly wallpapered. Even the dustcovers on the furniture picked up the soft colored light. Her attention fell on the bed, where a large white sheet had been draped across the mattress.

Caroline tensed. The bolts of cloth were no longer on the bed where she had left them half unrolled. And she couldn't help but notice that there was something different about the sheet covering the bed. And it wasn't only the lighted, orange shadows splayed across it. There seemed to be a lump of sorts beneath the cover.

"The portraits . . .?" she whispered, her heartbeats becoming anxiously erratic. Had Gavin placed them there after she was last here?

But this lump in the sheet did not look like a stack of painted canvasses. It was more rounded, as though it might be a . . .

Caroline paled. Her fingers began to tremble wildly. She stared at the lump, now seeing that, yes, it did have the shape of a body, tiny though it was. Just the thought made an icy sensation crawl up the nape of her neck.

She laughed nervously. Lord, this place did work on her imagination! A body indeed! What on earth could she be thinking?

A cold sweat of fear covered her skin. She had not convinced herself at all that what she was seeing wasn't real. Her knees felt rubbery as she moved slowly toward the bed, knowing that she had to see just what it was that hadn't been there before.

As though in a trance, Caroline set the candle down on the table beside the bed. She then moved her hands toward the sheet, fearing the discovery, yet knowing that she *must* look.

Coldness twisted her gut like a knife as she lifted the sheet and discovered the still form of little Sally.

"No!" Caroline screamed, choking back tears, her gaze frozen on the lifeless, tiny form. Sally's eyes were closed in death's sleep and her golden hair spread about her head like a halo.

Panic seized Caroline. She turned and began running blindly from the room. She scrambled down the stairs, stumbling in the darkness, not stopping until she found herself outside. Tears scalding her cheeks, she turned away from the house and just as she did she ran into what appeared to be a solid wall of steel but was quickly revealed to be the solid chest of a man.

Her gaze jolted upward. Her breath was snatched momentarily away from her when she saw who it was. "Elroy!" she gasped. "Oh, Elroy, I found . . ."

Elroy leaned his full weight onto his cane and grabbed her sharply by the wrist. "You've been inside St. Clair Manor, haven't you?" he said in a low snarl. "You've *seen,* haven't you?"

A slow, paralyzing fear washed through Caroline when she saw the hard brilliant glint in Elroy's eyes, and slowly understood what he had said. "Elroy, no," she softly cried, shaking her head in disbelief. "Don't tell me that you already know about . . . Sally. That would mean that you . . . that you . . ."

"That I *what*?" he growled, tightening his hold on her wrist, sorely paining her.

"Elroy, not your own daughter," Caroline whimpered, wincing when he jerked her closer to him. "Why, Elroy? I don't understand!"

Elroy released Caroline and gave her a shove back toward the house. "Get back inside," he snarled. "It's too bad you had to come snoopin' again. You'd have been spared. Don't you ever learn? You don't belong here. You belong at Twin Oaks."

"Why should you care where I am?" Caroline asked, stumbling as he shoved her again. She looked from side to side, thinking of escape. With his lame leg, he wouldn't be able to catch her!

But when she turned sideways and began to run, he thrust his cane out and tripped her. She fell to the ground in a painful heap, panting. Elroy jerked her back to her feet and held her there as he glared down at her.

"I wouldn't try that again," he warned, his steel-gray eyes boring through her. His lips were set in a cold, straight line; his face was void of color. "Not if you don't want to join Sally beneath the cold sheet."

Caroline stood momentarily transfixed in place, gaping disbelievingly up at him. She had never liked him, had even at times suspected him of many things, but she had never truly thought him capable of such a ghastly deed as killing his own daughter. And why had he? Had Sally been that much of a burden to him?

But it was now clear where Elroy had been the long, lonely night while Rosa had been half crazed with worry. All along he had been at St. Clair Manor with his daughter.

Caroline wondered just how long Sally had been dead . . . and how she had died. There had been no visible wounds on her body . . . not even *blood*. Caroline had seen enough in those few moments to at least know that!

Now fully aware that she might be the next victim, Caroline felt a resurgence of strength. Determined to get away from Elroy, she began slapping at him with her free hand. Her feet got tangled in the hem of her skirt and in the lace of her petticoats as she tried to kick him. When she finally succeeded in wrenching her wrist free, she swung around to run away, but stopped abruptly as she felt the sudden cold tip of a knife thrust against her throat. She gasped and stood completely still. . . .

"Now you'll do as I say or I'll cut your throat," Elroy threatened. "I got a lot of practice durin' the war. Don't think I'd hesitate at cuttin' you. You ain't nothin' but a Union bitch anyhow. I'd only be a doin' my duty for the Confederacy."

Caroline paled. "You wouldn't," she said, shaking her head. "The war is over, Elroy. You can no longer do anything for the sake of the Confederacy. If you kill me, you'd most surely hang."

"I will anyhow," he grumbled. "Ain't my daughter dead? It won't be long 'fore her death is discovered. What then, Miss Burton? What then?"

Caroline tightened her jaw and straightened her back. "You should have thought about that before you killed her," she said sourly. Her eyes wavered. "Lord, Elroy, how could you have?"

He pressed the point of the knife just barely into her flesh, making her wince. "I didn't mean to," he confessed. "But no matter. No one'd believe me. It's done, ain't it? She's dead."

He nodded toward the house. "And if you don't do just as I say, you'll be dead too," he said flatly. "Now go on in. I think I just might acquaint you with the tower room. You ain't been there snoopin' yet, have you? There are only two keys to the room. And I've got one of those two."

His words soaked into Caroline's brain. He had a key to the tower room? How? And did that mean that he also had a key to the manor? It must, or else how had he gotten in with Sally?

A chill went through Caroline as she slowly began to fit the pieces together. If Elroy had a key, then couldn't it have been he who had killed Lucky and Princess and planted them in the parlor? Had he been the one to move things about, to confuse her? But what would have been his motives?

But he did have the keys. He had to have already used the one to enter the house to bring poor Sally there. There was no other way to get in. She knew; she had looked herself. And Gavin had made sure that all entries were safely locked. He had even boarded up the cellar door.

Caroline's insides grew even colder as she realized that Elroy was now taking her to the tower room, which she knew had been locked! How had he managed to get the keys? Just how often had he been there when she had felt a presence while she looked for the portrait?

She was shaken from her fearful thoughts when Elroy gave her a shove and then quickly followed her, again placing the knife to her throat.

"Didn't I say go on inside?" he growled. "Move. Now. Or I might just make a pincushion outta you with this knife."

"All right," she said softly. "I'm going. But someone is going to wonder where I am. Rosa is already frantic, wondering where you and Sally are. And when Gavin finds out that I'm missing, he'll start searching and he'll look here first."

"He won't find you for days," Elroy snarled, his cane banging up the steps to St. Clair Manor. "By then, I plan to be gone."

"But what about Sally?" Caroline dared to ask as out of the corner of her eye she saw Elroy open the door, thankfully dropping the knife from her throat.

"When I'm safely away from Charleston, I'll send word to Rosa," he said, his words void of emotion. "She can then come to St. Clair Manor and get Sally. If she finds you too, then you'll just be lucky."

"But why, Elroy?" Caroline asked, as he shoved her toward the dark staircase. "What have I ever done to you? Why are you treating me like this? Is it only because I found Sally, or have you planned to harm me all along?"

Elroy suddenly stepped around to face her. He glowered down at her. "You're askin' too many questions. You just go on up those stairs until you reach the tower room. Then maybe we can talk. But I plan somethin' else more excitin' for you later."

His low, throaty laugh filled Caroline with a new sort of dread. She swallowed hard and flinched when he again placed the knife to her throat. She was beginning to remember another knife, another time, but the memory just wouldn't fully materialize in her mind's eye. Surely it was only the nightmare that had begun to trouble her. In the nightmare, hadn't she been fleeing from a man with a knife? Hadn't he even gotten so close to her that he had placed it to her throat just as Elroy was now doing? But surely there was no connection. Though she had at one time thought the nightmares to be a warning of some sort, she had to believe that she wouldn't dream about something *before* it happened. That only happened in books. . . .

Half stumbling, Caroline moved up the stairs. With no candlelight to guide the way, she felt as though she were walking in a dark, endless tunnel, filled with shadows menacingly lurking, ready to pounce out at her. The silence was deafening, broken only by the sickening thud of Elroy's cane. And as they drew closer to the upstairs landing, Caroline could hear Elroy's breaths quicken. She had to believe that so close to where his sweet daughter lay in death's sleep, he surely felt remorse for what he had done. His reason for having done it was still a mystery to Caroline. And would she ever know? After he had his fun with her, wouldn't she be just as dead?

"Just move on," Elroy warned, urging Caroline up the stairs, past the second floor of the manor. "You're movin' just a mite too slow. Are you thinkin' your lover just might happen along? You'd better hope not. I'll not play games with him. I'll just use the knife instead of playin'."

"Lord . . ." Caroline whispered, perspiration lacing her brow. She was glad that she had come alone and that she and Gavin hadn't planned a rendezvous for this evening. For if they had, Gavin's life would also be in danger. But wasn't it anyway? Just how long would Elroy wait around before leaving for good? Did he even plan to wait for Gavin?

Her mind went numb when her outstretched hands discovered the tower room door. She swallowed hard as Elroy inched her aside and she could hear him fumbling with the lock, cursing low in the darkness.

And then a soft trail of light fluttered out as Elroy finally managed to unlock the door and pushed it open.

"Get on in there," Elroy spat, shoving Caroline. "And don't think you'll get away, 'cause I'm goin' to see to it that you cain't."

Caroline's eyes adjusted to the soft light, thankful that night hadn't yet fully fallen in its shroud of black. While there was light, there was hope. . . .

"I'll just rip up some of these old bedsheets and that should hold you," Elroy said, jerking a yellowed sheet from a box of many that had been stored in the tower room. Leaning his full weight against a wall, he began tearing the sheet apart, all the while keeping his eye on Caroline, watching her like a cat, ready to pounce.

"Like I said," he grumbled, "don't you get no ideas of tryin' to leave. I might be half-crippled, but I've learned how to make allowances for that. I'm still swift on my feet."

He nodded toward her. "If you'd like to test my abilities," he chuckled, "there's the door."

Caroline's heart raced. She inched back away from him, against the wall. Out of the corner of her eyes she could see that the tower room was cluttered. There were all sizes of boxes; books piled here and there; odds and ends of furniture, mostly broken; and many items that were covered with dustsheets. And though she had wondered if the portrait were there, she didn't dare take her eyes off Elroy to take a closer look. The dusk was causing the tower room to take on an eerie cast, and Caroline's insides grew numb, as she realized that she would more than likely be spending the night there.

The plaster wall that she was now standing against was cold to the touch, and reeked of mustiness. The floorboards were unpainted, covered with dustballs. And the windows were hazed over with grime.

The wind howled outside, around the corners of the tower, sounding ghostly. How could she stand a full night in this forbidding place? She had feared even entering it again, much less having to spend a night bound there in total darkness! Oh, why had she come again? And, oh, poor Sally!

"Elroy," she suddenly blurted, "how? How did Sally die? You . . . you said, that it was an accident. If so, why hide it? Everyone would surely understand. Even Rosa. She's your wife. She loves you. Don't you know of her sacrifices? She left her duties as mother to work at Twin Oaks to make life possible for you and your family. Surely she would understand, Elroy."

Elroy limped toward her, this time without the assistance of his cane, looking grotesque as his lame leg swung clumsily away from his body. His foot made a strange splat as it hit the floor.

"Lay down on the floor," he ordered, his gray eyes cold. "Now!"

Seeing his knife thrust into the waistband of his breeches, Caroline knew better than to argue. She inched down onto the floor, dying a slow death inside as she felt the clammy iciness of the boards against the flesh of her arms. And then she cringed when Elroy's calloused fingers dug into the flesh of her wrists and he began wrapping small strips of cloth around them, binding them together.

Fear quickened her heartbeat when he lifted the dress of her skirt and then her petticoats to reveal her legs. She knew that he had rape on his mind.

She watched him, terrified, as he also bound her ankles. And then she breathed more easily when he brushed her petticoats and dress back down over her ankles and took her by the waist and lifted her into a sitting position against the wall.

"Now that ought to hold you," he grumbled. He sat down beside her and removed his knife from his waist. "None of this would have been necessary had you stayed away from St. Clair Manor. None of it."

"You knew that I came here. Often," Caroline softly argued. "You had to know that I would find Sally."

Her heart did a strange flipflop and her eyes grew wild and wide. "No," she gasped. "Elroy, you . . . you didn't purposely place Sally here, did you? Oh, no. Tell me that you didn't murder her. But it wasn't an accident, was it? You wanted to frighten me. It was you who killed Lucky and Princess, wasn't it?"

"I didn't purposely kill my own daughter," he said, his eyes wavering, showing emotion for the first time over her loss. "It was an accident."

He stabbed away at the floor with his knife. "If Sally would have only left me alone," he mumbled. "She was with me constantly. I had to be with her too much. When I gave her the sleeping potion, I only meant for her to sleep."

"Sleeping potion . . .?" Caroline barely whispered.

"I gave it to her many times before it killed her," he said thickly. "Guess this last time I just gave her too much. Damn. Damn!"

"So that's what was wrong with Sally," Caroline said, remembering so much. "Elroy, how could you have drugged your own child like that? You're . . . you're a beast."

Elroy glared at her. Again he placed the knife to her throat. "Be quiet!" he shouted. "You just be quiet."

"And hiding her, keeping her away from Rosa?" Caroline persisted, recoiling as she felt the sharp point of the knife piercing her flesh.

"There was no other way," he growled. "Rosa wouldn't have ever understood. You don't, so why should she?"

"Elroy, please . . . take the knife away from my throat," Caroline softly begged, feeling a slow trickle of blood warming her flesh. "Please?"

"Why didn't you stay away from St. Clair Manor?" he grumbled, dropping the knife down away from her. "I thought finding Lucky would be enough. I thought you'd get scared and never come back. But you didn't. So I killed the cat. When I brought Sally here, I had thought she would be safely hidden away, at least until I let Rosa know about her."

"Why would you want to scare me away from St. Clair Manor like that? Why? Why would you want to frighten me at all? I've been kind to you and your family just as my uncle has through the years."

He again began stabbing the floor with his knife, his face twisted into an insane smile. "I have many reasons," he snarled. He glared over at her. "You think you're too good for me. I could always tell when you were with me. You looked at me as though I were nothing."

He moved his face closer to hers. "But, lady, I've

got somethin' to tell you." He laughed. "You're not good for anything. You're nothing but a damn Yankee from the North . . . a Union bitch."

He nodded toward his lame leg. "Just take a look at my leg," he said thickly. "It's all your fault. It's everybody's fault who sided in with the Northern bluebellies."

Caroline sat aghast, listening. All along he had been watching her . . . surely planning to do something to get even with her, and just because she was from the North? He was insane. Surely insane . . .

Dropping his knife to the floor, he rose on one knee before Caroline. His hands framed her face, his lips came dangerously close to hers. "You didn't like my flirtin' with you, did you?" He laughed harshly. "Thought you was too good." His lips brushed hers in a quick kiss. "Let me tell you, lady, it's just my way when with beautiful women. But when you openly rejected me, believing that I was seriously flirting with you, I decided to get back at you. You rejected me because of my lame leg and lack of money and position, didn't you? I'm not Gavin St. Clair, all rich and powerful, and with two perfect legs, am I?"

He tightened his hands on her face. "Am I?" he shouted. "You only make eyes at men who can give you something out of life. You only flirt with men whose bodies weren't maimed by war, don't you?"

Fear lacing her heart, Caroline swallowed hard. "No," she said, wincing when his fingers dug into her cheeks. "You're . . . you're wrong, Elroy. You're wrong."

Smiling wickedly, he drew away from her, his eyes devouring the swelling curve of her bosom. He grabbed and molded a breast, his eyes gleaming. But he drew away when he felt her flinch and emit a low moan of disgust.

Grabbing his cane, he pushed himself up from the floor. "I killed Lucky and Princess and planted them in Gavin's house for you to find," he chuckled. "I knew how often you were coming here. I wanted you to believe that it was Gavin who was trying to scare you away, so you would reject him."

"Well, as you see, it didn't work," Caroline said icily, trying to keep the shakiness out of her voice. She couldn't let him see how truly frightened she was. She didn't want him to know that he was *capable* of frightening her! "And how did you get the keys to St. Clair Manor to do your ghastly deeds?"

A faraway look came into Elroy's eyes. He went to a window and peered from it. "Before the war I was the stablehand and handyman at St. Clair Manor for George St. Clair," he said thickly. "I had the run of the place. I kept the keys when I left to fight for the Confederacy. When I returned, Mr. St. Clair was dead. Rosa and I were lucky when your uncle took us in, so to speak."

"And this is how you repay my uncle?" Caroline hissed. "By treating me so terribly?"

Elroy swung around, his face dark with hate. "I never liked ol' Daniel," he said, walking toward her. "He was nothin' but an ol' geezer with lots of money."

He bent to a knee before her and traced the outline of her lips with a forefinger. "An ol' geezer with a pretty niece," he chuckled.

Then he reached for another strip of sheet. He placed it to her mouth. "I'll just have to gag you," he said. "Don't want you screamin' once I leave."

Caroline felt the dryness of the rag on her lips, and smelled the odor of mildew on it. Her eyes were wild, her heart thundering. But she was helpless. Utterly helpless . . .

"You should've never interfered in my life," Elroy spat, again rising to his feet. "But since you have, you've got to pay." ·

He began lumbering toward the door. "I'm leavin' now," he said. "But I'll be back in the mornin'. I've got things to do before rapin' me a Northern bitch."

Caroline cringed at the words. She shuddered at his crazed laughter, which echoed through the house as he left the room and descended the stairs. She listened until she couldn't hear him any longer, then tried slowly to survey the room but it was now too dark to make anything out. Tonight, as never before, darkness had arrived too quickly for her. It was as though a giant hawk had suddenly swooped down over the tower room, spreading its wings, making dark shadows appear ominously in every hidden groove.

And then a wary moon began creeping up behind the tower and a scattering of stars became visible through the windows. When the moon drifted behind ragged clouds, Caroline had never felt so alone. . . .

# Nineteen

$F$ighting against the nightmare that was again surfacing inside her brain, Caroline moaned in her sleep, thrashing her head from side to side on the hard, cold floor on which she now slept. But nothing would keep the nightmare from coming, and adding to the terror of having to sleep alone in the tower room, fearing what the next day might bring for her. She moaned again as her frightening dreams completely engulfed her. . . .

The rain beat against Caroline's face with such force, she could scarcely see the boards as she struggled to pull them away. But her fingers continued to claw at them, desperation urging her onward. She flinched as the tall weeds thrashed against her legs, like blows from a whip. She sobbed, taking a frantic look behind her, discovering the assailant only a few yards away from her . . . running toward her with a knife held poised before him.

With a quick jerk of her head, Caroline looked forward again, letting the bright flashes from the lightning guide her fingers onward . . . pulling . . . tugging, until finally with a sudden surprising ease, the boards began to fall away, one at a time.

Laughing hysterically with her final triumph, Caroline pulled the doors open and stepped inside, finally feeling safe as she hurriedly shut the doors behind her. She sighed with relief as her trembling fingers found a bolt lock. And just as she had it slid securely

in place, shouts of obscenity began outside the door.
Her nerves jumped, keeping time with the loud banging of fists against the door.

Caroline slumped against the wall, breathing heavily, brushing the wet strands of her hair out of her eyes.
She peered through the darkness, trying to see the
interior of this place that she had tried for so long to
enter. She cringed. There was an unfamiliar aroma in
the air as her hands began to work their way around
the rough exterior of the wall.

She began to inch her way around the room, her
hands now discovering the soft strands of hay spread
all about her. And then she was slowly recognized the
smells that burned into her consciousness. Horses.
Straw. Aged wood. Grain. Dried and rotted horse
dung. She now knew she was in someone's stable, a
stable surely no longer used, for the aroma was that of
mold, even death.

Several bright flashes of lightning reflected through
the cracks in the walls around her, finally making it
possible for Caroline to see, if only for a moment. But
a moment's length of time was all that it took for
Caroline to move her eyes quickly around her. Her
eyes widened in disbelief when she saw something so
grotesque it threatened her sanity.

Plunging her body backward, she landed hard
against a wall. She put her fingers to her throat and
began to sob hysterically, still able to see before her
closed eyes the long, straw-colored hair twisting and
curling through the opening in what once was the face
of a person.

Then Caroline almost quit breathing, trying to
listen more carefully. The voice outside the door had
faded away to an almost inaudible whisper. But she
could hear her name being called, a small child's
voice pleading for her to open the door.

But Caroline now had only one thing on her mind.
She had to take another look about her. Surely it had
only been her imagination, possibly the lightning
playing tricks on her eyes.

She crept to her knees and began crawling toward where she had seen the horrible sight. Once again there, the bright flashes of lightning revealed it all to her. Yet now instead of seeing a skull, she saw blue eyes looking upward at her through the ground, so glassy and staring, surrounded by strawlike hair of gold. . . .

Caroline's subconscious state couldn't bear the dream any longer. She began to scream, riveting herself quickly awake from her nightmare. Her head dully ached, her heart thumped wildly, a cold sweat of fear was wet on her brow. She blinked her eyes nervously and jumped as lurid, forked lightning split the sky to accompanying crashes of thunder and rain coming down in sheets outside the tower windows, drawing her fully awake.

Sobbing, she recalled the glassy eyes, the hair of straw. She could still hear the voice shouting her name. But who? Where? This was the first time her nightmare had taken her this far.

Oh, why . . .? she thought to herself. Wasn't it enough that she was a prisoner to a madman? Why must the nightmares plague her now?

Struggling, she moved herself into a sitting position, squinting her eyes, trying to see about her, but morning seemed far away. Between the flashes of lightning, she was sitting in pitch blackness. She tensed when the wind howled about the tower. She struggled with the bindings at her wrists and ankles and tried to work the gag from her mouth. But all these efforts gained her was a tired numbness. And when she felt herself begin drifting again, she fought it, but she couldn't stay awake. Sleep. It burned at her eyes. Her body slumped over onto the floor. Her eyelids felt heavier, heavier. . . .

At first, Caroline slept in a sort of drugged stupor, no thoughts or images at all playing across her mind. But in a short while she began to toss fitfully around on the floor. A dream was surfacing. It was very clear to her. She was in her Aunt Meg's yard in southern

Illinois. The cherries were ripe above her head but she couldn't reach any. The cherry tree was too high for her to climb.

A girl of five, she was too small. And she was afraid of getting her new dress dirty. She just held her favorite doll more closely to her, singing a lullaby, the doll's blue eyes staring upward at her, looking so real.

"Your hair is so pretty, Nancy," Caroline said to her doll, smoothing down its straw-colored strands of hair.

But suddenly the doll was no longer in Caroline's arms. Her twelve-year-old cousin Todd had grabbed it from her.

"You give me back my doll, you naughty boy," Caroline cried. "You're going to get her all dirty."

Todd laughed sarcastically, his gray eyes mocking her. "Want to see what I'm going to do to your doll?" he said, carrying the doll toward the back of the yard and the stable with the boarded-up double doors.

"What are you going to do?" Caroline asked, trying to pull the doll from Todd's grasp. But her attempts were futile and she felt Todd's bony fingers twisting her wrist until she began to cry.

"I'm going to tell Aunt Meg," Caroline said, jerking free, starting to run away.

"If you do, you'll be sorry," Todd's voice rang after her, stopping her.

Caroline had already grown to be frightened of him. In her three weeks' stay at her aunt's house, he had constantly picked on her. He had hurt her many times by kicking her or poking at her, bruising her in places unable to be seen by her Aunt Meg.

"Okay. I won't tell," Caroline said, walking back toward Todd. "But please, give me my doll."

Her pleading fell on deaf ears. She froze on the spot, watching Todd carrying her doll by its hair on toward the unused stable. And when he stepped behind it, out of her sight, Caroline began to run after him. When she turned the corner of the stable and saw him acting as though he was going to pull the doll apart, Caroline picked up a stick and began to hit Todd with it, causing him to drop the doll to the ground.

Todd turned and tried to grab the stick away from her. "Give me that!" he demanded.

"No!" Caroline shouted.

"You'll be sorry!" Todd said, grabbing her by a wrist. But the sudden appearance of a dog running toward them with a white froth seeping from the corners of its mouth made him stop.

"God!" Todd gasped. "A mad dog!"

Caroline whirled around and saw the dog. He seemed to be running sideways, seeming to have been injured, possibly by a passing carriage. Its eyes were glazed, its mouth white with some sort of foam. Its bark was terrifying.

Screaming, Caroline grabbed her doll from the ground and began to run beside Todd. They ran back around to the front of the stable. The house was much too far away to reach safely before the dog would most surely attack.

"The stable!" Todd cried. "We must get inside the stable! Caroline, forget your damn doll and help me get the boards off the doors!"

Trembling, Caroline dropped her doll and began working with the boards, the barking of the dog now drawing closer. Her fingers were fast becoming raw. But finally the boards began to fall away and when Todd threw the doors open, Caroline desperately reached for her doll, grabbed it, and hurried on inside with Todd.

Breathing hard, she watched, mortified, as Todd closed the doors behind them. But that wasn't keeping the horrible growls and barks from reaching inside the old, unused stable.

"Todd, I'm afraid," Caroline said, hugging her doll to her.

Todd went to Caroline and yanked the doll away from her. He threw it onto a thick bed of straw and then turned and wickedly eyed Caroline, his face almost grotesque in a crooked smile. He grabbed

Caroline by the wrists and began forcing her to the floor.

She looked up at him, never having seen him look so threateningly ugly. "Todd, quit!" she screamed. "What do you think you're doing? You're hurting me. And you're getting my new dress dirty! Why are you always so mean to me?"

"I'm not being mean to you, Caroline," Todd said thickly, lowering himself on top of her. "I like you. Really I do. I like the color of your hair. It's so pretty and soft."

Caroline tossed her head back and forth, trying to keep Todd's fingers from touching her hair.

"Get off me. Let me up, Todd. I will tell Aunt Meg. I will," she shouted. But she then grew silent as she felt the cold blade of Todd's pocket knife against her throat.

"Now, you won't tell nobody nuthin', do you hear, cousin?" Todd growled.

Fear had Caroline completely in its grip. She lay quietly while Todd's cold fingers began to pull her dress upward.

"Todd, what . . .?" she began . . .

Muffled screams held inside her by the gag at her mouth awakened Caroline from her nightmare. Sweat poured profusely from her brow, though she was completely chilled from the cold of the night. Tears soaked the gag at her mouth, as she sobbed, so relieved to be awake and away from what the nightmare was just about to reveal to her.

Oh, Lord, had she been raped? Had her cousin Todd raped her? Was that the reason for her nightmares? The stable! Her aunt's boarded-up stable! It *did* resemble the one behind St. Clair Manor. Apparently the sight of the St. Clair stable had brought to her consciousness what had been so gratefully removed after her traumatic ordeal those long years ago.

Trying to recall that dreadful day again, she couldn't remember it all. She knew that she should be glad but also knew that until she did she would never be fully free of the dread that she carried subconsciously around with her. It seemed that going to the stable would be the only way to rid herself of these tormenting nightmares!

Only a distant rumble of thunder could now be heard. The storm had moved on out to sea. Morning was now awakening, casting a faint splash of pink through the misty tower windows. Caroline groaned as she squirmed up to a sitting position, every bone in her body aching from her thrashing about through her troubled dreams. But though she was aching, she was determined to get herself free. With daybreak, who was to say when Elroy would return? And when he did, what was her fate to be?

Bending herself almost double, Caroline managed to get her fingers to her bound ankles. Now that she had some light to work with she saw the loose ends of the torn sheets where they were knotted. Her fingers worked, her back pained her from the stretching, but finally she managed to untie the hateful knots and soon had her feet free.

And now her wrists. Elroy was foolish for having tied them in front instead of the back. At least she could see the knot, and possibly find something with which to loosen it.

With weakened knees she rose to her feet. She stood there momentarily to get her balance, and looked slowly about her. Among all of this stored debris, surely she could find something to help untie the knot. She had to get away. Now! She kept listening for footsteps, knowing that at any time Elroy could return. It was too much to hope for Gavin to arrive to rescue her. Even if he did come to St. Clair Manor, she wouldn't be able to alert him. Her mouth was gagged! Only by untying her hands could she ever get that dreadful gag from about her lips.

With the strength back in her legs, Caroline began tiptoeing around the room, looking for anything that might have a sharp object projecting from it. She silently thanked the morning sun as it began stream-ing through the window, giving her an even better look about her.

And then something caught her eye. Her heart skipped a beat. Standing at the edge of the room, behind an oak bookcase, were the portraits! In Caro-line's desperation to escape she had completely for-gotten about her interest in them. And at first glance she knew that her search had truly ended, for the face staring back at her in its angelic sweetness belonged to her Aunt Amelia, who was indeed wearing her be-loved cameo necklace.

Caroline felt a strange dizziness sweep over her with the realization that she had been right all along. Though her Uncle Daniel would never have believed it, his wife had posed for the portrait behind his back. And by the look in her Aunt Amelia's eyes, she had greatly enjoyed the moments away from her husband!

Shaking her head and turning her eyes away, Caro-line felt a great sadness for her uncle who had sorely loved a woman who had betrayed him.

Slowly turning around to study the portrait, Caro-line wondered if her aunt had loved Gavin's uncle. Just how often had she met him at St. Clair Manor? Sitting for a portrait would take more than one day.

And did this disloyalty to her husband have any-thing to do with Amelia's strange disappearance?

Though relieved to have finally found the portrait, Caroline could not feel victorious. She knew that only one mystery had been solved by this discovery. She still didn't know why her aunt had disappeared, or where. . . .

And now Caroline was in danger herself and had to brush all thoughts of her aunt from her mind and concentrate on getting herself free.

Turning her back on the portrait, she again let her eyes scan around the room, searching for something, anything that could free her of the cloths about her wrists!

Her pulse raced as she saw a fireplace poker lodged

between two boxes of stored books. Her heart beating anxiously, she went to the poker and placed a hand to it, testing its solid strength. She smiled to herself. The poker was strongly lodged in place, giving her full use of its sharp end. Pushing up against the tip of the poker, she began trying to work it into the knot. She worked carefully, sweating, her wrists straining against the cotton fabric.

Finally, her eyes glistening with tears of relief, she managed to get the tip of the poker snugly into the knot. Barely breathing for fear that the poker would slip free, she worked with it until she saw the fabric loosening. Eyes wide, she watched as the knot came untied. She wanted to shout for joy when she eased her hands free. Had it not been for the gag she probably would have shouted and that could have been a kiss of death. For if Elroy was anywhere near, he would know that she had just been set completely free. . . .

Hurriedly, she removed the gag, running her tongue over her dried, parched lips. She ran toward the door and placed her ear to it, listening. Upon hearing no sound, she edged the door slowly open and gazed intently down the staircase.

But as usual, only darkness met her wondering stare. She knew that she would have to take a chance, for freedom surely was only a few brave footsteps away!

Lifting the skirt of her dress and her petticoats, she descended the stairs, safely reaching the second floor landing. There, she couldn't help but look back toward the closed door behind which lay the secret of a child's death. An ache stabbed her heart as she thought of Sally and her sweetness. It was almost too much to bear to think that she was now dead . . . and because of the utter stupidity of her very own father!

But Caroline had to hurry onward. Elroy might even be in there.

Almost afraid to breathe, she tiptoed on down the stairs, sighing with relief as she reached the first floor, and fled on through the house to the outdoors. As she ran softly across the lawn, something drew her to a sudden halt, transfixed, her gaze fell upon the stable and its boarded-up doors.

"Lord, I must . . ." she whispered. If she didn't now, she never would. She *must* go inside the stable. Surely by doing so she would be set free of her tormented dreams.

Seeing no signs of Elroy, she felt that she was safe enough, at least for awhile, to hurry on to the stable. And even when Elroy did decide to return to the tower room, he would have no reason to search for her at the stable after finding her no longer where he had left her. He most surely would believe that she would hurry back to Twin Oaks, to tell Rosa everything.

However, the way things were, Caroline didn't believe that she would be safe at Twin Oaks. Perhaps she should even hide in the St. Clair Manor stable until she heard Gavin arriving on horseback. She knew that he always wore a pistol. Surely he could take care of Elroy once and for all!

But then her heart plunged. How could she get inside into the stable? The doors were boarded up. And remembering her nightmare, she could recall just how hard it had been to remove the boards. Her fingers ached just when recalling her moments of sheer terror as she had tried so desperately hard to rip them off.

But perhaps she could find something with which to pry the boards off. Breathless, she hurried behind the stable, searching for anything that she might use as a tool. And then a glint arising from the grass drew her attention. Was she actually seeing an ax? It was too perfect! Surely she could pry the boards away with that!

She grabbed the ax, and determinedly slipped the rusted blade behind a board. Grunting and groaning, she worked at loosening the board until she heard the sound of splintering and crackling of wood.

Dropping the ax to the ground, she began pulling at

the one loosened board with all her strength. As it popped off, the others fell away with an uncanny ease. Caroline felt a strong sense of déjà vu, having only a short while ago dreamed the same scene. Fear of what she would find behind the doors filled her with paralyzing dread though she knew that her only discovery would be the horrible memory she had buried in her subconscious long ago. What she had already recalled of her past in her latest nightmare caused her to fear knowing the rest, but she knew that she must.

"I truly must," she whispered, trying to gather the courage to go on inside. She had to believe that the fear of the unknown was probably even more terrifying than knowing. And only she could put it all in place for herself. She was so close. There was no turning back.

Looking back over her shoulder, she was relieved to see that Elroy wasn't either in the yard or at any of St. Clair Manor's many windows. Holding the ax in one hand in case she should need a weapon, she began pulling one of the double doors open. Not wanting to attract any undue attention to the stables, Caroline only partially opened the door, just enough to squeeze her way inside.

The aromas of aged straw and rotted horse dung met her as she entered, making her nose curl. She narrowed her eyes, trying to see through the gloomy semidarkness.

But what she was seeing had nothing to do with the present. Just being inside the stable was enough to stir the most unpleasant of memories of her past. She was remembering another stable . . . another time . . . another place. And it was as it had been in her latest nightmare. She found herself reliving that day in her Aunt Meg's stables. . . .

She dropped the ax on the straw-covered floor and covered her mouth with her hands, stifling a sob as she recalled how her Cousin Todd had almost raped her that day while holding a knife at her throat. If the sudden thundering of a train on the railroad tracks that lay only a few feet from her Aunt Meg's stable had not frightened Todd so terribly that he had fled from the stable, she would have been brutally robbed of her innocence at the age of five!

She knew now that the grotesque, glassy eyes and the hair of straw that had frightened her so in her nightmare had belonged to the doll that she had carried with her the day of the near rape. Only now did she understand her full fears of that house and its boarded-up stable.

Tears splashed from her eyes. The experience with Todd had been so horrible she somehow had managed to block it from her mind. Until now . . .

A creaking behind Caroline made her turn with a start. Her insides froze when she saw Elroy silhouetted against the light at the door, leaning on his cane. The glimmer of a knife shone in his free hand, and a low, wicked laugh filled the dark spaces of the stable.

"Elroy," Caroline gasped, taking a step backward. "Oh, Lord. . . ."

"Thought you'd get away from me, didn't you?" He laughed, stepping into a splash of sunlight, which illuminated his full facial features for Caroline. "I don't know how you managed to get yourself free, but now that you have, I guess it makes it even easier for me to do what I've been wantin' to do since that very first day I saw you."

Caroline backed away from him. "Don't touch me," she hissed. "You're nothing but an animal. I won't let you touch me."

He waved the knife in the air for her to see. "Yeah?" he chuckled. "And what do you expect to do about it?"

Remembering the ax, Caroline desperately searched for it with her eyes. When she saw it lying closer to Elroy than to herself, her hopes waned.

But she forced herself to look brave, though her insides were a quivering mass of jelly. "If you turn and leave, you really won't have done anything wrong,

Elroy," she said. "The death of Sally was an accident. You won't get arrested for that. But if you rape me, that's a different story."

"I don't plan to only rape you," Elroy said, edging closer to her. "I plan to make sure nobody ever finds you to accuse me of a rape."

Caroline paled. "You're planning to kill me?" she gasped. "Elroy, surely you're not planning to do that. You're not a murderer. Why start now? Please reconsider all of this that you're doing. Elroy, your future will . . . will . . . be ruined."

"It already is," he shouted, placing the knife to her throat as he finally reached her. "Now get down on the floor. I don't want to waste no more time talkin'."

Caroline stood her ground. She felt that it didn't matter either way. He was going to kill her eventually, regardless of what she now did. "Never," she said, placing her hands on her hips.

Elroy threw his cane aside and shoved Caroline, knocking her to the floor. She lay there, momentarily stunned, and when she was able to fully focus her eyes again she found Elroy straddling her, his lips lowering to hers.

"No!" she screamed, finding the strength and courage to give him a hardy shove as she again suddenly remembered another attempted rape . . . another time. "It will not happen even this time! I won't allow it!"

When Elroy fell next to her in a puzzled heap, Caroline reached for the ax. And just as he raised his knife into the air for its death plunge, she brought the ax handle down upon his head.

Scrambling to her feet, she watched as he crumpled and fell into a shallow pit in the stable's earthen floor. She cringed when she saw the blood seeping from his head wound. His breathing seemed too shallow and his eyes were closed. He definitely seemed unconscious. But she had to be sure.

She inched her way toward him and touched him with the handle of the ax. He didn't stir. She bent to take a closer look and check for a pulse, but something else caught her attention out of the corner of her eye, something that caught the light of the morning sun and glittered enticingly at Caroline.

An object was sticking up through the ground. Its shine seemed like that usually found in jewelry. But surely it was not. Not here.

Dropping the ax to the floor, Caroline crawled closer to the shining object and brushed some loose dirt away. Her insides went cold. "God!" she gasped. "It can't be. But it is."

Her fingers trembled violently as she reached for the gold chain. And when she saw the cameo which hung from it, she knew that she had just found her Aunt Amelia's necklace. . . .

# *Twenty*

*I*gnoring Elroy lying behind her, Caroline crept closer to the necklace, in her mind's eye seeing flashes of the portrait and how beautifully the artist had captured the likeness of her Aunt Amelia. Her aunt's cameo necklace had stood out prominently in the painting, hanging lustrously around her aunt's tiny slender neck.

Caroline remembered her aunt's love for her cameo necklace and knew she wouldn't have willingly parted with it. And she had been wearing it the day of her disappearance. So how had it gotten in George St. Clair's stable? Caroline was afraid to know the answer to that question.

Her fingers touched the lovely face on the cameo. Breathlessly, she tried to pull the necklace from the earthen floor of the stable. Her brow creased with a puzzled frown—the necklace wouldn't come free of the mixture of dirt and aged straw. It was attached to something!

A hand suddenly grasped Caroline's wrist, turning her insides to ice. A scream froze in her throat as she realized that she had forgotten about Elroy.

"Caroline, darling . . .?" Gavin said suddenly from behind her.

Caroline looked up into the dark eyes that always sent her heart to spinning. "Gavin . . .?" she whispered.

She relaxed her hold on the cameo and rose quickly

into Gavin's warm embrace. "Oh, Gavin," she murmured. "Thank God you've come. It's been so horrible."

"What's happened here?" he said thickly, his fingers weaving through her hair, his gaze locked on Elroy, who lay sprawled behind Caroline. "Why are you here? And what has happened to Elroy? Why is he here?"

Caroline turned her head and lowered her eyes. She shuddered upon seeing Elroy and clung to Gavin more tightly. "I hit Elroy over the head with the handle of that ax," she sobbed.

"Why was that necessary? I don't understand what either of you are doing here in the stable," Gavin protested. "It's been boarded up for years. When I saw the one door open, I knew something had to be wrong."

"Elroy followed me here," Caroline softly cried. "He had tied me up in the tower room after I found Sally."

"Good Lord," Gavin gasped, his cheeks flaming. "Sally? Who . . .?"

"Elroy killed his daughter, Sally," Caroline blurted out, her eyes wild as she looked up at Gavin. "I found her inside St. Clair Manor. Elroy . . . he hid her there, Gavin. I found her."

She laid her cheek on Gavin's powerful chest and closed her eyes, tears stinging their corners. "And he killed my uncle's dog and cat," she sobbed.

Gavin was absorbing all that Caroline was saying, yet not understanding any of it. He eased her away from him and held her gently at arm's length. "Caroline, what are you saying?" he said thickly. "Why *would* he?"

Caroline furiously shook her head back and forth. "I don't know," she cried. "The reasons he gave were . . ."

A low groan from Elroy interrupted Caroline's words. She swung away from Gavin, raised her hands to her mouth, and watched, terrified, as Elroy rose up on an elbow. His eyes were glazed and blood still curled from the corners from the head wound. He began kneading his brow, again groaning.

"What . . . happened . . . ?" he groaned, seeing Gavin and Caroline through a blurred haze.

Then as he began pushing himself up to a sitting position, his gaze fell upon the exposed necklace. He gasped loudly, his eyes now cleared and able to make out the cameo.

"No!" he said beneath his breath. "It can't be. . . ."

Desperate, he crawled closer to the necklace and began hurriedly covering it with dirt.

Caroline watched, momentarily transfixed in place, as Elroy buried the necklace. Why? What could the necklace mean to him that he felt the desperate need to hide it?

"Stop that!" Caroline shouted. She went to Elroy and pulled at his shoulders. "What are you doing? I'm sure that's my aunt's necklace. Why don't you want me to find it?"

Gavin gently pulled Caroline away from Elroy. "Caroline, let me," he said, urging her aside.

Trembling, Caroline watched as Gavin grabbed Elroy by his shoulders and jerked him to stand before him. "I think you've much to explain here," Gavin growled. "Now where do you wish to begin?"

Caroline edged her way around Elroy and Gavin. She fell to her knees and brushed the loose dirt aside to uncover the necklace. Remembering how it had seemed attached to something earlier, she gave it a hard jerk and sighed with relief when it came free of whatever had held it, coming easily to rest in the palm of her hand.

She turned the cameo over. Her insides quivered when she read the inscription engraved in gold on the back, "To Amelia, my love, from Daniel."

As Caroline had known from the very instant she had seen it, the necklace was her aunt's. Now there was no doubt about it. Softly sobbing, she clasped it to her heart and slowly rose to her feet, eyeing Elroy warily.

"So? Are you going to start talking?" Gavin said tightly to Elroy. "Or do I have to finish what Caroline started? She seems to have struck a powerful blow. But believe me, mine would be harder. I doubt if you would walk away from it."

Elroy's steel-gray eyes moved to Caroline and to the necklace that she was holding. He paled, his eyes wavering. He then looked toward the spot where the necklace had been found, noticing how the ground had settled where he had dug ten years ago. If the necklace was that easily exposed to the naked eye, then soon the rest of what he had buried would be uncovered.

He knew that Caroline, with her love of mysteries, would not let him get away with lying about his interest in the necklace. The past had finally caught up with him. . . .

"I just couldn't scare either of you away, could I?" he snarled. "You just had to come snoopin'."

"What the hell are you talking about?" Gavin snapped angrily. "This is my place. I have a right to be here, to do whatever I wish. And I damn well wouldn't call it snooping."

Elroy glared at Caroline, hate heavy in his eyes. "She sure as hell did enough snoopin' for the both of you," he growled. "Just couldn't leave it alone, could you, you Northern bitch? You just had to keep comin' back for more. When you found Lucky, wasn't that enough? Why'd you have to keep coming?"

"It was you who shot Daniel's dog?" Gavin asked, tightening his grip on Elroy's shoulders. "You did it to frighten her away from St. Clair Manor? Why would you want to do that, Elroy? What did she ever do to you to deserve that?"

"I did it to scare the both of you away," Elroy spat. "Why'd you decide to come back to St. Clair Manor, Gavin? All these years that you left it vacant, why now? Isn't the townhouse mansion in Charleston enough for you? You have to have two places now as your uncle did back in the days before the war? I remember those days when he'd leave for months to live in Charleston for the social season. But things ain't the same today, Gavin. You ain't got no plantation planted with cotton. You ain't got no slaves to do the plantin'. Why would you even want to come back to St. Clair Manor? I'd have been safe had it not been for you and Miss Snoopy here."

"How is it that you know anything of my uncle's activities?" Gavin half shouted. "You speak as though you knew him quite well. How is it that you would?"

Caroline edged closer to Gavin. "Elroy was employed by your uncle," she half whispered. "He was not only your uncle's handyman, but also his stablehand. He even still has the keys to the house. Didn't you know? Don't you remember seeing him around while visiting your uncle?"

"He what?" Gavin stormed. "No. I don't remember him. I rarely came to St. Clair Manor once I broke free of my uncle. First there was law school, then there was my retreat . . . the townhouse, and then the war."

He gave Elroy a shove, then stepped closer to growl into his face, "Go ahead. You were saying?"

"She said it," Elroy said, half cowering. "I worked for your uncle. That's how I knew him."

"What else did you know?" Gavin asked, "Why were you afraid for me to live at St. Clair Manor? Why didn't you want Caroline here?"

Elroy gave the settled ground a quick glance. He swallowed hard and looked slowly around, feeling almost dwarfed by Gavin's powerful stance.

Gavin doubled a fist into Elroy's face. "I'm waiting, Elroy," he growled. "Tell me now or regret it."

Elroy flinched and raised a hand to his face. "All were accidents," he stammered. "My daughter. Amelia Burton . . . Grace Wilhelm. I didn't mean to kill them. It just . . . happened. Amelia and Grace felt they were too good for me. I just knocked them around a bit. Could I help it . . . if . . . I hit them too hard?"

Caroline's head began to spin. She clasped the necklace more tightly, now almost too afraid to look toward the spot where she had found it. Surely Elroy hadn't . . . !

She listened, feeling sick inside as his each word was spoken.

"I didn't want you to move back to St. Clair Manor for fear that you might uncover the graves here in . . . in the stable," Elroy confessed. "The first time I saw you come to the manor, I began fearing discovery. It was only by chance that old man Burton hired me on, giving me the opportunity to keep an eye on things at St. Clair Manor. But I should have known that the bodies would be found sooner or later. Rosa and I should've moved clean out of the Carolinas. That's where I made my first mistake."

Caroline's insides were weak. She felt as though she might retch. She turned away from Elroy, not wanting to have to look at him any longer. He had just confessed to killing her aunt . . . and another woman. And their graves lay only a few footsteps away. . . .

Elroy continued his morbid confession, a tale of jealousy and murder. "When I worked for George St. Clair before the war, I saw many beautiful women coming and going from St. Clair Manor, coming here to pose for their portraits," he said. "I became jealous of the old man and his money. Wanting to prove that my virility was worth more than money, I lured some of the women here in the stable where I successfully seduced them."

"You raped them?" Caroline said, spinning around to boldly face him. "You raped my aunt?"

Elroy chuckled beneath his breath. "That wasn't necessary," he said huskily. "Your aunt and the other women came willingly. Seems they were lacking in their love lives at home."

Caroline's eyes flamed in sudden anger, remembering her uncle and the special relationship that he had thought he had with his wife. "So you changed that, did you?" she hissed. "You and my aunt?"

"It was only short-lived," he growled. "When I found out that your aunt and Grace Wilhelm felt they were too good for a serious relationship with a mere stablehand, and only wanted the sensual pleasures that I skillfully gave them, I lost my temper and beat the hell out of them!"

Gavin kneaded his brow, glowering at Elroy. "So you buried them in my uncle's stable to keep an eye on their graves. Nobody would discover them since you were in charge of the stable. Isn't that right, Elroy?" he said, his voice strained. At one time he had even suspected his uncle of being responsible for the missing women after it had become common knowledge that some women had disappeared. So when he had found the portraits he separated them, hiding some in one place, and some in another. He had known that the one was of Caroline's aunt. He had feared that she had seen it that one time when he had caught her looking through the window! If she had ever questioned him about it, he wouldn't have known what to say. He didn't have any more answers than she. And now that he did, he was relieved to know that it hadn't been a St. Clair responsible for any of the disappearances or deaths.

"The damn war changed everything," Elroy said. "It meant me having to leave St. Clair Plantation, and when I returned the old man was dead and the plantation was not inhabited by anyone. When I saw you there that first time I knew that I must first try to frighten you away, or in the end kill both you and Miss Burton."

"You damn well won't get that chance now," Gavin stated flatly. He withdrew his pistol from his holster and aimed it at Elroy. "I think the authorities in town just might be interested in hearing the same story that you just told us."

Caroline shook her head with grief. "Aunt Amelia,"

she whispered. "All along she's been this close to Twin Oaks. She was murdered."

She raised her hands to her throat and stifled a sob, silently thanking God that her Uncle Daniel was not alive to learn the truth about his wife. Had he known before his death, he would have never been able to rest in peace.

And then panic seized Caroline as she remembered Rosa and what she was soon to find out. First that her daughter was dead, and then that her husband was some sort of demon. How could Rosa not have known the type of person to whom she had been married?

Yet Caroline thought she perhaps understood. Elroy did have a charming side, which was mostly hidden except for whenever he wanted to use it to his advantage. When with his wife, surely he charmed her to death! That could be the only answer.

"And Sally," she blurted out. "Someone must be told about Sally. And who is to tell Rosa?"

Gavin took a step toward Elroy and stuck his pistol into Elroy's ribs. "How could I have forgotten that you also killed your daughter?" he growled. "You're going to get the hanging that you deserve."

"Like I told Miss Snoopy, that was an accident just like the others," Elroy said thickly, his eyes lowering. "I didn't mean to kill Sally. I just gave her too much medicine to make her sleep. I didn't know I was givin' her too much. I didn't. I'm damn sorry about that. I . . . I . . . loved my daughter."

"A monster like you couldn't love anyone," Caroline said in a low hiss. "You were ready to rape and then kill me. You can't deny that, Elroy."

Gavin snarled as he grabbed Elroy and shoved him toward the door.

"My cane . . ." Elroy said in a low whimper. "I can't walk good without my cane."

"Then stumble," Gavin said dryly. "And when you do, I'll just laugh."

"How could you?" Elroy whined. "You know that I

got wounded while fightin' for the Confederate cause. You fought for the same cause. How could you laugh at someone who'd gotten wounded while fighting bravely?"

"I doubt if you've ever done anything bravely," Gavin said, giving Elroy another shove, this time out and into the harsh rays of the sun. "Anyone who'd kill two defenseless women and even his own child is anything but brave."

Caroline lingered behind. She went and stood over the spot where she had found the necklace. She felt drained of emotion now that she realized how wrong she and her uncle had been about Amelia. Yet, Caroline knelt and placed the necklace onto what she now knew to be her aunt's grave. Though she knew the graves would soon be dug up by the authorities, it seemed only fair that Amelia should have the necklace with her. It had apparently meant something almost spiritual to her aunt, though Caroline would never understand this, for if Amelia had loved her husband so much that she never parted with the necklace, why had she let a deranged man like Elroy make love to her? Surely her Aunt Amelia had been forced. Caroline would never believe anything different. She just couldn't!

Yet her aunt had willingly posed for the portrait and had done so knowing that her husband wouldn't approve!

Spiritless, Caroline scraped dirt over the necklace. Then she rose and walked from the stable, wishing that she hadn't uncovered the mystery at all. Like her Uncle Daniel, she would have been better off not knowing.

Stepping out into the brightness of mid-morning, Caroline looked toward Twin Oaks, wondering how she would have the courage to tell Rosa the truth about everything. But she knew that she must. It would be almost inhuman to let a complete stranger break the news first about her daughter, and then her husband. Would such a hurt ever heal? Could Rosa even live with the emptiness that had just come into her life? Caroline had seen Rosa in almost hysterics over her daughter. But she had to know. And soon.

Gavin walked ahead of Caroline, holding Elroy at gunpoint. He turned his head and gazed at her with a heavy-lashed look. "Are you all right?" he asked hoarsely. "You've just had quite a shock."

"Yes," she murmured, falling into step at his side. "I'm fine."

She eyed him wonderingly. "But, Gavin, I have to ask you about some portraits that I saw that first day we met," she murmured. "I saw them through the front parlor window. Did you know? I've suspected that you knew and were purposely hiding them."

"I thought that you saw them," he said thickly, his eyes now focused back on Elroy, who stumbled ahead, panting. "Yes, I felt the need to hide them. I knew one was of Amelia Burton, one of the women known to be missing those many years ago."

"But why did that worry you?" Caroline persisted, lifting her skirt as they made their way around the lagoon toward Twin Oaks.

"My uncle was known to be a bit on the peculiar side and a womanizer," he confessed. "When I knew that he had painted two of the missing women, I became suspicious, but never let on. He had treated me so kindly, I just couldn't do anything to show my lack of trust in him."

His eyelids grew heavy. "This is why I couldn't let anyone see the portraits," he said thickly. "Only after I had removed some to my townhouse and the others to the tower room did I feel free to ask you to help me restore St. Clair Manor. I see now that I was wrong about my uncle. I wish I had known long ago. I didn't treat him fairly. I stayed much too much at the townhouse in Charleston. That is why, Caroline. I guess in a sense, I was not brave enough. I couldn't face up to what might be true or to what might just be suspicions."

Caroline locked an arm through his free one. "I,

too, at one time thought your uncle might be responsible for my aunt's disappearance," she murmured. "I did see the portrait and I have since been searching for it."

Gavin's eyes widened. "You have?" he gasped.

"Since that very first day we met," she replied, laughing softly. "I couldn't rest until I knew if the missing portrait had something to do with my missing aunt."

"And now you know," Gavin said, giving Elroy a nudge with his pistol.

"Yes," she sighed. She looked toward Twin Oaks and caught the outline of Rosa standing in an upper window, watching their approach. "And now someone else must be told. Rosa. Oh, Lord, how I will hate the next few moments. How can I tell her?"

"You don't have to," Gavin grumbled. He nodded toward Elroy. "Let him tell her. His punishment for having done these things will start then."

"Yes, even then," Caroline said, sighing deeply.

# *Twenty-one*

*T*he morning sun glittered onto Spanish moss, making it appear like gold lace hanging from the branches of the live oaks. The air, sea-seasoned and flower-scented, was moist and sweet. The lawn gleamed lush and green, the azaleas coloring the landscape as Caroline and Gavin casually strolled hand in hand, Twin Oaks casting a shadow behind them.

"Happy, darling?" Gavin asked, his gaze sweeping over her loveliness as the silken folds of her lace-trimmed dress rustled about her.

"Never happier," Caroline sighed, smiling warmly up at him. It had taken awhile, but the discoveries at St. Clair Manor were finally fading away inside Caroline's consciousness. She was no longer plagued by nightmares. She had met her past head-on when her dreams had fully revealed the one ugly day of her childhood.

Now she only looked to the future, and sweet it was, now that she was Mrs. Gavin St. Clair and soon to be the mother of Gavin's child.

She looked at Gavin, secretly longing for a son that would be a mirror image of his father. As always when silently admiring Gavin, Caroline's heart swam with pride that he was totally hers.

"Darling, you're so quiet," Gavin said, drawing her from her silent reverie. "Is something troubling you?"

"No." Caroline softly laughed. "I'm just enjoying being with you again. Your business keeps you from me much too much. I just hate being alone."

Gavin leaned a hand to her abdomen and touched it tenderly, even almost meditatively. "In a few months you won't ever be alone again," he said hoarsely. "You will have our child to keep you company."

Feeling delicious inside, Caroline placed one of her hands over his. "Yes," she murmured. "Our child."

Gavin urged her hand to his lips and gently kissed her palm. "At one time I would have argued a pleasant future for us," he softly said. "When we first met you seemed to run hot and cold. I guess I shall never understand why."

Caroline's eyes wavered: she did not want to be reminded of any of the gruesome past. "It's all over now," she sighed. "Why must we talk about it?"

"Yes. Elroy seemed to have been the sole cause of all our doubts of one another," he said. "But we won't be bothered by him any longer. Damned how he decided to take his own life. Hung himself with his own belt. But he was better off. At least he didn't have to die with an audience watching."

A tremor coursed along Caroline's flesh. "Poor Rosa," she murmured. "It took so long for her to get over the double tragedies."

"But she has," Gavin confirmed. "And because of you. She is now even looking forward to having a baby around the house. Perhaps our child can take the place of her daughter."

"I'm sure it can't entirely," Caroline sighed, "but perhaps it can help."

Caroline swung around to face Gavin, holding his hands. "Do you mind living at Twin Oaks?"

"It is best for all concerned," he said dryly. "St. Clair Manor was full of ghosts . . . ghosts of both our pasts. Anyway, we still have the townhouse in Charleston," he said, his eyes lighting up. "I like how we've chosen to live there in the winter and here at

Twin Oaks in the summer. It makes entertaining more practical during the social season."

"And I loved having had the chance to renovate the townhouse into the lovely showcase that it now is," Caroline sighed.

Gavin laughed. "Well, at least I got you to renovate one of my mansions," he said, his eyes full of warmth. "You gave me a time trying to get your assistance at St. Clair Manor."

"It so reminded me of my Aunt Meg's house. If not for that one month spent in Illinois with my Aunt Meg, things would have been so different for me," Caroline sighed, snuggling as Gavin drew her closer. "My cousin Todd was such a demon."

"Come to think of it," Gavin said, his dark eyes wide, "where is Todd now? Whatever happened to him?"

"Oh? Didn't I tell you?" Caroline said casually, her face void of expression, her voice flat.

"No. What?"

"Todd had a way of teasing my uncle's prized bull," she said, looking blankly up at Gavin. "Well, one day, Todd went a little too far with his proddings and teasings. The bull turned on Todd and tore him to pieces."

"Well, I'll be damned," Gavin said, shaking his head.

Caroline looked at Twin Oaks. Freshly-painted, the three-story mansion rose from among the live oaks like a tall magnolia, making her proud. Even the interior had been freshly painted and wallpapered and all the rooms emitted the aroma of newness as new furniture had been brought in to replace the old.

Pride and happiness for Twin Oaks swelled inside Caroline's heart, but she worried that it was not the same for Gavin. She had seen him silently looking toward St. Clair Manor many times. Even though a new family was renovating it, she knew that a part of him still lingered there. The manor had born his name for more years than not.

"Do you miss St. Clair Manor now that you've sold it?" Caroline asked. "Can you truly say you're happy living at Twin Oaks?"

"The only things that I miss are the few years in my youth when I shared cotton season with my uncle," Gavin said thickly, glancing over at St. Clair Manor and seeing its utter darkness. It seemed that the family who now owned it only came by day. Did they also feel the ghostly presence that had seemed to linger in the dark shadows after the discovery in the stable? Would it always be there, haunting everyone who tried to love the old place?

He couldn't help but think that, yes, somehow, it would be a place where you felt wickedness hovering about you. Much wickedness had been born there. But thank God it hadn't been his uncle's doings, only Elroy's.

"You helped with the planting? Or the harvesting?"

"Both."

He looked into the distance, where the cotton fields lay wasted far behind St. Clair Manor and drew Caroline to his side. "But St. Clair Manor is a thing of the past," he sighed.

"Yes," Caroline said, closing her eyes. She accepted his lips as they consumed her in a gentle kiss, always hungry for their sweetness.

Having brought St. Clair Manor into the conversation, Caroline was again fighting against the memories, seeing images flashing before her closed eyes—the portrait . . . the cameo necklace . . . the boarded-up doors . . . the knife at her throat. . . .

But somehow, thankfully, these thoughts were now slipping away from her, perhaps forever this time, as though Gavin's kiss were willing them away.

# About the Author

Cassie Edwards resides in the friendly town of Mattoon, Illinois, with her husband, Charlie. When Cassie isn't writing, she loves to swim, cook, and read. As a teenager, her first love was reading Gothics.

# FLAMES OF PASSION

☐ **LOVE BETRAYED by Patricia Rice.** Beautiful Christina MacTavish was an innocent when she first encountered Damien Drayton, the "Yankee Earl." But Damien, who had come from revolutionary America to claim his legacy in an England he hated, wanted her only as his mistress. Her innocence crumbled under his desire as she realized that to surrender to his passion was treason ... but to refuse it was impossible....
(400232—$3.95)

☐ **LOVE'S REDEMPTION by Kathleen Fraser.** Surrendering to love's sweetest sin, beautiful, red-haired Hilary Pembroke blazed with feverish desire in the forbidden embrace of the handsome, rugged Virginian she had resisted for so long. She was ready to risk her very soul for an ecstasy that was sure to damn her ... or to deliver her to the sweet salvation of love....
(140400—$3.95)

☐ **SATIN AND SILVER by Jane Archer.** At the poker table, Shenandoah was known for her icy composure ... but now she was aflame with longing for a man who was leading her into certain danger. Rogue would stake anything on his desire for this precious lady gambler ... and dare everything to possess her forever....
(141121—$3.95)

☐ **UNDER THE WILD MOON by Diane Carey.** Katie was Will Scarlet's prisoner, yet she moaned with pleasure as his gentle touch made her forget that he was one of Robin Hood's bandits. For although he had taken her by force, he was keeping her, now, by love. Tonight a deep primeval rhythm would unite them so that no sword, no prince, could part them—now or forever....
(141547—$3.95)

Prices slightly higher in Canada

**Buy them at your local
bookstore or use coupon
on next page for ordering.**